This book is dedicated to my family.
You know who you are, even if you don't always want to admit it.

ISBN 978-1-7334624-0-2 (E-book)
ISBN 978-1-7334624-1-9 (Paperback)

Library of Congress Registration Number: TXu002161720

Any references to historical events, real people, or real places are used fictitiously. Names, characters, and places are products of the author's imagination.

NEW BEGINNINGS

Janet Olson

THE PROGRAM

It wasn't always this way. The program was only a few years old, after all. I don't think the government designed the program Youth of America Help a Nation to be a punishment, but punishment it was for some of us.

I guess you could say it all started in fourth grade when Swahili was introduced into our school's curriculum. Swahili class was where I met Daniel Morelli. We bonded over our mutual love of cars and we also shared a good friend, Engen Malone. Dan asked me out in middle school, but I wasn't interested in dating him. Thankfully, we were still able to hang out without any awkwardness.

The middle of junior year, I asked Dan to come over to study for an upcoming Swahili test. We were the only two in the house. That night sent me down a different path than the one I'd planned to travel. My parents could have been knocked over by a feather at my actions.

Several years back, my Gramps had worked for the United Nations. In fact, it was Gramps who encouraged my parents to enroll me in YAHN. He said it would be an awakening. The application went in a few days before the deadline and I was accepted.

I knew my parents were going to miss me the six months I was away. Were they disappointed in me? Sure. Did they think I would burn in hell as a sinner? No, they were beyond cool parents; they just put too much stock in Gramps' opinion. They must have really wanted to teach me a lesson because the program wasn't free. In exchange for my suffering, YAHN would be $20,000 richer.

Sixteen kids from Minnesota were selected to go to Africa, but only four of us were placed in Mukono District. We had met one another two weeks earlier at the YAHN orientation. I happened to already know one of the volunteers, Engen Malone. Engen would be working closely with a child who was autistic. Krista was placed in the Village Teaching program. Dorian (Dee) was placed in the Community Outreach program, and I would be in Orphan Outreach.

Since it was a three-day orientation, Engen and I got to know our roommates and our prospective jobs pretty well. The orientation took place in Minneapolis, not too far away from our houses. We spent most of the time together as a group, watching videos and getting lectured on African culture, history, and politics. We were educated on the type of plants to stay away from and what insects were dangerous. It was strongly suggested that we only eat food from the Volunteer Center or a restaurant, nothing from the open markets.

After the informative and terrifying orientation, I could safely say there was only one thing I wanted less than to go to Africa. The program was six months long, so that meant I would be having my baby there.

WHAT HAS LEFT

Maybe this is a good time to introduce myself. My name is Ida Denmark. I'm seventeen years old. Up until three and a half months ago when I was cursed with this pregnancy, I considered myself a well-adjusted girl with a decent head on my shoulders. Some considered my apathy and overall sense of aimlessness to be lazy, but I was fine with it. Dan's nickname for me, "Idle", pretty much sums me up.

I met Janelle and Engen in preschool. We each shared the same interest – nap time. Janelle had the uncanny ability to fall asleep as soon as her head hit the pillow. Engen couldn't fall asleep without sucking his thumb. Me, I liked observing them both too much to sleep. Back then, the things we learned about each other we learned together. Engen discovered at the same time I did that Janelle was precious. Janelle and I learned together that Engen was kindhearted, and they both knew that I was lost.

My idleness set in around the time I suffered my first panic attack in the ninth grade. Shortly after that first attack, it was like I'd lost interest in everything: sports, reading, leaving my house. My sister Marilyn thought I was destined to become a hermit. Maybe she thought this because my dream after graduation was to stumble onto hidden treasure, buy a house in the country, and cut myself off from humanity.

After the first attack, I'd moped for an entire month before my mom took me to a shrink. According to Dr. Lilly, anxiety was my issue, so she suggested to me some calming exercises. I decided to quit soccer. I wanted a quiet mind to hopefully help prevent more panic attacks, and sports made me feel violent. Shortly thereafter I ditched Dr. Lilly, deciding that I had a pretty good therapist in Janelle. *Had*, because she recently died in a motorcycle accident. I can't stand it, and I'll never get used to her not being here. It feels like a pencil eraser is constantly rubbing away at my heart. Her passing, this pregnancy, *and* the Africa mess are three absolutes that still haven't sunk in. The idea of leaving my home is sickening. Janelle's death is forever. The pregnancy is soul-crushing.

Ever since Janelle died, Engen has barely spoken to me. When I mentioned my possible YAHN punishment to Engen, he seemed indifferent. The next night, Engen got into a fight during the championship hockey game. The opposing team, the Titans, were losing by five goals. Three Titans fans decided to retaliate by harassing our cheerleaders, namely Engen's on-again-off-again girlfriend since the ninth grade, Brittany Welch. According to eyewitnesses, Engen barreled toward her taunters and beat the crap out of them. He was working on putting the third guy in the hospital before the security guards were able to pull him away.

There were no charges pressed against Engen, for the three douche bags were all over eighteen and facing their own charges for verbally harassing a minor in front of hundreds of witnesses. Engen's attorney, my father, had gotten Brittany and her dad to agree not to press charges against the three creeps as long as said creeps agreed not to go after Engen for any damages. They gladly accepted the offer. As for Engen, his parents enrolled him in YAHN a week before the cutoff date of the summer cycle.

This would be the first time that coed rooming among the volunteers was allowed. The program was still fairly new and only three states participated: Minnesota, California, and Florida. There were supposed to be eight boys and eight girls from each state, but somehow Minnesota ended up with nine girls and seven boys. The mistake was a mystery.

The apartments we'd be staying in were tiny, and could only accommodate four people. Bert, the Minnesota coordinator, saw Engen as the likely candidate to bunk with girls. Engen had three sisters and was already friends with one of the girls, yours truly. Ultimately, the final say rested with Krista and Dee's parents, since mine were already madly in love with him. After spending an hour with Engen at a coffee shop, their parents were convinced of his honorable character and signed the consent form. Therefore, Engen who'd been slated to volunteer in Jinja was swapped out for Mukono. If not for him being placed with me, my brain may well have suffocated. Even though we weren't exchanging a lot of words these days, he was still the epitome of home to me.

◆ ◆ ◆

It was two days before my flight and I was sitting at the dresser in my bedroom. Dan was over, cursing YAHN with the same litany of complaints: "How good of a worker will you be when you're eight months along and can't bend over? Do they still expect you to work if your back hurts?"

Dan rubbed his fingers back and forth across his forehead, a nervous habit of his since birth, and knelt in front of me. "I'm going to miss these gorgeous brown eyes, long brown hair, and sweet freckles."

"You just described me along with three other girls in our homeroom alone," I replied smugly. "Look at them if you miss me."

"You know how I've always felt about you. And now we have this," he remarked.

Dan rested a hand on my flat belly and leaned in for a kiss just as the wood flooring outside my room creaked. He sprang away and scrambled over to sit on my bed. Not only had it saved me from turning away from one of his kisses for the umpteenth time, but it cracked me up how worried my parents were of Dan and me hanging out in my bedroom. I mean, the worst had already happened. It's not like a person could stock up on pregnancies. It was also funny how Dan held out hope that it might happen again, even after I told him it'd been a one-time thing.

My eyes settled on a photograph of Janelle perched on my dresser. I got lost in the thought of how her legs never tanned like the rest of her body when I heard Dan sniffle. I got up from the chair at the dresser and sat next to Dan on the bed. He had tears in his green eyes.

Dan was the one who wanted the baby, so I agreed to have it for him. I also knew for a fact that Janelle wouldn't have wanted me to terminate it. I cared a great deal for Dan, however, sitting next to him was the closest I came to showing comfort. I wasn't good at emotional stuff. You'd think my best friend's death would've opened the floodgates inside of me. Instead, it seemed to shut me down further.

"As if you're missing the start of senior year for Africa," Dan scoffed.

"I'll have to keep up with my studies once school starts up again in September." I bit my lip. I still hadn't coordinated with Principal Andrews on how to do that.

Dan sighed. "I gotta get to work. Paul invited me to dinner, so I'll see you later."

My nine-year old brother Paul is delightfully odd. He's obsessed with missing children. His bedroom walls are papered with photos of abducted kids. One time, my older sister Marilyn took me and Paul out to lunch at this taco joint near our house. A man had been there with his kids, and good old Paul got it in his head that all four kids had been kidnapped. On our way out, Paul stopped by their table, glared the man down, and assured the children that he would do everything in his power to return them to their families. It was the funniest thing I'd ever witnessed.

Dan's eyes shifted to my belly. "You two be good."

I swallowed a sarcastic remark on how fetuses weren't well known for randomly escaping the womb to go set fires to abandoned buildings, and instead settled for, "We will."

Four hours later, I could tell that Dan was questioning his decision to return. During dinner, my dad grumbled about Dan being a bastard, and Gramps glowered at him with his very expressive eyes. My mother's cooking wasn't worth that.

I kicked Dan out ten minutes after dinner, because I wanted

to visit Janelle's parents before I left for Africa and time was running out. After rejecting Dan's offer of a ride, I set out on foot for the two-block walk to Janelle's house. I kept my head down and twirled a dandelion between my thumb and forefinger. I liked to test myself to make sure I could still find her house without using my eyes.

A few moments later, I stopped and turned my head sideways to see the familiar raised cement. I stepped onto the walk just as the screen door banged shut, and my head snapped up. I saw the side of Engen's smiling face as he said goodbye to Mr. and Mrs. Lyndahl, and I was overcome with a feeling of tenderness toward him. The YAHN orientation had been rough. He'd stayed by my side whenever possible; we just hadn't talked much.

Engen's eyes swiveled around to mine and his smile faded. I dropped the dandelion, hating that I used to be the reason for his smile, not the disappearance of it. Head lowered, he walked toward me. I continued to trudge up the walk, eyes firmly fixed on the Lyndahl's garden. We passed each other in slow motion, it seemed. I felt his warm fingers grasp my pinkie finger at the knuckle, and as he kept walking, his hand slowly ran down the entire length of my finger.

I half-glanced behind me in time to see his foot crush the discarded dandelion.

I know how you feel, I thought to the weed.

I rapped on the screen door. I'd spent the walk preparing myself for the inevitable misery I'd see in Mr. and Mrs. L.'s eyes, along with the slumped shoulders and hands that were so weak they could barely hold a coffee mug to their lips.

Mr. L. answered the door. He was 6'1, slim as a rail, and bald.

"Hi," I greeted, careful not to meet his eyes. The failure to protect his daughter had a haunting way of reflecting out of them at all times.

"Evening, Ida," said Mr. L. "You and Engen just missed each other."

"I miss him all the time now it seems," I said, trying to sound nonchalant.

I walked in and closed my eyes at the absence of smell. When Janelle was alive, some sweet aroma was always in the air, sugar cookies or Rice Krispie bars. The untouched grapefruit half that sat in front of Mrs. L. on the kitchen table didn't even emit a scent.

Mrs. L. let the curtain fall back in place. "Engen's still not speaking to you?"

"No." I pulled out a kitchen chair and sat. The cushion was warm. *Engen.*

"A tragedy born from a tragedy," she mused.

"Oh, Mrs. L.," I said consolingly. "The two are hardly comparable."

"I made him promise to call you this evening." Her hand flew to her cardigan. She closed it at the throat as if she were cold.

"Would you like something to drink, Ida?" Mr. L. asked.

"Water, please." I shook my hair back.

"Your hair is so beautiful." Mrs. L. gave a sad smile. "She envied it."

I took the water glass from Mr. L. "Thank you."

Mr. L. kissed his wife's cheek. "I'm turning in."

"It's only seven-thirty. We aren't going to see Ida again for half a year."

Mr. L. took off his glasses and rubbed a spot with the corner of his shirt. "Dear, I am tired."

"Goodbye. I'll call you guys from Africa every now and then," I said, before Mrs. L. tried to persuade him again.

"I would love that. Bye, Ida." Mr. L. bowed his head to me.

Ever since Janelle died, Mr. L. stopped using the word "good".

"Engen told me that you plan to disappear after high school; he seemed pretty distraught over it." Mrs. L. looked up from the bottom of her water glass. "I'd like to disappear, too."

"I know." Man, it was dark in this house.

"When something horrible happens to a person you love, it changes you." Her eyes were wide with grief. "You haven't changed."

"You have no idea what's going on inside of me."

"I am perfectly aware of what's going on inside of you." Her eyes dropped to my midsection.

"I wasn't referring to the baby." I took a drink of water and thought about how if it wasn't for her daughter, I wouldn't be in this pregnancy predicament. I certainly didn't feel like discussing that with Mrs. L., though.

Mrs. L. stood. She held out the bowl with the half of grapefruit and asked with her eyes if I wanted it, but I shook my head. She brought the bowl to the garbage can and threw away the grapefruit followed by the glass bowl.

"Engen blames me for what happened to Janelle," I blurted out.

Mrs. L. came back to the table, interest written in the lines of her forehead.

"She told me she was going on a date with an older guy who drove a motorcycle," I explained. "The only thing I told her was that she was crazy to go out with someone who hung out at a pool hall all day."

"Honey, Engen blames himself for not being a more attentive friend. Bill blames himself for owning that pool hall." Mrs. L. gazed at me as if seeing me for the first time tonight. "I blame Jamison. Why didn't he give her his helmet?"

"Because Jamison's a dick."

"And yet, he's alive," she murmured.

"He's in a coma."

"If he woke up, there'd be a trial. Bill and I wouldn't survive that."

Mrs. L. and I talked for another ten minutes before she told me I should go so I'd be free to take Engen's call in private.

TRYING TO LOSE DAN

Gramps is clean cut, distinguished, and still has all his own teeth. He's not stooped over from lack of calcium, and he could probably bench-press my body weight. He's also a hard man to interact with. I prefer Janelle's grandpa, Bernard, who asks questions like, "What did you say?" and "Who are you again?" Bernard outlived Janelle. It wasn't right, in my opinion.

I was named after Grams. She died six months before I was born. As far back as I can remember, Gramps has never called me by my name. To him, I am Kid, Girl, or my personal favorite, The Middle One.

I was mentally drained after my visit with Mr. and Mrs. L., so when I walked through the front door and Gramps nabbed me for a chat, I felt like liquid.

"It's a good thing you're doing this," he said in what I hoped was conclusion, "otherwise, you'd wind up resenting that baby."

I scoffed. "Africa, though? It's a little extreme."

He gave me a look that said I was daft. "You need to be awakened from this soft life."

I stirred my sugar-free peach iced tea with my finger. "I just can't help but think that what Americans are doing over there is interfering."

"You were too young to remember Uganda's water crisis of 2025--"

"I remember," I interrupted. "It was the reason you were away for two years."

When Gramps returned from Africa, he'd brought back a package for me. The tag read "to: You, from: Africa." Inside was a multicolored braided necklace. I chose to wear it as an ankle bracelet, and still do to this day.

"The people were thankful for the assistance," Gramps said.

"So, they have water now?"

"Yes. They actually have running water where you're staying. It's probably even clean."

"That's a shame."

Gramps gave me a stern look. "You haven't lived long enough to be this cynical."

"My best friend died seventeen weeks ago," I explained.

Gramps banged his hand on the table. "And mine died seventeen years ago."

Gramps then proceeded to drone on about the political situation in Africa. It was like being back in that orientation. How come the only conversations he started with me were either boring or cutting?

◆ ◆ ◆

School was depressing the next morning. Along each corridor were signs wishing luck to me and Engen on our "great adventure", not to mention our peers were out of control with their derisive comments.

"Hopefully you won't come back with malaria, I," Jeremy Waters taunted during lunch.

"Or HIV," Lindy Malone, Engen's youngest sister, quipped.

I shot a glance Engen's way to see how he was receiving all this. He caught my eye and gave me a what-are-ya-gonna-do shrug.

Brittany, who was currently "on-again" with Engen, intercepted the shrug, gave me a snooty look, and hugged Engen's arm to her side. She was jealous of the fact that he and I would be sharing a bedroom for six months.

Dan put his arm around my shoulders and squeezed, just as I was taking a drink of milk. It spilled all over the front of my shirt.

"I thought the milk didn't come in until after the baby was born," Brittany yelped.

The whole table, aside from Dan and Engen, erupted in laughter.

"Easy," Engen warned her.

I excused myself. I was about to turn down the hallway to the restroom when I overheard my name.

"And did you know Dan is, like, working two jobs in order to support the baby?" asked Tawny. "I don't think Ida even has one."

I snorted softly. I'd worked for my dad at his law office for over a year now.

"Dan is, like, totally gonna forget her once she's gone," chimed in Trish.

"How? He, like, likes her a ton," said Tawny.

"Amelia's going to make him forget. She's wanted him ever since she moved here from New York, like, two years ago."

Most girls wanted Dan. He was 5'11 with short brown hair, green eyes, and thanks to basketball and baseball, a rockin' body. Up until now, Dan hadn't bent to Amelia's advances. Maybe I should say something to encourage it.

I found an opportunity later that evening after dinner. Dan was helping me pack some things that I'd suddenly come to realize I didn't want to be without for six months.

"Amelia's going to seduce you when I'm gone," I informed him.

Dan calmly ran his fingers across his forehead. "In order to seduce a person, the one seduced has to be willing to give in to the seduction."

I fiddled with a piece of yarn on my blanket. "Since you and I aren't a thing, you should ask her out."

Dan watched me sort through my pictures of Janelle. "Oh, I see what's going on here. You pushing me to date Amelia...Engen breaking up with Britt after school today...you two plan on finally hooking up out there."

I lightly touched the other piece of jewelry I never took off, my best friend necklace from Janelle. I'd given up having a relationship with Engen due to Janelle's multiple pleas for me not to date him.

"Me and nobody is the plan," I answered. "You should date other girls, though."

"We'll see. We're due at my house for farewell brownies with my mom." Dan's eyes twinkled. "She works at nine, so we'll have the house to ourselves."

"Yes to the brownies." I stood and followed him to the door. "No to whatever else you're thinking."

As I followed Dan out of my bedroom door, I noticed that his jeans just barely covered his butt even with a belt on. He'd been so worried about me and the baby that he'd lost weight. One gains and the other loses, isn't that the way it usually works?

YO-YO

My family and I were saying our goodbyes in the living room the next morning at three-thirty. The flight was at six a.m., but I needed to get to the airport by four in order to check in with the YAHN group, get the boarding passes, and go through security.

"A yo-yo for a yo-yo," Paul said, and handed me the small toy Dad had given him on his fifth birthday. It was the same yo-yo Gramps' dad had given Gramps when he was a boy.

"Thanks, Pauley." I turned the yo-yo over in my hand, touched by the gift. "Are you sure?"

"The YAHN pamphlet said to bring toys and games to share."

I smiled. "That it did."

"Befriend the natives. Make eye contact." Paul made a 'v' with his fingers, and pointed from his eyes to mine. "Let them know that you know them. I don't want my niece to get kidnapped before I meet her."

Paul was convinced the baby was a girl. I had no clue what it was, nor did I care.

"Thanks for the advice, Pauley, it wasn't eerie at all."

Paul nodded solemnly. "A scared parent is a vigilant parent."

I pulled Paul into a hug. When he squeezed me, a tear slipped out of my left eye. Before I could form another thought, my face was pressed against Dad's chest.

Dad kissed the top of my head. "I'll miss you, pal. You be careful."

My lips were squashed against his shirt, muffling my voice, "I will."

He let me go and my sister moved in. Marilyn accuses me on a weekly basis of faking the pregnancy because I'm not showing at all. With my thin body type, my doctor predicted I could make it to twenty weeks before I began to show. Marilyn stared solely at my midriff and broke down crying.

"Are you sad because I'm leaving, or because I'm knocked up?" I asked.

Marilyn bridged our distance by placing a hand on my shoulder. "I'm sad because I don't think you're going to get anything out of this extraordinary opportunity."

"You're probably right." I turned to my mother, and my bottom lip trembled. "Please don't make me go."

Mom hugged me. "I'm sorry, but you need this. It's not right for a girl your age to long for solitude. You need to find a reason to...be."

I sniffed. "To be what?"

"That's what I hope you'll find out."

I went over to Gramps and was rewarded with, "Try not to be such a smart ass over there."

I swallowed my disappointment. "Got it."

Gramps took me by the shoulders and made me look into his faded brown eyes. "You'll be in good hands. Otherwise, I never would've sent you."

"Right."

I went and stood by Dan, who was giving me a ride to the airport, and turned to take in my family. Mom was enveloped in Dad's arms, while Gramps had one hand on Paul's shoulder and the other on Marilyn's shoulder. It was a nice image to take along.

Dan waved goodbye to my family, and we walked out to his car together. When we got in, he said, "Don't forget to send me the next ultrasound picture."

"I won't."

"Do you have your yellow fever certificate?" he asked.

"Yep."

"You're going to have to show it before you board the plane."

"I'm the one who told you that."

We drove the rest of the way in silence. When we got in line at the airport drop-off, Dan said, "Hey, Paul mentioned that you told your parents your phone won't accept calls in Africa. Why'd you do that?"

"They agreed to this whole thing, therefore they don't get to talk to me."

Dan peered at me curiously. "Sometimes I don't understand you."

"I know," I whispered.

A uniformed officer rapped on the window with his knuckles and tapped his watch.

"I'll see you when I return," I said.

Dan flung the car door open. He tried to get out of the car but forgot his seat belt was on. He fell back inside, unclasped his seat belt, and then with a huff, exited the car. He slammed the door shut and kicked it. It was hard not to laugh as I grabbed my carry-on and joined him outside. I kept my eyes on Dan as he opened the trunk to get my suitcases for me and then slammed it closed.

"Something wrong?" I asked.

"I told you I was coming to Africa for the birth."

"I'll tell you what I told my mom, I don't need you there. I have Engen."

Dan signaled to an attendant that we needed a cart for the luggage. "I love you, Ida."

Uncomfortable after hearing those words, I watched the nice man load my luggage.

Dan cupped his hand around my neck. "I know you feel something, otherwise you wouldn't have given it up to me."

"Always the poet," I quipped.

He smiled widely. "Don't work too hard."

Dan drew away from me and started toward his car. He gave me one last wave before he got in the car and drove away. I took the cart with my luggage and moved through the sliding glass doors into the airport. It wasn't busy, but the feel of the airport made my stomach turn. I felt an arm slide through mine.

"Boo," Krista whispered in my ear.

"Hi." I noticed my roommate was only carrying a small purse.

"Traveling light?"

"My luggage is over there." She pointed to the group we were walking toward. "You're the last to arrive."

"Were you brushing your teeth? You smell minty."

"You like?" Krista blew in my face. "My breath didn't smell so great after I threw up every ounce of food I've consumed since the age of ten."

I understood that notion; my stomach had been churning ever since I found out I was going to Africa.

"Morning, Engen," I greeted, when we reached the group. I nodded at Dorian. "How's it going, Dee?"

"Alright," she said, tossing her long black hair over her shoulder. "Krista and I were hoping you'd be able to get him to talk."

I sat down in the chair next to Engen, and rested my head on his shoulder. His letterman jacket felt scratchy against my cheek.

"Nice of you to join us," Engen said, trance-like.

A kid from Shakopee clutched his hand to his heart. "He's alive! It's a miracle."

Krista gave him the middle finger. "Go to hell, Dex."

"I got my ticket right here," Dex replied, holding up his passport.

I may not have been in the mood to smile, but I did appreciate his clever response. I lifted my head off Engen's shoulder and gazed at the dimple on his chin.

Engen set a hand on my cheek. "Last night I lied when I told you I was scared."

"You're really terrified?"

"No." He stared into my eyes. "I'm actually--"

Before Engen could finish his personal remark, there was a loud clap. I tore my eyes from Engen's and glanced over to see our coordinator, Bert.

"Is there anything we need to go over before we get our boarding passes?" Bert asked loudly.

"Are you leaving us in Amsterdam?" Dex asked.

"Yes, Mr. Brandis," Bert confirmed. "The Ugandan coordinator, Akiki Ogunwale, and the groups from Orlando and Sacramento will join us in Amsterdam. Anything else?"

Everyone shook their heads no.

Bert clapped his hands. "Grab your stuff, and we'll get the boarding passes."

Engen obediently stood and slung his two jam-packed duffel bags over one shoulder. "Give me your bags. You shouldn't do heavy lifting," he reminded me.

"I have that." I pointed to the cart. "Dan have a little chat with you?"

"He gave me a list. I draw the line at foot rubs. Deal?"

He held out his fist and I bumped it with mine. "Deal."

I found it amazing that Dan and Engen were still friends, considering Engen had beaten the crap out of Dan after finding out I was pregnant. Brittany broke up with Engen on the grounds that he shouldn't have defended another girl's honor. It only lasted two days before she was begging him to take her back.

"Say, I," Krista cleared her throat. "Why can't you carry anything heavy?"

"She dislocated her shoulder," Engen said at the same time I said, "I have a hernia."

Engen abandoned me and followed Bert.

I faced Krista and Dee. "Hernias are the worst."

"Huh," Krista said, disbelief marring her features. "And your shoulder?"

"You're not going to believe this," I tee-heed, "two nights ago I was moving some furniture and pop, out it went."

Dee crossed her arms. "That's pretty unbelievable."

I shrugged. "Fortune's fool, that's me."

"Denmark. Colten. Tran. Now!" Bert shouted.

I made a U-turn with my cart. I didn't miss the glance that Dee and Krista shared, though. Whatever. If they wanted to think I was a lying, hernia-laden freak, I could live with that. I pushed the cart at a jog until I caught up with Engen. He was impressively tall. I was five-feet-eight and eyeline with his chest.

He gave me an amused look. "Wasn't it *you* who came up with the hurt shoulder bit?"

"I panicked."

Since I wanted to keep it under wraps for as long as possible, Engen and I had discussed the previous night that we needed a way to keep our stories consistent in case we had to explain away any pregnancy-related issues.

"Do you want to change it to a hernia?" he asked.

"Naw. Hernias are for dads."

"What else did we say last night?" he quizzed.

"We stick together no matter what. For the next six months, we're our only connection to home."

His smile immediately comforted me. We were familiar to each other and we were going to need that familiarity in the alien land that awaited us.

We received our boarding passes, made it through security, and arrived at the gate just in time to board the plane.

THIS ISN'T PERMANENT

The flight to Amsterdam was boring as hell. Krista sat next to me, and an old guy with hairy ears sat next to her in the aisle seat. I had to get up and go to the bathroom so often that he graciously offered to switch spots, which put me right across the aisle from Engen.

I played games on my phone, then watched a movie to pass the time. It was one of my and Engen's all-time favorite comedies. Each time a scene came on that I knew he'd found funny, I'd glance over at him, or I'd catch him out of the corner of my eye watching me for my reactions. I was so confused by us now. Engen didn't speak to me outside of Janelle's house yesterday, yet he'd called me shortly after I left the Lyndahl's and we talked for a half an hour. Now he was sneaking glances at me like I was the new girl in town and he was too shy to talk to me.

If Engen and I had been our old selves, if this had been pre-Janelle's passing, the two of us would be annoying the passengers with our joking, back and forth banter, and laughter. We both had various friends, and loving families, yet I was the only one Engen wanted to converse with. He believed that my words were careful, therefore, worth listening to. I genuinely felt *heard* by Engen. That being the case, you wouldn't think Janelle's death would've had the power to alter our interactions, yet it did. Engen blamed himself for Janelle's death. He was the last person she had seen before her date with Jamison. Engen knew that Jamison was in his early twenties, and was leery of him wanting to date a high school girl, so he told Janelle he wanted to meet Jamison before she went anywhere with him. However, Engen wasn't paying close enough attention to Janelle that evening, otherwise he would've known that she already had a date planned with Jamison.

I watched Engen across the narrow aisle until he made eye contact with me. "You didn't take her from me," I whispered.

He nodded slowly. "What terrifies me is that one day you might see things differently," he responded.

"Never," I disagreed, as I took in his face. "My God, I wish you could see it."

"What's that?" he asked.

"What I see when I look at you."

When we disembarked in Amsterdam, I immediately broke into a sweat. Wave after wave of people swam around me, and I was bobbing in the middle of an ocean surrounded by sharks. I also happened to be blocking the exit. My fellow passengers were anxious to enter the airport to stretch their legs, but mine wouldn't move.

A powerful arm took mine. Engen led me off to the side, positioned my back against the floor-to-ceiling window, and stood in front of me with his hands on my shoulders. He was so tall he blocked everyone from my sight. I shakily clutched his forearms.

"Focus on my eyes. It's just me and you now," he soothed. "Take a deep breath."

The gray of his eyes reminded me of the color of the wolves' coats at the zoo near home, and the sincerity displayed in them sent a ripple of serenity over me. I was forced to blink as the sweat from my forehead ran into my eyes.

"This isn't permanent," he said calmly. "You will get out of this airport."

My gaze drifted. He shook me, and my eyes snapped to fixate on his again.

"These people will go away. This isn't permanent." He kneaded my shoulders. "Say it."

"This isn't permanent." The sweat pooled on the back of my neck.

I wasn't a diagnosed agoraphobic, but my fear of unknown, overrun places had gotten bad enough over the last few years that Engen knew what to do to calm me down before my breath left me completely.

He ran his sleeve across my forehead to wipe away the sweat.

"Thank you," I said sincerely. "I feel better now."

"Let's go find a quiet area," Engen suggested.

The flight from Sacramento came in soon after ours. The kids looked like us, bleary-eyed and rumpled.

"I need to find a milkshake," I announced to Engen. "Want anything?"

"Naw. Do you need help navigating through the crowd?"

I shook my head. "As you reminded me, this isn't permanent."

"No, but *this* is, me and you." Engen cupped the side of my neck with his right hand. "Lately I've been distant, but the way I feel about you hasn't changed. *Won't* change."

I felt a stirring in my chest as I circled a hand around his left thumb. "I never told anyone that you sucked this thumb until the age of ten," I said reminiscently.

"And I never told anyone the reason you slept with Dan," Engen said while his right eye twitched.

"I didn't know you knew." My eyes closed in shame.

"It's adorable that you think there's something I don't know regarding you." He affectionately ran his thumb along my wrist.

I gave him his hands back and wagered a glance at Dee and Krista. They both eyed me warily, and who could blame them? First there was the shoulder/hernia incident, and then the mild panic attack. It's a good thing I wasn't here to make friends.

I was alone with my milkshake all of thirty minutes when Engen messaged me that the Orlando flight was in, and the Ugandan YAHN representative wanted to address us. I made it back just in time to hear:

"My name is Akiki. For the next six months, myself along with the supervisors at your respective job sites will be the ones you come to if you need anything."

"Could this guy talk any slower?" Krista whispered.

"Tell me about it." I took a sip of chocolate shake.

"You were selected because you stood out as mature young adults," Akiki continued. "If we take things one day at a time, we will all have a positive experience."

"I'm so sick of the word 'experience,'" Dee commented.

I nodded, and without taking my eyes off Akiki repeated, "Tell me about it."

"And you are?" Akiki asked.

Akiki had a lazy eye, so Dee and I both assumed he was talking to the other and didn't answer.

He stood in front of me. "You would be...?"

"Ida Denmark, sir."

"Denmark," he responded crabbily. "My colleague speaks often of your grandfather, Ransom. He was a great help to our village some years ago."

Forty-six pairs of eyes studied me curiously as Akiki went back to the front of the group. Great. What I've always wanted, to be the center of attention.

◆ ◆ ◆

We landed in Entebbe International Airport at 11:05 a.m. I was impressed that the airport was enclosed. I'd expected to land in a field somewhere with cows and goats grazing. We collected our luggage and were separated into three groups: Mukono, Wakiso, and Jinja.

As soon as I stepped outside my lungs clogged. It was extremely hot and humid. I inhaled and smelled a mixture of motor oil, charcoal, and jungle. As we waited for our bus, I took in the scenery. There were lots of buildings and hotels that looked like they would fit in in America.

With my middle finger and thumb, I peeled my t-shirt from my neck and fanned myself. I glanced around and saw that Krista's face was the same shade of red as a lobster, and Dee's hair was sticking to her forehead.

"Come and make yourselves a name tag," Akiki said.

Everybody surrounded Akiki except for Engen and me. We shared a pained look. Krista bounded back a moment later and stuck a name tag on my shirt above my left breast, then handed Engen his.

"Did you write this?" Engen asked Krista.

"Yep. You're welcome," she replied.

"You replaced both the e's in my name with i's and added a hyphen." Engen pursed his lips and held the tag out for me.

Sure enough, in thick black marker I saw, 'Ing-in.'

"That's how it sounds to me," Krista said grumpily.

"My name *sounds* like it has a hyphen in it?" he asked incredulously.

Krista stuck her tongue out at him.

"Here come the buses," Akiki said. He then addressed the two additional groups, "The YAHN representatives on your buses will give you your instructions."

"Real buses," Krista exclaimed as she boarded.

The exhaust from the buses was making me ill. "I expected one of those rickety things with livestock on board," I said.

"We require buses of this size to hold the luggage," Akiki explained.

I sat down in the back row. Krista plopped down next to me. Engen stuck out his lower lip in a pout. I shrugged apologetically. He picked the seat in front of mine next to one of the Orlando kids, Marco, while Dee sat next to one of the Sacramento boys.

After the luggage was loaded, Akiki announced from the front of the bus that we'd be stopping at the bank in Mukono Town. One bumpy ride later, we exchanged a portion of our U.S. dollars for shillings. According to what we learned in orientation, with our housing and meals already paid for, the average volunteer shouldn't need a whole lot more than one hundred thousand shillings of spending money for the *entire* six months. That was only fifty dollars. If you planned on buying clothes, souvenirs, or additional snacks, then you would most likely need more. Not foreseeing a want to purchase any keepsakes from here, I opted for the one hundred thousand shillings.

Money being exchanged, we continued on our way.

On the bus, Akiki handed out maps along with directions from the town to our apartment, and from our apartment to our work assignments. I heard yelling, and craned my head to look out the back window to see four little kids running after the bus. More kids joined in every few blocks, all smiling and shouting.

"Does anyone know what the children are chanting?" Akiki quizzed us.

"Mzungu," I offered, when no one else spoke up.

"Correct. It means white person." Akiki grinned, showing his yellowish teeth. "For those to whom this applies, keep in mind this is not a derogatory term. The kids love white people."

Krista was their girl, then; she had the palest skin and blondest hair out of us volunteers. She surprised me by whipping out a camera and taking pictures of the kids, which only caused them to shout louder.

I rested my head against the soft backing of the seat and closed my eyes. Fifteen minutes later, the bus stopped in front of a square, two-level building which held four apartments. Next door was another apartment building mid-construction. Our bags were unloaded by the driver as all of us volunteers gawked at our temporary environment, dumbfounded.

"There must be some kinda way outta here," Engen sang softly, in his best Jimi Hendrix voice.

I looked at Engen and almost smiled at his fondness for extremely old music.

Akiki handed each of us a key card to the building. It would log our scan-in times, and ensure we were keeping to curfew. The card would also allow us access to the Volunteer Center, or VC. We were instructed to bring our luggage inside, and then meet back outside the apartment building so we could hitch a ride to the VC. There, we'd have lunch and get ready for our village tours.

My apartment was one of two on the bottom floor along with

the restroom for the girls, key card required. The guys' apartments and bathroom were on the top floor. It was so hot here, Akiki said that most volunteers showered twice a day. He also said not to be surprised if the bathrooms were crawling with cockroaches. The hallway was so narrow that we had to walk single file. My, Engen, Krista, and Dee's apartment was the first one, so the girls behind us had to wait for us to enter before they could get to theirs.

It wasn't until I walked into the apartment that I wanted to cry. The duffel bags slipped off Engen's shoulders and fell to the floor. The living room held two loveseats, one purple and one white, a coffee table, and a window air conditioning unit. Off to the right, the kitchen contained a small, round table with four wooden chairs and a mini fridge. It was also close to 105 degrees in here.

Krista gave a huff at our meager surroundings and stepped down the short hallway which had two doors directly across from each other. Dee followed her. Krista opened the door to the right and gasped. Engen and I picked up the rear. He opened the door to the left, and inside we saw two single beds with mosquito netting, a tiny nightstand with a lamp and alarm clock separating the beds, and a small closet completing the room. This bedroom was easily half the size of my bedroom back home.

Engen put his arms around me and held me to his chest. After four seconds I couldn't tell whose sweat was whose anymore, so I gently pushed away. I had the urge to run, but there was nowhere to go. I put my hand to my forehead and found it sticky. I turned around slowly, walked back to the living room, and sat down on the purple loveseat.

Engen stood in front of me. "Are you okay?"

I massaged my temples. "There are no words for this moment."

"You're right." Engen attempted to peel his sweaty shirt off his skin. It made a slapping noise when he let it go, and the material stayed plastered to his chest. "I need to change clothes or

I'm going to die of whatever the opposite of hypothermia is."

Engen entered the hallway just as Krista was exiting her room, tears flowing down her face. There wasn't enough room for both of them to pass at the same time, so Krista screamed in frustration. Engen backed up and let her through first.

Krista sat on the white loveseat and scowled at the inside of our apartment with contempt. "How can they do this to us? Don't they know we're not used to living destitute?"

"You were at the orientation, so you know that Akiki isn't going to approve of that look." I gestured at her outfit which consisted of short shorts and a sports bra that exposed all of her belly.

"If we're not on assignment, it's only 'recommended' that we don't dress slutty," Krista paraphrased.

Dee joined us in the minuscule living room and inspected the air conditioning unit. "The a/c is up as high as it goes," she informed us.

Krista screamed again. "I hate my mother for this."

"Maybe you shouldn't have stolen her credit card for the tenth time and bought tons of stuff with it," Dee pointed out.

"What can I say? I have a problem."

"Therapy used to solve these kinds of problems," I interjected.

Dee scratched her eye. "Maybe this will work better than therapy."

Krista stared at her. "Says the girl who was sobbing into her teddy bear three minutes ago."

Engen reentered the room wearing brown and white checkered shorts, and pulled a gray tank top down over his abs. Krista whistled.

"We should go meet up with Akiki." Engen looked at me expectantly.

"Probably." I didn't feel like moving just yet, so he gave up and went without me.

"Ladies, did you see the six-pack on our roommate?" Krista asked, thunderstruck.

"Of course, we have pulses," Dee replied.

"Maybe this won't be so horrific after all," Krista said with a sigh, and followed after Engen.

Dee closed one eye. "Aren't you going to change, I?"

"Nope."

"You've been wearing that outfit since yesterday," Dee reminded me, rubbing at her closed eye.

I thought about the thing growing inside me. "No matter what I wear, I'm going to be uncomfortable."

Dee blinked like a rat. "I should get these dust particles out of my eye."

We left the apartment. To our right was another apartment and a staircase, and to the left was the bathroom and the door we'd come in. When I opened the restroom door, a cockroach roughly the size of my thumb scurried toward me. Two girls were hopping around and trembling. I brought my heel down hard on the roach and twisted it repeatedly. The squishing didn't have the desired effect, which was a painful death, but at least the roach sped away from us.

We exchanged a quick introduction. The brunette's name was Eve and the redhead's name was Bianca. They each entered a stall.

I motioned for Dee to enter the last stall, then gaped at the three small showers with timers, and two sinks. For seven, normally eight, girls. They were seriously out of it here.

MEET THE NEW BOSS

The Volunteer Center was ridiculously nice. The temperature was cool, there were white tiled floors, pristine-looking bathrooms, a gym, computer lab, and a cafeteria containing one long table. Now I was even more pissed off over our living arrangement, knowing that there *were* nice things here.

The entourage of little kids had followed us. They weren't allowed in the cafeteria, but they could watch us through the giant window in the hallway.

According to Akiki, his colleague Lev was tied up with a crisis. Since Lev was one of our tour guides, we had to sit around after lunch and wait for him. What we knew concerning Lev was his age, nineteen, and that he'd been the only white kid who'd ever been adopted from New Beginnings Orphanage. He was now in charge of said orphanage, therefore he'd be my boss.

Krista was making me look at the dust under her fingernails when the yelling started. The kids in the hallway were going bonkers over something. I glanced up when I heard Akiki say, "At last. Welcome, Lev."

As Lev walked toward the table, I noticed that he was dressed like a regular teenage guy, in a plain white t-shirt and dark blue jeans. His feet were bare and he had short, wavy blonde hair. His waist was slender and his arms were muscular. Thanks to the heat, his t-shirt clung very nicely to the lines of his abdomen. I was pretty sure I was breathing while I tried to calculate the distance still between us. Krista squealed, telling me she, too, was appreciating the appearance of the male walking toward us.

Akiki motioned to all of us. "Lev, meet our newest recruits."

"Good afternoon," Lev greeted in a voice that was deep and slightly accented.

His thumb tapped against his thigh as he scanned our faces. I must have been a little dazed because when his eyes found mine, they locked on me and lit up. If I didn't know better, I'd say he seemed relieved to see me.

Lev's eyes cut away from mine and he continued, "I apologize for my tardiness, but before we head out, I'd like to introduce myself to each of you."

The volunteers stood. Lev headed straight for me, but Akiki stopped him and made him start at the front of the table. Lev shook hands with each recruit and asked where they were stationed. My face flushed, and I turned away from him. My eyes met Engen's. He appeared troubled, so I shot him a wink.

"Ida?"

I was impressed that Lev knew my name, until I remembered that I was still wearing a name tag. I shifted my eyes, followed by my head, toward the smooth voice. Lev was positioned not three feet in front of me. My mouth fell open when I noticed his blue eyes. I'm talking *blue*. His tanned, toned arm extended toward me. He wore a multicolored braided bracelet on his wrist that was identical to the necklace/ankle bracelet Gramps had given me so long ago.

Puzzled that we both had the same bracelet, I glided my tongue between my dry lips. Lev's eyes widened. I was going to shake his hand, but stopped. What was I thinking? I couldn't touch him; my hand would betray me in a heartbeat.

Lev's whole body seemed to sigh. "It's so good to see you here."

"Um...thanks," I replied. It was an odd greeting, but maybe that was how they did things here.

Lev didn't seem offended that I hadn't accepted his hand. Interestingly enough, he seemed amused. He returned his hand to his side. Damn it! I'd missed the opportunity to touch him. The urge to reach out for him was so great that I had to clasp my hands behind my back, military style.

"I look forward to working with you. How--"

Lev was interrupted by Akiki's elbow nudging him in the ribs. He pressed his lips into a thin line and moved on to greet Krista.

I, meanwhile, pretended to be interested in a tree outside the window that looked like it'd been planted upside down.

Krista tugged on my sleeve. I think she asked me a question. She probably expected me to respond. Instead, I watched a smiling Lev shake hands with Engen. For some unknown reason, it made me uneasy.

After the introductions were made, Akiki informed us that we would split into groups for the short village tour. Engen, Krista, Dee, and I formed a semicircle.

"Lev's an absolute dream, isn't he?" Krista yelped.

Dee blushed and nodded.

"He seemed like an airhead to me," Engen remarked.

Krista zeroed in on me. "You totally shut down when Lev tried to shake your hand."

Engen raised his eyebrows at me.

"I'm tired, guys, give me a break," I said.

I was surprised Krista didn't try to extract more out of me until I realized that Lev was sauntering toward us. He was accompanied by a pretty girl with dark eye makeup, black hair, and a grumpy expression on her face, as well as a scrawny boy wearing thick glasses.

"Meet Megan and Stuart," Lev said to me. "The three of you will be working at the orphanage together."

Megan popped her gum. "'Sup?"

"Hey, Megan. How's it going, Stuart?" I shook their hands.

Lev watched me and Stuart clasp hands, with an arched eyebrow.

"Please call me Stu," Stuart requested solemnly.

"You got it. Call me 'I'."

Ugh, why did I say that? Lev seemed entertained, anyhow. His lips were wiggling around like they itched.

"'I' must be short for something." Stuart's tone implied that if it wasn't, he wouldn't be associating with me further.

Saying 'I' was short for 'I don't want to be here' didn't seem like something Lev would appreciate.

"Ida," I said.

"As in the lame state Idaho?" Megan asked in a bored voice.

"Nope, as in the lame human girl's name."

Engen put his arm around me and drew me to him. "Your name is awesome."

Lev eyed Engen's arm. "Nice to see you're already getting along."

I ducked out from under Engen's arm, leaving him looking confused.

One of the women that had been holding the kids back from mauling us stepped forward to take Dee away. It turned out she was heading in the opposite direction.

"Let's get this tour started," Lev said. A guy appeared out of thin air at his side. "This is my buddy, Eze."

Eze was approximately seventeen. He had the darkest skin I'd ever seen, a closely shaved head, wide nose, and honest smile.

"Which one of you is going to be working with the special needs child?" Eze wanted to know.

Engen lifted his pointer finger.

"I'll be taking you into the house to introduce you. I'm a friend of the family..."

Eze went on to say some more stuff, but since Lev was penetrating me with a most admiring gaze, I couldn't pay attention.

"How is your Swahili?" Eze asked Engen.

"It's pretty good, thanks to this one." Engen stuck a finger through my belt loop and tugged me closer. "I thought the family spoke English?"

"The family does, but Buvama has not yet learned. If that is going to be a problem for you, we could switch you with someone." Eze focused on me. "Perhaps her."

"Whoa." Lev placed his hand on Eze's chest. "Let's see how it goes before we talk about switching. Besides, Ida won't know anything regarding Buvuma's autism."

Eze kept his eyes fixed on Engen. "You *are* familiar with it?"

I couldn't stand the way Eze was glaring at my friend. I angled myself forward so I was in front of Engen. "He's read all the literature."

"He reads?" Eze asked.

"He's beyond capable of taking care of that kid." My fists shook. "So back off."

Eze and I examined each other. His eyes reflected only kindness so my fists relaxed.

Lev rubbed his hands together. "Okay, let's do it."

When we got to the door leading outside, Lev held it open and let everyone walk ahead of him. I was calming myself down from the confrontation with Eze, and was the last one out the door. Lev fell in step beside me.

"Ida?" Lev said my name like he was relishing it.

I slipped my hand in my front jeans pocket to grasp the yo-yo from Paul. "Yeah?"

"How was your flight?"

"Never-endingly boring."

"I bet," he chuckled nervously. "Man, I can't believe--"

Akiki's hand landed on Lev's shoulder, and he whispered something in his ear.

"Fine," Lev relented, and called for Stuart and Megan to follow him.

I gaped at Akiki, confused.

"In case you have forgotten, we have an additional stop on our tour," Akiki said meaningfully.

The doctor. The sad thing was that for a moment I *had* actually forgotten.

The rest of the group was ahead. I casually picked up the pace so it wasn't too obvious that I was trying to ditch Akiki and his moldy breath.

I caught up with Krista and she put her arm through mine.

"Don't you think it's beyond weird that Lev knew your name?" she asked.

"Considering I'm wearing a name tag, no."

"But you're forgetting that yours truly made it."

I peeled the tag off my shirt and held it up to see the lone letter 'I' printed on it. "Process of elimination. How many of the volunteers' names could begin with the letter I, besides Engen?"

"Ha. Ha," Krista said. "I get the shivers just remembering how slowly Lev ogled you. It was like he knew you."

I'm glad I wasn't the only one who'd noticed that. "Well, he doesn't."

"But you'd *let* him, wouldn't you?"

I was done with guys getting to know me, for the rest of my life. I was thinking about paying attention to where we were going, but the horde of kids had crowded us again. Only two were wearing shoes, all of them had on cut-off jean shorts, and not one wore a shirt. Their arms were long and skinny as they mimed taking a picture with a camera, so they must have recognized Krista as the photographer from the bus.

Engen checked behind his shoulder, I guess to make sure I hadn't been snatched up by a lion. A kid swung from each of his arms. He was the only person in Africa apart from Akiki who knew I was pregnant. I could probably keep it under wraps for an additional eight weeks if I was lucky.

After ten minutes of walking, we left Krista in the care of her supervisor, Telly, at the community center, and continued on the tour.

Nearby, I saw a woman hanging clothes to dry, and another repairing a roof on a circular hut. A door was open to a neighboring hut, and I saw a woman nursing a naked baby while yelling at two other children.

"Hey." Engen took my elbow. "Back at the VC, why'd you duck away when I put my arm around you?"

"Did I?"

"Feigning stupidity. Real cute." Engen held a hand out. "Am I allowed to hold your hand?"

I slapped his hand away. "Don't even think about it."

Engen snickered and tickled my waist.

A few minutes later, we stopped in front of a hut with a young boy around 10 years old sitting outside in the dirt. His hair was patchy and he had oversized teeth that jutted out from between his lips. One eye was slightly bigger than the other.

"Buvama, this is Engen." Eze lifted his hand to indicate Engen.

"He is going to be taking care of you."

The boy rocked back and forth and didn't even bother trying to focus on Eze. The door to the hut opened, and a sleazy-looking man walked out of it. Before the door swung shut, I caught a glimpse of a woman wearing only a t-shirt. When she saw me looking in, she gave an unabashed nod, took a puff off a cigarette with one hand and caressed her pregnant belly with the other.

Engen knelt down. "Hey there, Buv."

Buvuma shrieked and flapped his crooked hands in the air. Engen recoiled and shot up to a standing position.

"Watch him while I have a word with his mother," Eze ordered.

While we waited, Engen tried to get through to Buvama, but he just covered his ears and rocked back and forth. It seemed like many painful ages before Eze returned and told Engen that Buvuma's mother was in no condition to meet him today. Apparently Eze's work here was done, because he turned and ambled away. Engen exhaled in relief.

Akiki glanced at his phone. "We are ahead of schedule, so we will go to the orphanage before your doctor visit."

I rolled my eyes in annoyance. Basically, we had separated from Lev for nothing.

I was so sick of walking, that when I saw the orphanage I almost fell to my knees in thanks.

Akiki held the screen door open. "Ida, come with me to the kitchen."

"I'll see you in a bit," Engen called.

I was appreciating how peaceful it was here, when we passed an office with a homemade wooden sign hanging from a nail. The name 'Lev Rosen' was carved into it. I chewed on my thumbnail. For some incomprehensible reason it made me swoon.

"Sherry will be here for one more week." Akiki pushed open the metal double doors. "She'll help you get acquainted with the kitchen. Sherry, this is Ida," Akiki introduced us.

Sherry appeared to be in her early thirties. She had brown hair and hazel eyes. I liked her immediately.

"Nice to meet you," I greeted, and extended my hand.

"Likewise." Sherry shook my hand exuberantly. "I look forward to showing you the ropes."

"Do you work for YAHN?" I asked.

"No, I volunteered through my church," Sherry said. "I'm going to miss this place like you couldn't possibly fathom yet."

"I'm pretty nervous," I admitted.

"I'd fear for your sanity if you weren't. Help me bring lunch out?"

I looked at Akiki. He nodded his approval. "Meet me out back in ten minutes."

"What should I do?" I asked Sherry, once Akiki had left.

"Grab a tray."

I picked up a tray with ten bowls of chicken, rice, and carrots, and followed Sherry. She bumped the door near the back of the kitchen open with her butt, and that's when I heard it: twenty screaming kids who somehow managed to sound like a hundred.

I followed Sherry to the end of the long table and set a bowl down in front of a kid who appeared to be five years old. He beamed at me. I handed out more bowls, and was met with a smile from each child. I was tempted to smile back, but then I thought of my small apartment with the cockroach-infested bathroom and the infernal heat, and I just couldn't.

When I set down the last bowl, I stuck the tray under my armpit and scrutinized the table. The girls were wearing green dresses, and the boys were wearing white shirts with green shorts. All of the kids were either bald or had buzz cuts. Seeing the children with food in front of them gave me a feeling of accomplishment even though I hadn't been the one to prepare the meal.

A little girl touched my elbow and motioned for me to lean over. I put my ear to her lips and she whispered, "You're pretty."

I gave her an awkward pat on the head. "So are you, kid."

I glanced up and saw Lev leaning against the wall by the backdoor exit, arms crossed, watching me intently. Engen was leaning against the opposite side of the door, watching Lev apprehensively. I shared Engen's uneasiness. As great looking as Lev was, I found myself unsettled by his staring.

Sherry slipped the tray out from under my arm. "It's time for you to meet with Akiki."

As I neared the door, I tried not to look at Lev, but failed. He smiled. I didn't. That made him smile all the more.

Engen wrapped an arm around my waist and whispered, "Doctor time?"

I didn't answer Engen right away; I was too concerned with deciphering the change in Lev's eyes the moment Engen's hand made contact with my body. "Yep."

Engen and I followed Akiki to his truck. We shared a doubtful look when we realized that one of us was going to have to sit right next to Akiki. We had a conversation with our eyes until finally Engen relented and got in.

The road was so bumpy that I ended up closing my eyes. Not five minutes later, the truck stopped. I opened my eyes and saw that we were parked in front of a shabby-looking one-story house. There was a rhino-shaped sign outside with the words 'Health Centre' painted on it. Two men smoking cigarettes were milling around nearby.

"No," Engen said forcefully. "No way is Ida going to be treated at this dump. Hell, the VC is more sanitary than this place."

Engen had read my mind.

Akiki appeared offended as he got out of the truck. "They provide excellent sexual health services here."

Engen shook his head determinedly. "Take her to a real hospital."

"Dr. Milton is expecting her," Akiki said. "Come along."

Resigned, I opened the passenger door.

"Ida," Engen said. "You deserve better than this shack."

"We haven't seen the inside yet," I rationalized. "Don't judge a book by its cover and all that."

Engen nodded respectfully, and followed me.

Akiki waved at the men that were hanging around nearby.

"Wtalo, how are you?"

"Fine, Uncle," Wtalo responded, even though his mistrustful eyes were on me.

Akiki turned to me and Engen. "I need to speak with my nephew."

I watched Akiki walk toward the men, and noticed that farther down the dirt road there was a neighborhood that appeared to have small, well-kept houses on each side of the street. I found that interesting, considering the building Engen was holding the door open to was disturbingly ugly.

Inside, the waiting room held a round table with magazines and ten folding chairs. It was crowded in here, but all the chairs were available. Engen and I stood in line to check in. It went fairly quickly because nobody seemed to be here to see a doctor. Each person spoke to the lady at the counter, she'd hand them a small bag, and then they'd leave.

When Engen and I approached the counter, the frazzled-looking nurse in navy blue scrubs said, "Come back tomorrow."

"Pardon?" I asked.

"We do not have any more condoms," the nurse explained.

"That's not why we're here," I said.

Engen snorted. "It's kind of why we're here...if you think about it."

Sure, it was funny in a twisted way, but I didn't feel like smiling. I kept my facial expression neutral as I looked at the unamused nurse and said, "I have an appointment."

"Name," the nurse requested.

"Ida Denmark."

The nurse searched her notes. And then she burst out laughing. "I get it now," she roared. "That was a good joke, young man."

Engen joined in the laughter. I slowly turned to look up at him.

When he saw the stern look on my face, his laughter abruptly ended and he cleared his throat. "Too soon?" he asked.

"Go right on in to room 2," the nurse instructed through her fits of laughter.

While Engen and the nurse bonded over my misfortune, I met Dr. Milton. He was mid-forties and roughly 4 foot 10 inches, I estimated. He had my chart from my doctor in Minnesota and seemed pleased with the way the pregnancy was progressing. He made sure I had prenatal vitamins, and told me he wanted to see me back here in a month. He gave me his card and said I could call him anytime with questions or concerns.

I told him not to hold his breath.

THE ORPHANAGE

"A wide variety of people looking to adopt visit New Beginnings every day," Lev addressed me, Megan, and Stuart in his office the next morning. "It's important that you be upbeat and helpful to everyone, including the children. As you may have learned in your orientations, a high percentage of orphans are not truly orphaned due to their parents dying, but have been separated from their families due to poverty or abuse. For the most part, the kids here are pleasant, but keep in mind that each of them have been traumatized in some way."

Megan, Stuart, and I nodded solemnly.

"Adoption is a serious matter," Lev continued. "We work by appointment; Stu, that's your area. Becky, my assistant, will be training you. Megan, you'll make sure the children are clean, clothed, and rested. Ida," Lev locked eyes with me for three beats before continuing, "you're in charge of preparing breakfast and lunch. In between meals, you'll be busy cleaning dishes and leading arts and crafts. Any questions?"

"What do *you* do?" Megan asked.

"Each morning I give the kids two hours of schooling. I perform background checks on clients, and decide which ones get to adopt our kids." Lev leaned back in his chair and twirled a pencil between his fingers. "I also determine which orphans on the waiting list are in the most need of being accepted to New Beginnings. I order and pick up supplies, and fill in at nearby orphanages if needed. Additional questions?"

We shook our heads, no.

"Alright, go get started," Lev said.

The three of us turned around and filed toward the door.

"Ida?" Lev asked.

I swiveled my head, followed by my body, to look at him. "Yes, Lev?"

He gave me a half smile. "If you need help, my door is always open."

"I appreciate that." I turned and came face to face with his door. I wagered a glance at him. "You planned that, didn't you?"

"I saw Megan nudge the door closed with her foot." He jabbed his pencil over his shoulder. "The calendar of a&c activities is posted on the wall behind me. If you notice a project coming up and we don't have enough supplies for it, let me know."

"Okay." I slowly reached for the doorknob.

"Ida?"

"Yes, Lev?"

"I think we're going to enjoy working together."

"Sure, maybe." I made another play for the doorknob.

"Ida?"

"Yes, Lev?"

"Nothing," he sounded breathless. "I just wanted to hear you say my name again."

I resisted the urge to roll my eyes, and made my way to the kitchen.

"Sorry I'm late, Sherry. Lev had something to tell me."

"Lev's a great guy. Take this sprinkler system." She pointed to the ceiling. "He had it installed last year, and paid for it out of his own pocket."

"Nice." I took in all the food that lay before Sherry. "What are we making?"

"Scrambled eggs, sausage, and toast."

"That sounds like a lot of work," I remarked.

"It's a treat in honor of you, Megan, and Stuart coming on board."

Sherry went on to show me that making food for twenty could not only be easy, but kind of fun. I noticed that there was a cart in the corner. I brought it over to the refrigerator, loaded twenty mini milk cartons on it, and wheeled it out. Later, I would officially meet these kids for arts and crafts, and I had a feeling they would scare me when they weren't shoveling food in their faces.

A quick hour later, Lev was helping me prep for the art project. There were four small circular tables with five small chairs at each. I set a piece of construction paper in front of each chair, and Lev set down the crayons.

"Are you nervous, Ida?" Lev asked.

I cupped my hand around my ear. "What was that?"

Lev took a step closer and put his lips near my ear. His breath was warm, and it sent a tingle down my spine. "Are you nervous, Ida?"

"Yes. And I heard you the first time; I just wanted to hear you say my name again."

"No fair stealing my lines."

I tacked photos up on the cork board for references as the kids assembled in the rec room in an orderly fashion, with huge smiles on their faces.

"Hey, kids," I greeted. "Your task for the day is to draw a person, or people that you admire. Some examples are hanging up on the board. As you draw, I'm going to walk around and get to know each of you."

The kids shuffled in their chairs and faced their papers.

I took the charms on my necklace in between my thumb and forefinger, and slid them back and forth along the chain as I made my way to the first table. I went up to the girl who'd called me pretty yesterday, and knelt down beside her.

"What's your name?"

She took the end of a crayon out of her mouth. "Asya."

"Who are you going to draw?"

"Lev."

"Is he pretty terrific?"

"Ah-huh." She nodded.

I caught Lev's eye. He was looking at me like I hung the moon. "What's your name?" I asked the young boy sitting next to Asya.

"Adroa."

"Are you nine, Adroa?"

He nodded. "How'd you know?"

"I have a brother your age," I answered.

"What's his name?" Asya asked.

"Paul." I put my hand to my throat and massaged it. "Who are you drawing, Adroa?"

"My sister, Kya. Some men killed her for no reason," he said mechanically.

The kids started gabbing about the people they knew who died. Janelle's demise was still too fresh, so I moved on to the next table. Two of the little girls were drawing Lev. Lenny was five and didn't speak English. His paper was blank, so I explained the project to him in Swahili. I craned my neck around to see if that dopey look was still on Lev's face, but he was no longer in the room.

Before I knew it, the older kids were off to change clothes before heading outside to play football, and the smaller kids were being ushered away by Megan for a nap.

I collected the drawings and cleaned up. When everything was in order, I grabbed a blank sheet of construction paper and sat down in one of the little plastic chairs. I took a crayon and started drawing Paul. I'd just finished Gramps and was starting on my mom when I heard a light knock on the door.

"Completing your own project? Now that's devotion."

I looked over my shoulder. Lev had one arm stretched straight above him, fingers hooked around the top of the door frame. Under the other arm was a soccer ball. My legs tingled; it had been way too long since I'd played.

He walked into the room and twirled the ball on his pointer finger. "Do you want to play football with me and the kids?"

Mentally I shook my head, but when I opened my mouth I said, "Sure. You have the wrong ball, though."

"No, I don't."

"Ah, so you're one of those."

"One of what?"

I turned back to my drawing and reached for a green crayon. "You call soccer *football.*"

Lev chuckled and pointed at Gramps. "Is he one of your her-oes?"

"I guess."

"Mine, too. His eyes need to be lighter."

My head snapped up. "No, they don't."

He raised an eyebrow. "You and Ransom have the same color eyes, and they're a much lighter and softer shade of brown. Like faded wood. Your eye color is the only facial feature you don't share with your mother."

It wasn't a surprise that Lev knew Gramps, considering he used to live here, but, "You know what my *mom* looks like?"

"I know what your entire family looks like."

Wordlessly, I sprang to my feet. Lev snapped me out of my shock by tossing the ball at my chest, and I caught it reflexively.

"Let's go," he declared with a grin.

HE KNOWS ME

Everyone was gathered in the dining room to say goodbye to Sherry. I passed out slices of the cake I'd baked her, and noticed that there were two left. I took both plates, two forks, and went in search of my hardworking boss. Lev was in his office, typing away on an ancient-looking laptop. I didn't want to bother him, so I slowly backed away.

"Come in."

I held out the small paper plate. "Cake?"

"Absolutely. Please, sit." He gestured to the chair in front of his desk. "I'm working on Sherry's review and I could use your input."

I sat, obligingly. "I've only worked with Sherry for a week. It doesn't seem right that my opinion be included in her review."

Lev looked at me as if deciding what to do with me. "I've only worked with you for a week. Would you like to know how many pages I could fill praising you?"

Considering I didn't have anything unfavorable to say, I decided it couldn't hurt. "I feel relieved that Sherry was here for my first week. Thanks to her, I feel confident that I can run the kitchen by myself."

"Insightful." He tapped his long fingers against the keyboard.

I picked up my plate, pushed my chair back, and stood.

"Where are you going?" Lev asked around his gigantic bite of cake.

"To the kitchen, so you can get back to work."

"You aren't disrupting me." He then said the one thing I wanted to hear, "I'm sure you're wondering how I know your grandfather."

I promptly sat.

"He was out here twelve years ago with the U.N. We were in the middle of a water crisis." Lev took a second bite. "In fact, the same table you draw at in the rec room is the last place I saw him in person."

"How did you know I was related to him?"

"If you only knew the number of stories he's told me about you." Lev shook his head. "I don't think that man has forgotten a single thing you've done."

"That's odd," I said reflectively.

"How so?"

"It just is." I took a bite of cake and almost gagged. "Ish. This is terrible."

"I know." He jubilantly took another mouthful. "Your first?"

"And likely the last." I dumped my plate into the garbage. "Were you and Gramps close?"

"Quite. After my parents died, I lived with him for a year. He used to take me to Lake Victoria on his days off. Shortly before he went back to America, I was sent to live here at the orphanage." Lev pointed his plastic fork at the remaining cake. "Did you forget to put sugar in this? It's completely dreadful."

"Stop eating it then," I instructed.

He laughed. "Ransom still enjoying retirement?"

"I guess. He builds model airplanes and works on cars, mostly. When's the last time you spoke to him?"

"How old were you when you quit ballet?"

"Ten."

Lev choked down a spoonful of cake. "When did you dye your hair black?"

"A year ago." I couldn't stand the grossed-out look on his face anymore, so, since he wasn't going to, I picked up his plate and tossed it.

He glanced in the garbage can and then shifted his eyes back to me. "When did you refuse to take that test, the SAT?"

I blew out my lips. "A month ago."

"Then it was a month ago when I last spoke to him."

My jaw dropped. "You two are basically still in contact?"

Lev smiled. "Basically."

So this was the guy from Africa that Gramps spoke to on the phone a few times a year. Paul was going to be so jealous when I told him I knew the mystery guy. I, on the other hand, was chafed. Aside from the recent chats regarding Africa, Gramps rarely spoke to me, yet he talked to Lev all the time *about* me.

"Why didn't he just adopt you if he loved you so much?" I asked, angrily.

Lev's breath faltered at my tone. "Did I do something wrong?"

"Of course not. Things with Gramps are complicated is all."

Feeling embarrassed, I turned to leave, and ran into a tall local girl. The first thing I noticed was her thick Afro. My eyes shifted away from the burnt orange color of her hair, and set upon two large brown eyes.

"Baba." Lev stood, clearly taken aback. "What are you doing here?"

"I thought I'd let you take me to lunch." While saying this, Baba surveyed me from head to toe, deemed me unworthy, and locked eyes on Lev.

I was going to make my escape when Lev grabbed the crook of my elbow and drew me to him. "This is Ida Denmark, Ransom's granddaughter. Remember him?"

"Of course." A change passed through Baba's bulbous eyes. "You just got here? That's too bad."

I nodded adamantly. "I agree."

Lev rubbed my shoulder. "Ida's a fantastic cook. I just had the best cake I've ever tasted in my life."

I looked up at him in appreciation of his joke. He was grinning adoringly at me.

Baba glared at me. "Looks like you could use some more cake. What do you weigh, forty pounds?"

"Thirty-eight," I answered.

Lev burst into honest laughter and held me tighter.

Baba pressed her lips into a semi-thin line. "Can we do lunch, Levy?"

"Um, Ida, did you still need me to go over that thing with

you?" Lev asked.

He didn't want to be alone with this girl. I recognized the signs from when I tried to blow off Dan.

"If you wouldn't mind, Levy, I mean, Mr. Rosen, I'd love for you to go over that information with me," I said, playing along.

"I guess I'll see you around then, Baba." Lev waited to let me go until she was gone. "I've tried to elude that girl for half of my life," he shared. "She just won't get the hint."

"I suppose you could do worse," I said, still feeling little ripples of sensation from where he'd touched me.

Lev was busy roaring with laughter, so I made my exit.

Just because I had "Gramps" issues didn't give me the right to take them out on Lev. It was Gramps' business that he chose to build an enduring relationship with an orphan as opposed to his own granddaughter. The way I'd handled my emotions during that conversation with Lev only increased my desire for solitude.

Lev found me later that day after a&c. I was sitting in the rec room working on another drawing of Paul. The subject of the kids' art project today had been someone who makes you laugh.

"You wanna play, or are you still mad at me for knowing Ransom?" Lev asked, giving me sad eyes.

"I was never mad at you," I replied. "It's hard to explain."

He tossed the ball back and forth between his hands. "Oh, one of those 'it's not you, it's me' kind of things. I get that brush-off line from the ladies all the time."

"Are you forgetting that I was an accessory to *you* brushing off a lady earlier today?" I went back to coloring in Paul's t-shirt. "Besides, I can't imagine there's a girl strong-willed enough to brush you off."

"It happened a week ago." He whistled and tossed the ball at me. "I tried to shake this gorgeous girl's hand, but was denied. Then to top it off, she went and shook a different guy's hand right in front of me. It was the ultimate rejection."

I threw the ball back to him on my way out the door. He pretended like the force of my throw caused him to stumble backward. I could tell he hung out with kids way too much by his style of playful mannerisms.

He jogged to catch up with me. "What do I have to do to get a smile out of you?"

I opened the door leading outside, and the heat hit me hard. "You could start by saying something funny."

"What?" he said in a falsetto tone. "I've used all my best material on you."

We made our way to the field. "I guess my personality is as dry as this weather."

"There *is* a smile in you, and I'll find it." He jogged backward to join the game. "I feel like winning today, so you be on Adroa's team."

I bit the inside of my cheek to keep from remarking on how I actually was a decent player, I just didn't want to get carried away and risk hurting the kids. I joined Adroa's side and was met with a chorus of groans from that team.

"Come on, guys," I complained to the kids. "I'm not that terrible."

We lost 10-2.

STALKED

The week passed without anything eventful happening, unless another run-in with Baba counted. Lev and I had been shooting hoops at the net attached to the New Beginnings' garage, our after-work tradition, when she showed up. Lev asked me to cover for him so he could hide. Turned out it was me she was looking for. She wanted to inform me that this was her home and that I had no right to interfere with her pursuit of Lev.

I'd laughed it off at the time, but then told Dee all about it on our way to the VC for breakfast. It was 5:30 that morning and the sun wasn't up yet. Dee had had trouble sleeping. Dee and her supervisor's everyday job was to make house calls to assess the needs of families affected by HIV and AIDS, and it was starting to wear on her mind.

I'd had trouble sleeping as well. My sleeping problem was attributed to what was going on inside my body. My mom had insisted I bring along one of her pregnancy books, so I'd stuffed that into my work bag. Later, I planned to read up on the light, consistent spotting I'd been experiencing, to see if it was normal or worrisome.

Dee threw her hair into a bun as we walked. "Sister Luisa told me there's going to be a dance in a few weeks."

I cringed. "Do you like those things?"

"It's not the type of dance you're thinking of in the gymnasium at school. It's outdoors, and there's going to be a bonfire." She trotted in front of me and grabbed my hands. "The four of us should go."

"Sure."

"I might see if they need help there, maybe serve drinks or something."

"Do you get extra credit for that?"

"No. Do you get extra credit for playing soccer every day?" Dee countered.

I felt my face warm just as a *clacking* sound reached our ears. Dee gripped my arm as we passed the stranger responsible for making the noise, noting that he'd mastered the art of cradling two semi-large rocks in one arm. He pointed his chin at me and crooked a finger, beckoning me over. Rock dude had unkind, brown eyes, and a leer that sent a shiver down my spine. However, I nodded back at him in acknowledgment and then faced forward.

Dee picked up the pace. "Why did you nod at him?"

"I don't know," I replied.

"I can't believe you aren't creeped out." Dee's whole body shivered.

"If he was a wicked guy, would he be standing underneath a light making a racket? No."

"Like my mom says, it takes all kinds to make the world go 'round."

It struck me as funny that the woman who spent all summer by her swimming pool drinking mojitos thought it took all kinds to make the world go 'round. I pondered that for a moment, and didn't even notice that the clattering sounded closer. Thankfully, we were nearing the VC.

Dee clutched her VC key card. "Do you think he knows we're volunteers?"

"Your designer jeans don't exactly scream 'native,'" I said, never too tired to point out the obvious. "If he's any good at being a criminal, he probably knows we're staying in the volunteer housing."

"Oh, you're so screwed."

"Me?"

"It was you he was looking at."

I guess it was up to me to take care of him, then. "What do you want, man?" I asked, while turning.

I came face to face with a sweaty, blonde guy wearing a white tank top and black jogging pants.

"I'd like a cure for HIV, malaria to be a thing of the past, and all the orphans in the world to be adopted by loving people. If all that were to happen, I wouldn't say no to a slice of key lime pie." Lev arched one eyebrow. "What do *you* want?"

"I'll have what you're having except I want the pie first." I clutched the right side of my ribcage, feeling out of breath.

"We're glad to see you." Dee reached in her purse and pulled out some lip gloss. "Ida was being followed by a scary guy."

Lev's eyes widened. "*Followed*?"

"I don't think 'followed' is the right word," I said.

"You're right," Dee agreed. "Stalked would be the more appropriate word."

"You're telling me there was a strange, potentially dangerous man following you, and your plan was to *confront* him?" Lev asked with concerned eyes.

"Yep." My eyes lowered to his chest, traveled down his abs, and rested on his thighs. Horrified when I realized that I was blatantly checking him out, I quickly changed the subject. "What brings you out this fine man?" I cringed at my error. "Fine morning?"

"Running. I try to get in five kilometers a day," Lev said, graciously letting my blunder pass.

"That explains it," Dee muttered.

Lev looked at me questioningly. Even though I knew she meant it explained why he was in such excellent shape, I shrugged.

Lev set his hand on the back of my neck. "Please be careful. I wouldn't be able to stand it if anything bad happened to you."

"Worried you wouldn't find a replacement gourmet chef on such short notice?"

His eyes smiled. "Exactly."

I watched him jog away and inadvertently sighed.

"You basically told Lev that he was a fine man," Dee kindly pointed out.

"That I did."

◆ ◆ ◆

Later that day after a&c, I went to the kitchen and wedged a stool between the fridge and the wall so I could have privacy while I perused my damn pregnancy book. Engen's boarding pass, which was doubling as his bookmark, fell out when I opened the book. I picked up the ticket, put it back where it was, and pondered over how it would have been easier to just call up the information on my phone, but it seemed to mean something to Mom that I learn about my pregnancy from the same book that she'd learned about hers.

I'd just found the section that referenced what I was experiencing, spotting, when I heard the door to the kitchen swing open.

"Ida? You in here?"

Megan! I lifted my butt and sat atop the book to conceal it. She must have heard the creak of the stool, because footsteps were nearing. I rested my elbow on the windowsill, set my chin in my hand, and gazed outside.

"What are you doing back here?" Megan asked.

"I was thinking that I wanted to paint this view."

"The busted-up garage?"

"You see a dilapidated garage, I see a thing of beauty," I deadpanned, as I turned to look at her. She was wearing a black tank top and wide black shorts that went to her calves.

"Our fearless leader is worried," Megan said, unconcerned. "He mentioned that he usually finds you in the rec room before the game."

"It slipped my mind."

"You look...raised." Megan lifted her black penciled-in eyebrows. "What are you sitting on?"

I made sure my knees were firmly locked together. "Nothing."

"I should call Lev back here so he can see for himself that I found you."

"Wait." I sighed. "I was reading a book."

"What book?"

"None of your business."

Megan turned toward the exit. "Hey, Lev!"

"This." I sprang to my feet and held the book out with both hands.

She cricked her neck, stared at the book in awe, and then at me. "Oluchi was right."

"Who?"

"This psychic priest lady I met."

I scrunched up my face. "I'd appreciate it if you didn't tell anyone."

"I take it you don't want the baby."

I grabbed my bag and stuffed the book in. "Who helped you figure that out? A shaman?"

I pushed the double doors open. Down at the end of the hall, Lev was pacing. He saw me and made an instant beeline.

I braced myself as he pulled me to his chest. "Whoa, this is unnecessary."

"You're always in the rec room when I come to get you for the game," Lev spoke into the hollow of my cheek.

I touched my fingertips to his back, sort of half-assedly returning his hug. "I was trying not to be so predictable."

"I'm still on edge from this morning when Dorian said someone was following you."

I pushed back from him. "I can look out for myself."

"I still worry." Lev walked out of the front door and held it open.

I followed him out. The soccer game was already underway. Lev turned around without warning, causing me to run into him.

"If something happened to you, I would be dev--" he wet his lips with his tongue, "deemed responsible. I don't want to lose my job because some volunteer got herself kidnapped."

I silently told my jaw that if it fell open, I'd rip it off. I wasn't going to react to being called '*some* volunteer.' I was some volunteer. And this volunteer was losing her mind by imagining she meant something more to him. Not that I necessarily wanted to mean more to him. OK, so the jury was still out on that one.

An hour later, I was ready to faint from exhaustion. I needed to reconsider this whole being physically active thing.

"I'm going to grab a shower." Lev stopped outside the employee restroom and eyed me. "Unless you want one first?"

I was dripping sweat. "I didn't bring anything along."

"I have a towel, soap, and shampoo. I even have an extra shirt if you want to get out of that one." He cocked an eyebrow. "Although, I do enjoy the drenched-in-sweat look on you."

"A shower would be great."

Lev opened the bathroom door. "After you."

He took a key out of his pocket and opened the middle locker. He unhooked a big brown towel and tossed it at me. It was slightly damp. When he went back inside the locker, I quickly put his towel to my nose and inhaled. It smelled wonderfully of honey and African sandalwood. I was overcome with a bout of lust. Lev handed me a fresh bar of soap. I psychotically wished that he'd given me a used bar until I realized that he'd use this one after me. There was only the one towel, so that meant he'd be using that same one after I did, too. I wondered if he'd considered this, and if so, did he find it as intimate as I did? I met his eyes. By the heat of his gaze I knew the answer was yes.

I brought the soap to my nose. "I'm going to smell all manly now."

"You think I'm manly?" Lev made a move to set his hand on the doorknob, missed, and since he was counting on the doorknob to support his weight, almost fell over. "You might want to lock this."

"I believe the main threat of intrusion is already in here."

Lev took the hint and left. I locked the door, got in the shower and thought of nothing but Lev throughout it. I dried off and glimpsed the open locker. There'd be no harm in taking Lev up on his offer of a clean shirt. I plucked a bright blue one off a hook, fit it over my head and almost passed out when I smelled the inside of it. Delicious.

I hung the towel over the shower rod, then plodded down the hall to let him know that the shower was free. I found him in his office with a short, twenty-something, blonde girl. Her hand was on his bicep and he was laughing hysterically. I swiveled around, my wet hair flinging beads of water every which way.

"Ida, come in," Lev said through his laughter. "Meet Matilda. She cooks dinner for the kids and not only stays overnight here a few days a week, which is a godsend, but sees the kids safely to bed. Well, most of the time it's safely."

The hand that was still on his bicep squeezed in delight, and they started laughing again. I noticed that Matilda was wearing a wedding ring. What kind of married woman goes around squeezing guys' biceps?

"Isn't Lev the best?" Matilda asked in a southern accent.

"Um...he's okay."

That caused Matilda to laugh louder, and Lev to stop. She was adorable with her heart-shaped face and cornflower blue eyes. I felt a burst of anxiety in my gut at the thought that maybe Lev liked her. Maybe he'd been pining after her and trying to break up her marriage for years.

I was for sure losing my mind.

"I've seen you walking home with that tall, handsome guy. Is he your sweetheart?" Matilda asked.

"Ah, no," I clarified. I watched Lev wander over to his desk and fool around with the stapler. "Engen and I have known each other since we were four."

"And nothing's popped up between the two of you in *all* that time?" Matilda persisted.

There'd been several instances where Engen and I'd gotten hot and heavy, but what business was it of hers? "Just friendship."

"Satisfied?" Matilda dragged her eyes back to Lev and stuck her hand out. "Paycheck please."

Lev's lips parted and his face turned apple-red as he handed her an envelope.

Matilda waved it in the air. "It was nice meeting you, darling."

"Ditto," I said.

As she walked past me, I caught a whiff of some flowery perfume that didn't agree with my stomach.

"Shirt looks good on you," Lev complimented.

Realizing I had nothing to say to him, I left to go clean up the rec room. I then went to the kitchen. As I stirred a pitcher of lemonade, I thought about how Lev was the most annoying person in the world; he was too cheerful and friendly. Since he wasn't going to stop being him, I had to start being me. I wasn't going to allow myself to think I was special to him.

I tasted the lemonade to make sure it wasn't too sour. It was.

"You're testy," Lev observed.

Startled over hearing his voice, I dropped the wooden spoon. I bent down to pick it up.

Lev set a hand lightly on my shoulder. "Are you ignoring me?"

I was starting to feel lightheaded at his nearness. I shrugged his hand off and found some sugar.

"You *are*." He smiled. "How fascinating."

Lev leaned against the counter and watched me. His hair was wet and slicked back, and there were wet spots showing through his t-shirt. Could he do anything that wasn't sexy? I turned away from him to rinse off the spoon.

Lev ran his fingers between my shoulder blades. "After you tell me what's wrong, do you promise to go back to ignoring me?"

"Matilda," I blurted out. I silently admonished myself that I'd allowed his reverse psychology to work on me again.

Lev put his forehead between his thumb and middle finger. "I cannot believe she grilled you about that friend of yours. What's his name, Edward, Edgar?"

I gave him my best I-wasn't-born-yesterday look. "It's not that."

"What then?"

She squeezed your bicep and made you laugh like a crazy person. "She gets paid to work here."

Lev laughed. "You kill me."

I tapped the spoon against his chest. "I think you're easily amused."

He ran his hand down my damp hair. "I'd pay you double Matilda's salary if I could keep you."

My breath caught at the seriousness in Lev's eyes as I said, "I'm going back to ignoring you now."

"I've been dying to ask you out, and I think I finally found the nerve," he declared.

I dropped the clean spoon.

Lev was grinning like a fool. "There's this dance... never mind, you're ignoring me, so there'd be no point, right?"

I turned away from him.

"Your wet hair is very becoming," he added softly, before leaving.

I tugged on my lower lip. Lev was curious to know if Engen and I were a couple. So curious in fact, he'd been discussing it with Matilda. I smiled and rubbed my cheek against my shoulder, feeling the cotton from the shirt that belonged to him. Perhaps I'd ignore him again tomorrow.

THREE WEEKS DOWN

"Honey, it's Mom. Your brother and Dan said they've been in contact with you, so I thought I'd give it a try. I hope you don't think that every time you confide in us we're going to ship you off to a foreign country." She laughed nervously. "Please call me. I miss you and love you dearly. Of all my children, you're the most mine."

"It's true." Engen laid on his stomach on my bed next to me, mirroring my position with legs bent, feet facing the ceiling. "Marilyn's like your dad and Paul's, well..."

"Paul's a mystery of epic proportions."

"His genius is misunderstood," Engen added.

"I want to talk to her, but I think it'd be the proverbial straw, and I can't break my back out here." I yawned. "From now on, will you listen to my mom's messages and then let me know the highlights?"

His eyelashes flickered as he looked at me. "Of course."

Engen's phone and mine were linked, so I could see that he had a message. "Wanna listen to yours?" I asked.

"Already did. Doug, not Brittany."

Doug was married to Engen's middle sister, Kaylee. He could be pretty overbearing.

"I wasn't going to judge."

His leg fell into mine. "Your ability to not judge is how we ended up in this predicament."

"Africa?"

"Nope." He shook his head. "The other predicament we're trapped in."

59

"We're in two predicaments?" I stared into his gray eyes and felt myself drift. "I wasn't aware."

He ran his bare foot up and down my ankle. "I can't wait until you're aware."

"You could just tell me what I'm meant to know."

Engen's tongue slipped through his lips, causing a shiver to run through my body. He opened his mouth, however, no words came out. I set my head on my arm, closed my eyes, and listened to the sounds of a flute drifting through the open window.

Engen cleared his throat. "You're my favorite part about life."

"Back at ya."

"But, I know I don't stand a chance after what I did last fall."

I hadn't realized I'd been holding my breath until it rushed out. I turned onto my back and sat up so quickly my head became dizzy. "I'd better go, I'm walking to work with Stuart."

I left the room, but stood outside the door with my back against the wall while Engen yelled muffled swear words into my pillow.

Why did things have to be so complicated? I thought, as I pushed off the wall. I exited the apartment and met up with Stuart outside. We didn't get far before Engen caught up with us. The three of us walked and discussed music before Engen requested, "Dance with me?"

A smile spread across my lips. "In this heat, on this dusty road, with those men arguing by that broken-down van, and that cow staring at us?"

"Yes, why not, for sure, and most definitely," Engen listed.

"I think it would make the cow jealous," I said in low voice.

In response, he put his hands on my waist and pulled me close. I slung my arms around his shoulders, and we slow danced by the side of the road.

"Um, Ida?" Stuart asked. "Should I wait?"

"No," I responded.

After Stuart took off, Engen asked, "Is it still cool if I bring Buv to the orphanage this morning for a visit?"

"You bet. I'll be the one in the apron, laughing maniacally as I pour arsenic in the kids' oatmeal."

"Ida," Engen said reproachfully. "You will *not* be giving arsenic to those children."

"No?" I raised an eyebrow. "What do you suggest, then?"

"Cyanide."

I slapped a palm to my forehead. "That's right, we have all that extra."

Complications temporarily forgotten, I set my head against Engen's chest and sighed in contentment.

By the afternoon, I was back to obsessing over my mother's message and coming to the conclusion that I was going to call her later, when Lev came into the kitchen and plopped down onto a stool like he owned the place.

Did he own the place? I shrugged and went back to washing the lunch dishes.

After a few moments of silence, Lev joined me at the sink with a faded dish towel slung over his shoulder. He picked up a plate and started to rinse it. His eyes shone brightly from the sunlight streaming through the window and his hair looked golden. I decided to focus on my chore instead of him.

After the dishes were rinsed, we fell into a routine: I dried, handed them to Lev, and he put them away. Occasionally we bumped elbows or hips. It all went unacknowledged, though. I started humming one of Paul's many made-up songs. Lev whistled to accompany my humming. After the dishes were dried and put away, I started to ask him if something was wrong, when Stuart's head popped into the kitchen.

"Lev, that Baba chick is here. She said you were expecting her."

"Thanks, Stu." Lev pulled the towel from his shoulder and set it on the sink, leaving his eyes on me.

I glanced out the window. The girl who Lev claimed to avoid for half his life, he was now *expecting*?

"I'd been having a horrible day up until now," Lev remarked, fondly, as he headed for the door. "Thank you for making it better."

I didn't see Lev for the rest of the day.

The next day he was absent as well. I went to visit Engen after the long, Lev-free day of work, and was just in time to join him and Buvama for a walk. Good thing I'd just pounded two bottles of Coke, otherwise I wouldn't have had the energy.

"Talk to a female about this," Engen implored. "We live with two. One of them is even sort of sane."

I'd been telling him about Lev helping me with the dishes yesterday.

"But you're a guy. You have first-person knowledge of what's going on inside that cotton ball you call a brain."

"Tell me why you care," Engen said peevishly, then yelled, "Leave that dog alone, Buv!"

"It was a peaceful moment for me," I explained.

Engen sighed deeply. "What were you and Lev discussing?"

"Haven't you been listening?" I slapped his arm. "Nothing."

"That's right. *Nothing*. So then—put that dog down, Buv!" Engen ran ahead to wrangle the small dog from Buv's tight grasp. I caught up with them and waited patiently for Engen to remember that he'd been in the middle of a thought.

"Okay, so then some chick showed up and Lev told you that you made his day."

"See, you aren't so terrible at this," I congratulated him. "Now diagnose the situation."

"I just don't see where the problem comes in."

"If *I* had the power to make his day so fabulous, why would he need another girl?"

Engen gave me a you-belong-behind-bars look. "You make me indescribably happy. I'd rather be with you than anyone else in the world. You're breathtaking and fun to be with."

I put a hand on my hip. "This isn't helping."

He flicked a mosquito off my shoulder. "You don't look pregnant at all. Your body's just as perfect as ever."

"Did you watch me change into my pajamas?" I asked.

His face turned red. "Are you referring to a *particular* time?"

"The other night when you said that I didn't have to leave the room to change, because you were so wiped out that even if you wanted to peek, you couldn't, because your eyes were incapable of opening?" I said in one breath.

"No. Maybe. Yes! Your boobs are killer. I've always had a thing for them. There was a time when you enjoyed the attention I bestowed upon them."

There was no denying that.

He gave me a lazy half-smile. "If what they say about pregnancy is true, your melons are going to get even bigger."

"By 'they' you're undoubtedly referring to medical professionals, not horny teenage boys, right?"

"Definitely the latter." Engen leaned over and kissed my flushed cheek. "Watching you change clothes is the purest thing I've done to you."

This was true. "Can we go back to when you were trying to help me figure out why Lev took off with Baba?"

"Right. That. You're hot, but you're not exactly warm, see what I'm saying?" He raised his eyebrows at me.

I had nothing to offer in reply.

Engen elaborated, "There are some guys who want a girl who'll take care of him, show him he's special and desirable. You aren't that girl."

I punched him in his kidney.

"Ouch! What the hell was that for?"

"The fact that you needed to remind me of *that night* twice in one week is why we're in this predicament."

"I wasn't including myself in that group of guys. You asked for advice, I was giving it." He rubbed his lower back. "I knew when I saw that empty soda bottle I was going to wind up getting clocked at some point."

"Bad!" Buvama shouted.

"Ida *is* awful, isn't she?" Engen encouraged.

"You taught him to say 'bad?'" I asked.

"No, his mom calls him that all the time."
Suddenly my problems didn't seem so awful.

DIRTY LAUNDRY

Since I was already doing something boring, collecting my dirty clothes for our building's caretaker Selma to wash, I decided now would be a good time to call Dan. With the eight-hour time difference between us, we had previously agreed on trying to touch base once every two weeks.

"Good evening," Dan answered.

"And a good morning to you," I responded, noting the sun shining brightly through his bedroom window.

We chatted easily for a few minutes before the conversation started to lag.

"What do you do on your down time there?" Dan wondered with a yawn.

"Play games and watch movies at the Volunteer Center, explore, have wild orgies," I replied dryly, throwing another dirty shirt in the laundry bag. "How is the golf course?"

Dan was spinning a hockey puck on his desk. "Boring and pointless."

"At least you're getting paid."

"Let's not talk discuss work. I'm sick of hearing about the orphans and your boss."

I sat down on my bed and started to braid my long hair. "I don't talk about my boss, do I?"

"Only every third sentence." Dan's hand slammed down on the puck. "I believe Lev's been gone for two whole days now."

Engen knocked on the door jamb. "Is your laundry bag ready?"

I shook my head.

"Well get on it," he ordered with a smile. "Hey, Dan. How's

MN?"

While the guys talked on my phone, I returned to my task. I was living out of my suitcase, which made the job harder than it should have been. Was there some rule that I had to wear clean clothes to work? It's not like I'd get in trouble. It's not like I had a boss who actually showed up. I continued to shove more clothes into the bag.

Engen tapped my shoulder, and I jumped.

"I was watching you act out your internal monologue on your face," Engen said. "Something bothering you?"

"No."

Engen took the laundry bag from me and tested the weight. "There's a ton of clothes in here," he commented.

"Isn't that the idea?"

"I suppose. Oh, and I accidentally disconnected with Dan. Sorry," he said with a cheesy grin.

"I forgive you."

Here's a piece of advice: never bag up your laundry unless your head is clear. Last night, I sent away every article of clothing I'd brought, apart from the pj's I'd been wearing, to be washed. My third week in Africa was coming to a close and I was desperately searching through Dee's closet for something to wear. I settled for a flowy peach skirt. Dee was a good four inches shorter than I was, so the hem barely graced my knees. I paired the skirt with a white tank top, pulled on a pair of Engen's white socks followed by my sneakers, and I was ready to go.

When I got to the orphanage, I noticed that the energy had somehow shifted. On my way to the kitchen I saw that the door to the storage closet was open, so I pushed it closed. With all the cleaning supplies in there, we were told to keep the door shut in case the kids wandered by and were in the mood to drink chemicals.

The door reopened. I turned around, walked back, and closed it again. I gave it a defiant nod and continued to the kitchen. It sprung open once more. When I turned around, I saw a blonde head sticking out. He hadn't seen me, so I walked back to the door and shut it.

"C'mon, it's dark in here," Lev grumbled, and opened the door. He was holding a small pad of paper and a pencil. Both items fell at the same time, and his jaw dropped. "Holy hell. I mean," his eyes were trained on my bare legs, "wow."

I bent down, collected his stuff, and handed it to him.

He lifted his eyes to my face and took his things. "You're stunning."

I nodded at the door behind him. "What are you doing in there?"

"Inventory." His eyes fell back to my legs.

"I'll just--"

Lev seized my hand and pulled me into the closet. Before I had time to check and make sure I'd brought my stomach with me, my back was up against a metal shelf.

I gave the brooms, pails, and sponges a once-over. "What am *I* doing in here?"

"Welcoming me back." He set the pad and pencil on the shelf behind me.

"Did you go somewhere?" I asked casually.

"I was gone for two days. Didn't you notice?" His tone was playful as he took a step closer to me.

"Maybe."

"I missed you," Lev whispered. "I almost called you a few times, but something always seemed to pop up."

"You're only supposed to call us volunteers if it's an emergency."

"Who said it wasn't?" Lev looked me up and down and gave a low whistle. "If I told you that you were incredibly sexy, would you report me to YAHN?"

"I'm wearing men's socks with a skirt," I scoffed. "If you think that's sexy, I'd have to report you to a psychiatrist."

"Wearing men's socks with a skirt is my newest requirement in a girl."

"You have requirements?"

Lev pressed his lips to my cheekbone. "It's a fairly new thing."

"How new?"

"Around forty-five seconds."

The door slammed shut, and I was startled into grabbing his waist. "It *is* dark in here."

Lev put his hands on top of my wrists to secure them to his waist. "I've had a few dreams starring you that started out similar to this."

"If it was this dark in your dream, how can you be sure it was me?" I challenged.

Lev touched his nose to mine, proving he didn't have a hard time seeing me in the dark. "Because it's always been you."

I tried to convince myself that I wasn't enjoying this. I sensed his nose on the top of my shoulder, followed by a sniff. "Are you...smelling me?"

"Mmmhmm. It's strictly for research purposes." Lev inhaled my hair. "Your scent will be a useful detail for future dreams."

"Well, if it's in the name of research, smell away, Mr. Sandman."

Lev laughed, put his arms around me, and held me to his chest. Feeling at ease now, I rested my head there. I concentrated on the sounds going on inside of his body: the thrum of his heart and his throat when he swallowed, before subtly stepping out of his arms. I felt around for the doorknob, twisted it, and flooded the room with light.

Lev blinked. "Is something wrong?"

"Absolutely not."

Lev eyed me sheepishly. "I should've told you that I'd be gone for a couple of days."

I waved my hand as if I were greeting him. "You don't owe me any explanations. It's no concern of mine what you do, or who you do it with."

The muscles in his jaw clenched. "Good to know."

Except that it didn't sound like it was good for him to know. "You did mention Tuesday that you were having a horrible day. You could've talked to me. I would never judge you or laugh at you."

"My mother's best friend passed away. She got the news Tuesday morning and called me to see if I'd go with her to pay her respects." Lev picked up the pad of paper and secured the pencil behind his ear.

I covered my heart with my hand. "I'm sorry."

"It was Baba's grandmother who died, and Baba was kind enough to give us a ride with her to Jinja."

I wished I didn't have firsthand knowledge of what Lev's mom was feeling. I choked back tears as a vision of a young, curly-haired Janelle with grape Popsicle all over her face sprang into my mind.

While I stood there feeling depressed, Lev seemed more than content with ogling me.

I jutted my thumb over my shoulder. "I should go."

"Stop by my office later so we can discuss any supplies you might need." He raised his eyebrows. "Among other things."

"I wasn't trying to break the nothing-above-the-knee rule. This skirt was a mistake."

"I disagree. I hope you'll share the story with me, though."

"Maybe the abridged version," I said mysteriously. "Bye, boss."

"So long, beautiful-smelling volunteer."

DREAMS SUCK

A very real dream involving Janelle caused my eyes to pop open, so I was staring at the dark ceiling. I turned my head to the left and saw Engen watching me from his bed, his right eye twitching.

His right eye involuntarily twitched whenever he was thinking of Janelle, and since I had a tendency to talk in my sleep, I had a feeling it was my fault he was awake.

I put my hand to my steaming hot forehead. "Sorry."

He sat up and put his feet on the floor. "What was the dream about?"

"It was a memory of one of our fake shopping trips." Janelle and I would try on the goofiest clothes imaginable, tell the salesperson to hold them for us because we'd forgotten our money, and then never go back.

"I remember those." Engen arched his back and scratched it.

I turned onto my side so I was facing him. He was smiling fondly at me. I let my hand support my head and described the dream, "I was trying on dippy outfits and Janelle was trying on normal ones. When I asked her why she'd waste our trip trying on clothes she'd actually buy, she said it was because she'd met a guy at her dad's billiard hall, and they were going out."

Engen clenched his fists. "Jamison."

"I told her she was crazy to date an older guy who played pool all day. Janelle said she didn't even like him that much," I recalled. "She just wanted to ride on his motorcycle."

Engen clutched his abdomen. "Please don't say any more."

"You asked," I reminded him.

"I was hoping it'd be one of the good times."

"Like when she slammed that baseball into your eye?"

Engen ran his pointer finger over his right eyebrow. "I took so much heat for having two girls for best friends."

I sat up and put my feet on the floor. Our knees touched. "The three of us used to play baseball and football for hours. It's not like we sat around painting your toenails or--"

Engen reached over and covered my mouth. "I wouldn't have had it any other way."

I swallowed. "You didn't talk to me at her funeral. I needed you. Not Morelli, *you*."

He touched a finger to my forehead. "I know how this mind operates, and you never needed me."

"I hate that you think that." I stood, turned, and sat next to him on his bed. "And it really pissed me off that you didn't need me after she died."

"I *always* need you. I shouldn't have abandoned you after her death." Engen took a deep breath. "I came here to repair what I broke between us."

"You're here because you *broke* those douche bags at the hockey game for taunting Brittany."

"I wasn't avenging her," he said, as if it should have been obvious. "We weren't even together at that time."

"Then why did you go so crazy?"

"After I found out you'd applied for YAHN, I begged my parents to allow me to enroll. I figured attacking Dan would be enough to convince them that I was heading down a dark path, but it wasn't." Engen took a deep, steadying breath. "The fight at the hockey game was a means to drive the point home to my parents that I wasn't going to get better without help."

"You had no way of knowing that we'd both be accepted, though."

"I didn't, but somehow Janelle did." Engen set his hand on my thigh.

My breath hitched at his touch. "She spoke to you?"

"Sure. You don't talk to her? Don't feel her?"

"Yeah, but it's just our imaginations."

"All I know is that we're here together." Engen tucked my hair behind my ear. "Flying to another continent doesn't even begin to scratch the surface of what I'd do in order to be with you."

I was angry at Engen for his carelessness. I stood. "I'm going for a walk."

Engen yawned. "I'll come with you."

I fished in my suitcase for a clean pair of jeans. "I wanna go alone."

"At least tell me what direction you're heading in."

I pulled my freshly washed jeans on under my nightie. Not gonna lie, the jeans were a tight fit. I picked a random spot on the wall and pointed at it. "That way."

"I'll never be able to sleep, knowing you're roaming around by yourself."

"I'll bring my phone." I changed the setting to 'vibrate' and slipped it in my pocket.

"Call me often."

I saluted him and left. When I got outside, I took a deep breath and decided to walk toward the doctor's office. There was a cute little neighborhood over there that might be worthy of further exploration.

I walked approximately a kilometer when I noticed a goat across the road. My phone vibrated. I reached into my jeans pocket. "Answer. Wasn't I supposed to call you?"

Engen sighed, perturbed. "Like that was going to happen."

"Well, I'm doing stupendous. Done." Engen's image disappeared. I kept the phone in my hand. It was too much work to put it back in my pocket.

"Where are you headed, goat?" I asked it. I heard a person snickering, but I continued walking. After I determined that I'd imagined it, I decided to hit up the goat again. "I can't figure out if you're following me, or if I'm following you."

More laughter.

"I told you she was funny," said a male voice, endearingly.

I spun around to see a woman holding Lev's arm. He was wearing jeans and a short-sleeved, collared shirt with the top three snaps undone. He was shoeless.

"You startled the poor thing, Lev," the woman admonished.

"I'm fine," I said.

"You were talking to a goat, dear," she was kind enough to point out.

I could tell by Lev's dancing eyes that he was trying not to smile. "Ida, this is my mother, Omo."

I knew Lev was adopted, so the news that this short, black woman was his mom didn't shock me.

"It's great to meet you." I extended my hand, only to realize that I was handing her my phone. I switched it to my left hand.

Omo took my hand in both of hers. "I feel I know you, seeing as how my son thinks all you do is worthy of retelling."

I decided to let that comment pass. "I was sorry to hear that your friend passed away."

"Thank you." Omo gave me a polite nod, and patted Lev's arm. "And thank you for walking me home, my son."

Lev bent over so she could kiss him on the cheek. "Goodnight, Mom."

I had the strangest sensation that I was melting.

Omo touched my elbow as she passed. "I want you to come over and see me very soon."

"Sure, does next Sunday--"

"Tomorrow afternoon."

"Ah...okay." I widened my eyes at Lev as she walked away. "Why were you telling stories about me to your mom?"

Lev ran a hand through his tousled hair. "I miss you when I'm not with you. Discussing you helps."

I watched as that dumb goat approached me and started gnawing on my silk nightie. I blew out my lips in exasperation at the goat's audacity.

Lev's face was purple with laughter. "Only you."

I put my hands on the goat's head and pushed him away. "I seriously doubt I'm the only person who's ever had their clothes chewed on by a goat."

Lev scanned my body. "What's with the outfit, anyway?"

"I didn't think I was going to run into my boss and his mom, or

I'd have dressed for the occasion." I stuffed a hand into my back pocket. "What were you walking her home from?"

"She works late hours at a nursing home, and I don't like her walking home by herself." He yawned. "Plus, her eyesight isn't great."

"I could pick her up," I offered. "I rarely sleep, and you look like you could use some."

From the look in Lev's eyes I thought he was going to kiss me. "That's a generous offer, but I couldn't let you do that."

"I wouldn't mind." My eyes dipped to gaze at his hips. "You're barely standing up."

He reached out and readjusted the strap onto my shoulder. "The only reason for me to go to sleep is so I can dream of you."

I groaned. "Where do you get these lines, and who do they actually work on?"

"Believe it or not, everything I say to you is untested material."

"I suppose a hands--" I cleared my throat, "semi-decent looking guy like you doesn't have to do any work at all. The ladies probably flock to you like goats to silk."

"So you *do* think I'm good looking," Lev said, with a gleam in his eyes.

"Your mom is going to wonder why you haven't gone inside."

"No she won't; I live over there." He nodded toward a house that was across the street and two doors down from his mom's.

"You have your own place?"

"Yep. If it was just my mom in her house, I would've stayed, but my uncle lives there as well, and it got suffocating." He tenderly ran his finger up and down the length of my arm. "Wanna come over?"

Unable any longer to withstand the desire in his eyes, I took off in the direction of my apartment. It was either that, or take him up on his offer. He followed, which seemed counterproductive.

"Running an orphanage must be pretty profitable if you can afford your own house," I said conversationally.

"My parents left everything to me in their will. I opened a retirement account for my mom, put enough aside for four years of college, bought my house, and the rest goes toward building a better orphanage."

Sherry had told me on my first day of work that Lev had paid for the sprinkler system in the orphanage out of his own pocket. As if I was drooling over that fact.

"I can find the way myself," I said after I heard Lev give a gigantic yawn.

Both of Lev's palms faced the early morning sky. "What kind of guy would I be if I didn't make sure you got home safely?"

"Why wouldn't I?"

"Because there are some people who wait for instances like this to attack women." He made a shooing motion with his hands. "Just pretend I'm not here."

I continued walking, feeling self-conscious of the way the material of my nightie clung to me. I hoped he wasn't looking at my butt. I stiffened my spine and tried not to obsess over how I was walking, which only made me walk weirder. I heard Lev chuckling. When I reached the door to the apartment building, I turned to shout good night to Lev, but to my astonishment, he was standing right in front of me.

I backed into the door, and tried my best to look casual. "Thanks for seeing me home...I guess."

"You're welcome...I guess." Lev reached up with his right hand, gently plucked the necklace from my sticky skin, and studied both charms. "Why is your heart broken?"

"It's a best friend necklace," I spoke to the exposed part of his chest. "The idea is that you wear one half and your best friend wears the other. I just happen to own both halves now."

"You don't have a best friend anymore?" he asked, sincerely interested.

"I'll always have her."

Lev gently set the necklace back, and tilted my chin so I was looking up at him. I hooked my finger over the next snap of his shirt, tempted to tug it loose.

"Before I came here, I was taught that Africans thought it impolite to look them in the eye, yet you always make me look at you," I noted.

"I adore your face," Lev said admiringly. "And I'm originally from Canada, so that rule doesn't apply to me." He shook his head slightly. "Perhaps we should call it a night."

"Be careful out there," I said as he walked backwards. "There's a psychopathic goat on the loose."

"I hear it only preys on American volunteers who wear jeans under their stunning nightwear," Lev replied.

I pretended to wipe sweat off my brow. "I guess you're safe then."

"In case you were wondering, you have the cutest butt I've ever had the pleasure of following."

I watched him walk away until I couldn't see his outline any longer. Then I smiled. While I found half of what Lev said to be corny, I appreciated his ability to say what was on his mind.

◆ ◆ ◆

Omo closed and locked the door behind her. She looked cute in her cheetah print scrubs and matching kanga. She was so gung-ho to hang out today, that even though she was called into work for the afternoon shift, she still insisted I come over.

"Lev said you received my message. I'm sorry to cancel our meal," Omo said sincerely, "but I could not say no to the extra money."

"No problem. I'm happy to walk you to work," I said.

We started on our way toward the nursing home. Omo put her arm through mine. We moved at a snail-like pace, and it wasn't like Omo was decrepit or anything, she just liked to walk slow.

"Your grandfather is a hero around here," Omo stated.

"I wish Gramps would've told me some stories about his time

here."

"He misses it."

"How do you know?"

"He and Lev talk often," Omo explained. "I used to be keen on your grandfather. He did so much for Lev."

"Like what?"

A man drove by on a motorized boda-boda with a small cushion on the back for a passenger, and showed us a nice toothless grin.

Omo patted my arm, dodging my question. "If I had not been married to Lev's adoptive father at the time, I may have asked your grandfather out on a date."

"Omo, what happened to your husband, Mr. Rosen?" I asked cautiously, hoping I wasn't overstepping.

"Nolan? He decided to move back to America. Lev and I loved him, but we refused to leave our home. Last I heard, he was living in Massachusetts."

"Lev has lost *two* fathers?"

Omo brought her hand to her chest. "It still breaks my heart. Lev blames himself for both."

"How so?"

"He believes he killed his parents. You see, Lev and his birth mother, Samantha, made it out of the building the night of the fire, but when they got outside, Lev realized he did not have his favorite toy. Then, while Samantha was helping a neighbor calm her children, Lev snuck back inside the burning building. Samantha went in shortly after to find him. The smoke was so thick Lev was close to fainting, when Ransom scooped him up and yelled for Samantha to follow him."

Omo stopped in her tracks. "When Ransom heard a loud noise from behind, he turned just as a burning couch fell through the ceiling. The impact caused him to drop Lev, and he toppled back into the fiery couch. It also divided them from Samantha. Ransom got Lev up, and beat the fire out of his shirt while running at the same time.

"Once they got outside, they ran around to the back of the

building, but Samantha wasn't there." Omo took a deep breath and resumed walking. "Then Lev's birth father, Anthony arrived. Ransom told Anthony where they'd lost Samantha. Anthony went in, and that was the last time Lev saw him. When the fire truck came, it was too late; Lev's parents were gone. Lev was brought to the burn ward in Kampala feeling alone, ashamed, and at fault."

After a few moments of reflection, I said, "Next time you go to visit their graves, I'd like to come with."

"They do not have graves."

I was shocked. Of course I hadn't expected a young Lev to make the funeral arrangements, but why hadn't the U.N. put up a marker of some kind?

"Does Lev have a place to go where he can feel close to them?" I asked.

"No, but I know he thinks of them often."

"Lev is kind of," I searched for the right word, "amazing. He lost his parents in an unthinkable way, yet he's so optimistic."

"He has a special place in his heart for you, Ida. He will be happy to know that you think good things concerning him."

My face flushed. "He's also immature, and can be truly annoying."

Omo giggled and opted for a subject change. "What do your parents think of you being here?"

"They think I'm a closed-off introvert. They hope that this place will somehow cure me."

"You do not cure your children, you nurture them. There is nothing wrong with wanting a little time to yourself," Omo assured me.

Omo was quickly becoming my favorite person in Africa.

FLIRTING AND FIGHTING

"You ready?" Lev asked, spinning the soccer ball on his pointer finger.

I had been in the rec room, holding my drawing in front of my face and zoning out. The subject of the day had been "Something you can't live without." The kids had chosen an object, which had been the idea, but I had drawn a portrait of Engen. Even though we'd gotten into a fight the previous day when I'd gotten back to the apartment after walking Omo to work, he was still the most treasured thing in the world to me.

"Why do you want me to play if you think I suck?" I asked Lev as I laid the drawing back down on the table.

He set the ball on top of my drawing and gently rubbed my shoulders. "I love watching you sweat."

"You're warped." My eyes closed at his touch. I rolled my shoulders under his hands. "That feels so good, Lev."

He leaned down and ran his lips over the top of my ear. "You have no idea how I've longed to hear those exact words from your mouth."

I wanted only one thing, for Lev to rub my shoulders for the rest of eternity. That's when I knew it was time to put an end to it. I stood and faced him. "Have you tried asking Stuart to play?"

Lev adopted Stuart's nasally voice. "Could you please call him Stu?"

I laughed.

Lev's mouth hung open, comically aghast. "I've been going out of my way trying to make you laugh, when all I had to do was an impression of *Stuart*?"

"I guess."

Lev plucked the ball from the table and tossed it to me, then reached over and pulled the headband out of my hair.

"You need to get out more," I said.

"Is that an invitation?"

"You spend too much time around kids."

"You don't know what I do when I'm not here." He'd been walking backward, and I didn't bother to tell him that he was going to run into the door. "Ouch."

I suddenly found myself curious to know what he did for fun. I passed him as he held the door open for me. "All I know is that you may look like a man, but you act like a child."

He put my headband in his hair. "Lucky for me, you love kids."

A gust of hot wind blew by as Lev and I made our way onto the soccer field where the kids were waiting for us to start the game. "Not really."

"Says the girl who draws her nine-year old brother all the time."

I grabbed my headband off his head. "Touché."

"What does too-shay mean?" Afi asked.

"It means that Lev just scored a point," I explained, fixing my hair.

"They're called goals," Afi stated with a roll of her head.

"Yeah, don't you know anything?" Lev quipped.

The kids erupted in over-exaggerated laughter.

"Too much time with kids," I chided.

He ran his tongue over his lips. "After lunch you should come with me to pick up the supplies in Seeta."

"I'll be busy washing the dishes."

"I'll help so you get done faster."

"Deal."

An hour later, I realized that when Lev didn't have the death of his mom's best friend on his mind, he did dishes the way he did everything else – childishly. He blew suds in my face and mashed them in my hair. It was just the kind of thing that would annoy me, but Lev made it charming somehow.

"Did you order any of the supplies I requested?" I asked, and ducked in time to miss a jet of water aimed for my head.

"You asked for stuff?" Lev pondered. "When?"

"Last Friday. You summoned me to your office to give you a list of supplies that I needed…"

Lev closed his eyes. "You were sitting across from me with your luscious legs crossed, twirling the hair at the nape of your neck and chewing on the end of your pencil. It was very hypnotic."

I constructed a beard on his jaws and chin with soap suds. "So, in other words you didn't?"

"Sorry, my mind has a tendency to wander when I'm around you. It's called Ida-itis." He wiped his lathered face off on my neck. "And I'm *not* trying to get help for it."

Taking his goofiness as confirmation that he ordered my supplies, I pulled the cork out of the drain.

Lev covered my hands in a dish towel and began to dry them for me. "Before we leave, do you have anything on you that you don't want pick-pocketed?"

I removed my phone and key card. "All set," I declared.

Lev grabbed a set of keys for the truck out of his office. I could tell he was happy because he was whistling. On our way outside, Lev inquired after Paul, and I happily launched into a recent anecdote. When we reached the truck, Lev paused in front of me, listened intently, and laughed endearingly at all the parts I'd also found amusing. When I was done with the story, he opened the passenger door for me.

"Ida!"

I peeked over Lev's shoulder. "Engen, hey."

Engen gave Lev a curt nod, then looked at me strangely. "You're done for the day, yeah?"

"I am," I answered, unable to decode his expression.

The sides of Engen's mouth crinkled. "Then what are you doing?"

"Going to Seeta to pick up supplies."

Engen's eyes adopted an agitated look. "You told me last week that you'd go with me to the bank and to pick out jeans for Buvama today."

"I forgot," I said repentantly, and turned to Lev.

Lev searched my eyes. "You're not coming with me anymore," he surmised.

It disturbed me to see the dejected look on his face. "Can we do this tomorrow?"

"I need some of that stuff *for* tomorrow, and the kids need to try on their shirts for the photo shoot next Tuesday." Lev faced the orphanage. "It's obvious you want to go with him, so I'll get someone else."

Lev jogged over to Megan. I couldn't hear what was said, but I saw her head bob up and down excitedly. The next thing I knew, they were walking toward me and Engen, both grinning broadly. When Lev walked up to me, he leaned forward and whispered in my ear, "See, you're easily replaced", then kept walking. I'd be lying if I told you my skin didn't crawl and my skull didn't go numb. I must have messed up pretty badly if it caused Lev to speak to me that way.

Engen put his arms around me, and I laid my forehead against his heart. I heard the truck door close and shifted my eyes toward it. I watched as Lev started the truck and slung his arm over the back of the seat. He turned around with a fake-looking smile on his face while he reversed. I tightened my arms around Engen. Lev saw us and slammed on the brakes. His smile faded, and his eyes, which always seemed a dreamy blue, now appeared chock-full of blue poison. I turned my face into Engen's chest while he stroked my hair sympathetically. I didn't look up until I heard the truck peal away. Feeling like I was unjustly reprimanded, I let Engen go and started walking toward our apartment building, hoping we would come across a matatu that was heading in the same direction as the bank.

"Ida, wait."

"Lev told me I was easily replaced."

"Nobody could replace you in a thousand years." Engen took my hand.

"Where will I work now?"

Engen gaped at me like I was a naive child. "I don't think he meant he was going to reassign you. He was just jealous that you chose me over him."

"Of course I chose you," I said emphatically. "Even if we didn't have plans, and you asked me for the first time right now to go with you, I still would've chosen you."

Engen squeezed my hand. "That's why no one could replace you in a thousand years."

◆ ◆ ◆

When Engen and I had gotten back from town the previous night, we'd grabbed a quick dinner and then swung by the orphanage to pick up my phone and key card. I'd been exhausted, but couldn't sleep because Engen snored all night. I managed to crawl my way into the orphanage a little past eight this morning.

"Miss Denmark, I must speak with you immediately," Akiki greeted.

I gave a tired wave. "What are you doing here?"

"I am getting the children ready for the day." Akiki held out his hands to ward off more questions. "The truck broke down shortly after Lev and Megan picked up the supplies last night."

"You're joking."

Akiki appeared to be in pain. "Lev spoke with a man who knows cars, and he said the problem is the alternator. On your application, you listed auto mechanics as a skill. What do you suggest?"

"The orphanage has another truck identical to the one Lev's using," I replied. "Take the alternator from that one and run it out to them in your car. Make sure you have a tool kit and some jumper cables."

"Can you help?" Akiki asked. "Becky has offered to cook the meal."

"Where are the tools?" I asked, my hands tingling at the idea of doing something I loved.

"In the garage." Akiki unwound a key from his key chain. "Let me know when you are ready to go."

I took the key from him. Nine minutes later, I had the alternator and jumper cables loaded in the back of Akiki's sucky old pick up.

"Why do you look so angry, Miss Denmark? You were not the one who was up all night guarding the supply trailer."

I should have been, though, I thought.

"Lev is my nephew. He did not do this on purpose to cause strife," Akiki opined.

I stared at the back of the truck in front of us that read *Danger Petrol* as I processed this information. Omo and Akiki were related. Ah, so this is the uncle Lev didn't care for, and the reason he moved out of his mom's house. It made perfect sense.

We had made it onto a real paved road, however the tires still kicked up dust like you wouldn't believe. I knew Krista had an issue with the sensation of driving on the "wrong side" of the road here, but it didn't annoy me. What bothered me was the constant zigzagging line of motorized boda-bodas. You couldn't turn your head without seeing one, and the drivers never turned *their* heads to look at the traffic around them. You also could not go over ten car lengths without a person on foot, boda-boda, or bicycle cutting you off.

After the longest fifteen minutes of my life, we arrived at the scene to see Lev and Megan sitting with their backs against the trailer. Megan's head was resting on Lev's shoulder as he looked fixedly ahead. They both appeared to be angry, tired, and hungry. I instructed Akiki to drive up to the dead truck so they were close enough to jump the battery. I leapt out of Akiki's truck and grabbed the tool kit and jumper cables from the bed. Lev shook Megan awake, and then jogged over to meet me.

Lev nodded to Akiki, and turned to me. "What can I do?"

"Grab the new alternator," I replied tersely.

Lev did as he was told.

I stopped in front of the broken-down truck, and set the tool kit down. The hood had already been popped, so I lifted it. Lev stood next to the truck with his arm propped against the hood, watching me work and passing tools to me when I asked for them. At least he knew not to talk to me. I handed him the useless alternator. He set it on the ground, then fitted the spare in place for me. After the new one was installed, I retrieved the jumper cables and hooked the orphanage truck's battery up to Akiki's. I leaned over to give Akiki, who was still behind the wheel of his vehicle, a thumbs-up and he started his truck. I got into the orphanage's truck, stepped down on the clutch, and turned the key. The truck started right up.

Lev unhooked the cables and closed the hood. "You're a genius, Ida."

I collected the tools and wrapped the greasy old alternator in the towel we'd used for transporting the working one. Lev took it and set it in the bed of the orphanage's truck. I laid the tool kit in the bed of Akiki's truck and saw Megan approach with an exasperated look on her face.

"Don't get me wrong," Megan began, "I like you, but I'm sick of discussing you. I'm riding with Akiki."

I clicked the rear bed door in place, and turned to see Lev leaning against the hood of the orange truck. Without its support, he probably would've passed out from exhaustion. It didn't stop him from looking at me like I was some sort of goddess, though. Deciding that riding with Lev would be better than being sandwiched between Akiki and Megan, I sauntered toward the orange truck.

Lev flattened his palms against the hood. "What else do you know regarding this vehicle?"

"Enough to write a manual."

He cocked an eyebrow. "Do you think you can you drive it?"

I shielded my eyes from the sun. "Blindfolded."

"Do you mind? I didn't get a wink of sleep last night."

"Neither did I," I mumbled, but climbed into the driver's side. I waited for Lev to get belted in, then followed Akiki, mentally preparing for the long, dusty drive home.

"You look crabby," Lev observed.

"Nobody looks happy while driving."

Lev smirked. "You have the most precious streak of grease on your cheek. May I?"

Out of the corner of my eye I saw Lev lick his thumb and move it toward me. I put my shoulder up to block my cheek. "What makes you think I want your saliva rubbed into my skin?"

"I was only trying to help."

The old alternator thumped up and down on the bed of the truck, that's how bumpy these stupid roads were.

"You can help by being quiet," I advised.

He put his arm around the back of the seat. "Watching you work on the truck was the sexiest thing I've seen. I hope you never wash your cheek, because each time I see that grease spot I can revisit that moment in my mind."

I licked my right hand and rubbed my cheek raw. Lev chuckled. "Exactly what do you find so funny?" I demanded.

"I can't believe you can change an alternator in an old truck, and you can hold your own during our basketball scrimmages, but you can't kick a ball down a field."

"If the circumstances were different, I'd be rubbing your face in the dirt every day," I said, confident that I had the soccer skills to take Lev on.

He snorted. "How do you figure that?"

"Your defense stinks, you never guard your left side-"

"That's not true."

"It is true! The kids are constantly flanking you." I shifted gears. "Monday - me and you, one on one," I challenged.

"You fix cars, you know more about the Superman Universe than I do, and you claim you can kick my butt at football." Lev turned in his seat, facing me. "Are you *trying* to make me fall in love with you?"

I kneaded the steering wheel with both hands. "Please don't make me vomit on an empty stomach."

"What happened to the girl who was all hot to kiss me?" He squeezed my thigh. "I miss her."

You replaced her, I thought, bitterly, still unable to let his "easily replaced" comment go from the previous afternoon.

Lev closed his eyes, and I thought he'd fallen asleep. I was admiring how peacefully his long eyelashes rested against his smooth, clear skin, when his eyes fluttered open. I quickly cut my eyes back to the road, but he laughed softly, and I knew I'd been caught.

"How do you know how to fix cars?" Lev asked.

"I've been taking classes at school since the seventh grade. Also, we have five cars at my house, and one always seems to be broken. Gramps and I fix them together. It's when we do all our conversing," I said, and then wrinkled my nose, wishing I hadn't added that last part.

Lev's brow furrowed in confused. "Ransom can carry on a conversation for hours."

I swept the sweaty hair off my forehead. "Maybe with you, but not with me."

"I have a hard time--" Lev started to say.

"He doesn't talk to me, okay?"

"Why are you shouting?" Lev asked curiously.

"You have me all worked up," I explained, flustered.

Lev made a pshaw noise. "What did I do?"

"The orphanage is down three helpers because of you."

He slid closer to me. "Believe me, I ran all the scenarios on how to get home last night."

"You could've called me, Lev. I would've found a way to bring the alternator out to you."

"In the dark? To a place you've never been?" Lev shook his head. "I couldn't have asked that of you."

"You could've." I braked behind Akiki, and faced Lev. "You could've asked that of me."

Lev rubbed his tired eyes. "I was a jerk yesterday and I want to apologize to you."

"Apologize for what, exactly?" I hated my shrilly voice as I feigned ignorance.

"You're stubborn."

"And you're exasperating."

Lev pressed his thigh against mine. "According to my mother, you think I'm amazing."

"With the kids. With me, you're impossible."

"So, the things I say have no impact on you?" Lev gazed sleepily at me.

"Which of your remarks was supposed to have had an impact?"

"When I told you that you were easily replaced." Lev hung his head. "You have to know that I didn't mean it."

"How would I know that?" I asked, huffily. "As my boss, I'm sure it's in your power to request a replacement volunteer."

We came to a stop. Lev put a hand on my face and made me look at him. "You thought I was threatening your *job*?"

"What else could you have meant by 'replacing' me?"

"I wanted you to think I meant your *company* was easily replaced. Your job will never be at risk." Lev put his arm around me. "I keep forgetting that you aren't like most girls, though."

"Meaning?" The car behind me honked, so I turned my attention back to the road.

"I can't seem to make you jealous." He put his nose to my neck and confessed, "I never needed help getting the supplies. I just wanted you with me."

"You have an extremely odd way of showing it."

Lev chuckled as I stopped the truck in front of the orphanage, so we could unload the supplies from the trailer.

"Thank you for coming to my rescue," Lev said.

I ran my palm around the wheel. "Yeah, well, I did it for Megan."

"You're going to lose so bad when we have our football match."

"Please," I dismissed. "I'm going to have you begging for mercy."

"You'll have me begging for something, but it won't be mercy," he said seductively.

I snickered, wanting to keep up the flirtatious banter, only first I needed to think this over. Was it a good idea to lead Lev on, knowing that I was not only pregnant, but leaving Africa in four and a half months? Probably not, however I also didn't want to run the risk of seeing him with random girls for the remainder of my time here. I knew all too well that seeing the guy you like with another girl due to pure stupidity was torture.

HANGING WITH THE VOLUNTEERS

"Why do you guys insist on calling me Stuart when I've asked you repeatedly to call me Stu?" Stuart asked dejectedly.

"If you'd only kept your trap shut, you'd be Stu," Engen stated.

I smiled and gave Engen a fist bump, appreciating his candidness.

I was sitting with a group of volunteers at the picnic table outside our apartment building. It was early evening, and either it was nice out, or I had grown used to the weather.

"A smile out of crabby Ida?" Stuart remarked. "The other day at the orphanage you were content as well. What's with you these days?"

"Promise not to laugh?" I inquired, playing with the bottle cap from my Coke.

"No," Dee, Engen, Stuart, Sheldon, and Megan replied in unison.

I decided to tell them anyway, "I'm starting to get some satisfaction from cooking for the kids. Watching them eat and knowing it was me that cooked the meal, is rewarding."

"That's the corniest thing I've ever heard," Sheldon offered.

Engen shot him a dirty look. "Keep your opinions to yourself."

"If you knew those kids, you'd understand," Megan said.

Stuart smirked. "This, coming from the girl who was sent here for practicing magic."

"So I mixed a few potions, no biggie. I also see pieces of the future." Megan peeled a small sliver of wood off the table. "Anyway, my parents couldn't deal, so they sent me here."

"Did it work? Have your powers faded?" Stuart wondered.

Megan made eye contact with each of us to make sure she had

our undivided attention. "No. In fact, this place has broadened my powers. I met a priest with psychic ability. She and I are getting together tomorrow afternoon. Do any of you want to come with?"

A chorus of, "No, nope, and uh-uh's," erupted.

Megan turned her heavily eye-lined gaze at me. "Ida?"

I smacked my lips together uncomfortably. "I'm busy."

Megan accepted the answer, but Engen pounced. "What are you doing, Ida?"

"I'mgoingtoLev'smom'shouseforlunch," I said.

The gang looked around at one another, bewildered. Engen was the only one who understood. Figures.

"When were you going to tell me?" he demanded.

"You aren't going to be around, anyway," I reminded him.

"Where are you going, Ida?" Dee inquired.

"To Lev's mom's house."

"Atrocious idea," Stuart sang.

I took a swig of my soda. "Why?"

"If you say something to piss his mom off, he could send you home," Stuart explained.

"Oh no, not *home*. That would be awful," I jested.

"The priest I hang out with sees the future. Ida isn't going anywhere," Megan said confidently.

"Wait, what?" Engen asked her.

Sheldon was mortified. "You talk to the priest about us?"

Megan closed her eyes. "Since you guys surround me, so do your auras."

"Megan, what do you mean Ida isn't going anywhere?" Engen asked, worried.

"I'm not supposed to discuss it, Engen, but I am sorry," Megan said compassionately.

Engen looked at me, swallowed deeply, and took my hand in his.

I rolled my eyes. As if he believed that nonsense.

Stuart peered at Sheldon over the top of his glasses. "Do you think Megan and Ida should be planting roots?"

I held out my free hand to prevent Sheldon from answering before he even began. "We're merely establishing acquaintances," I assured Stuart.

"Maybe you see Lev as just an 'acquaintance,' but you aren't aware of the way he watches you. *You* don't have to listen when he raves about you." Stuart wagged his thumb back and forth between himself and Megan. "We do."

"Stu, what are you saying?" I asked.

"So it's 'Stu' now that she needs information," Stuart said in disbelief, looking around the table at the others. His eyes swung back to mine. "I don't know what you did to Lev, but he's completely lost in you."

"I did nothing to Lev."

"Keep it that way," Engen pleaded and squeezed my hand.

I met Engen's gray eyes and saw real fear in them. I imagine my eyes reflected the same anxiety less than a year ago, when we fought and I begged him not to leave me. If only he'd turned around and saw that fear, would he still have gone to Brittany's house?

Hardening my heart, I tore my eyes away from Engen.

Stuart leaned forward. "I tried to ask Lev an important question yesterday, but you happened to be nearby playing with Tunisia, so did I get an answer? No. All I got was drooled on."

"Are you honestly blaming me for Lev's submandibular gland?" I asked Stuart, and then had to hide a smile at the thought of Lev's internal organs. I was grateful to them for helping him live.

"I'm more practical than that," Stuart answered. "Just try not to be so attractive all the time."

Engen growled at Stuart, "Watch it."

"Save it, Engen. I heard you and Marco discussing Ida's looks, among other things, the other day," Stuart said.

I choked on my swallow of soda, wondering what reason Engen could have for discussing me with Marco?

"You truly don't see how severely Lev wants you, do you?" Stuart adjusted his dark framed glasses. "How do you feel about him?"

Maybe if Stuart wasn't being such an ass, or if Engen wasn't boring holes into me with his eyes, I could admit that right now I was missing Lev so badly it felt like my stomach lining was wearing away.

Sheldon raised his hand. "If I may?"

"What?" Engen and I yelled, testily.

Sheldon smiled broadly, overjoyed that he finally had our attention. "In my opinion, the whole point of this program is to plant roots."

All except Sheldon grimaced in disagreement. We may like the people we've met, but we weren't ready to plant roots yet.

DANCING

The rest of the week went fairly quickly. Tuesday was the photo shoot at the orphanage. When I showed up at work, I was immediately overwhelmed by the vans parked in front. The screen door was propped open as people filed in with lighting and camera equipment. I carefully worked my way between them to get inside. I had gotten so used to our little ways here that this seemed like an intrusion.

I peeked inside the rec room. I saw cameras, strangers, and the kids, who looked fantastic in their matching powder-blue shirts. I smiled proudly. In my biased opinion, they were the perfect group of kids to photograph in order to promote adoption.

It was now Friday, the day of the one-on-one soccer match.

Lev entered the rec room with a toothpick in his mouth and the soccer ball under his arm. "You ready?"

"Almost."

Lev checked out my drawing. "Paul and the curly-haired girl again. Why don't you draw some different people for a change?"

I paused, feeling my eyebrows stitch together in a strange realization. "I don't remember what they look like."

"That's depressing."

I stood and walked around the table. "Save your tears for the field, Rosen.

Lev tossed the ball at me. "Is that trash talk?"

"Intimidated?"

"Hardly." He reached out and pinched my elbow.

I grabbed his wrist before he could take it back and held it in both hands, inspecting the bracelet on it. It looked *exactly* like the one Gramps had given me. I let him go, picked up my drawing, and said, "Let's set some ground rules. It's just me and you, no kids, got it?"

"Eventually I would like kids." Lev's eyes flashed mischievously. "But for now, I'm happy with it being just us."

Talk about hitting close to home. "First one to get past the other to score a goal wins. Anything else?" I asked.

"The stakes."

I let my drawing slip from my hand into the recycle bin. "Gloating rights."

He stared at my drawing, thoughtful. "I have a better idea. The loser owes the winner a favor. I can name anything at any time and you have to agree to it."

"When *I* win, *you'll* have to do whatever I say."

"You trust that my request will be," he traced my clavicle with his finger, "innocent?"

I twirled the ball on my finger like a basketball. "No, but I still agree."

"That's incredible."

We walked to the field, bumping hips the whole way. It was terribly childish, but I couldn't stop smiling.

I tossed the ball to Adroa. He ran the ball out and set it down in the center of the field. Lev and I each stood three feet from the ball, facing off. Lev hopped back and forth, shaking his hands out. I was relaxed and confident.

"Are you sure you want to lose in front of all the kids?" Lev taunted.

"I won't lose."

Adroa blew the whistle.

This was going to be easy.

"You want the shower first?" I asked, after the match. It had only lasted two minutes, but we were both drenched in sweat.

"No, I'm heading out soon." Lev walked with me inside. "Are you going to that dance tonight?"

I stopped in front of the employee restroom. "I think my roommates are making me."

"You ready, sweet thing?" Matilda came from behind, and put her arm through Lev's.

"Yep," Lev answered. "I hope you don't mind that I'm dirty and sweaty."

"It was bound to happen to us both today anyway." Matilda turned at me. "Ida, you look utterly worn out."

I covered my heart with my hand and pretended to look touched. "Thank you."

"I'll wait for you outside," Matilda told Lev, as she strolled back down the hallway.

"Thanks for the game, Lev." I could hear the sourness in my voice. "You really had me going for awhile there."

"You always have me going."

I watched him walk away, puzzled. Why did Lev insist on flirting with me when he clearly intended on getting involved with someone else?

◆ ◆ ◆

"You want to go to the VC with me and Dee to play some Foosball before dinner?" Krista asked me.

"Sure," I said, finishing a letter to my mom. "Is Engen going to the dance?"

"He said he would if you did. No big shock there."

Krista flopped down on Engen's bed. "Do I have a chance with him?"

I ground my back teeth together. "I think he's still hung up on his ex."

"He's hung up on somebody, alright," Krista mumbled, watching me.

"Will there be a lot of people at this dance?" I wondered, ignoring what she was insinuating.

"How many people do you consider a lot?"

"Five."

"That's right. You hate crowds." She rolled her eyes. "You and Lev lock lips yet?"

"No, he has other things going on." I told her about Matilda. Krista gave me a sympathetic look. "Do you still hate it here?" I folded the letter and placed it in an envelope. "For sure."

"What do you hate the most?"

These were questions we asked each other at least once a day. "That it hasn't rained since we've been here. You?"

"How the kids in my class don't seem to be learning anything from me."

This was the first time she hadn't complained about something superficial. I was shocked, yet proud of her for taking an interest in her work.

I stood up, stretched, and caught a glimpse of a groundnut stain on my shirt. It was Engen's old mechanic shirt from his job at Jake's Auto, and the smudge was right next to his name, which was stitched into the shirt in cursive. I unbuttoned it and decided to go for a sexier look, so I changed into a black satin corset-style number that zipped halfway up the back. It went well with the dark blue distressed jeans I was wearing.

I brushed my hair to the side. "Will you zip me up?"

She obliged. "This top is hot. Can I borrow it sometime?"

"Absolutely," I said, even though Krista didn't seem to be in short supply of cute outfits. Tonight, for example, she was wearing a navy blue floral print romper.

Krista fluffed my hair. "There. Perfect."

I sprayed some perfume in the air and walked under it. Krista indicated I should enter the hallway first. I heard her steal a quick spray from the bottle as I made my way to the living room to see Engen, sitting with his feet propped up on the coffee table.

"Ready to go, friend?" I asked.

"Where?" he replied, bored.

I threw a leg over his stretched-out legs and sat down on his shins. "To the VC to play Foosball, eat, and then go see the dancing."

Engen stared at my chest. "I thought the dance was Friday."

"This is Friday." I snapped my fingers next to my face.

He dragged his eyes upward. "Did you win that game against Lev?"

"I did."

"I wish I could've seen you play. It's been so long."

"Shake a leg, I," Krista said.

"Wait." Engen's smile faded. *"You're* going to the dance?" he asked me.

I set my hands on his thighs and propelled myself forward so I was straddling his lap. "Better than being in this apartment, right?"

He set one hand on my waist; the other hand rested on the side of my neck as he gazed at me. "Not if I had you here."

"If you need to talk, we can stay."

"Then what *would* you two do tonight when Dee and I are trying to sleep?" Krista asked sorely.

Dee nodded in agreement as she threw a short, burgundy chiffon kimono wrap over her champagne-colored shirt. The wrap just graced the hem of her white shorts.

With his eyes locked on mine, Engen asked Krista, "Will there be a lot of people there tonight?"

Krista threw her arms up. "You two are so creepily connected."

The girls left.

"There's going to be a bonfire," I told him.

Engen pulled me to his chest. He held me, breathed me in, and then sighed. "Whenever we were together, I was deliriously happy. Were you?"

"Unspeakably," I agreed, my chest tight.

Engen may not have *officially* been my boyfriend, but from age 13 till 15 it seemed like he was. Up until ninth grade that is, when Engen was tired of keeping us a secret and wanted to go public. I didn't think that was a good idea. I didn't tell him the reason was Janelle; if I had just told him, he would have understood. Instead, he allowed Brittany into the picture to light a fire under me, which only succeeded in making me mad, but only for a month. After that, we were back to not being able to keep our hands off each other...up until last October, that is.

"I haven't seen myself once since that last time with you," Engen said, mirroring my thoughts.

"I see you quite often," I assured, my face smushed into his gray Budweiser t-shirt. "What's going on with you?"

"I feel...adrift, and I needed to hold you for my sanity." He eased up on his embrace. "Will there be marshmallows at this fire?"

"Doubt it." I stood, my legs between his. "Anyway, I gave up marshmallows." Janelle, Engen, and I had spent many evenings dedicated to roasting marshmallows in Engen's backyard. Without her, it seemed pointless.

"I didn't know that." Engen leaned forward to give my exposed hip bone a kiss.

The feel of his mouth caused every hair on my body to stand straight up. I swung my leg back over and helped him stand. "Because you stopped talking to me."

He kept hold of my hand as he slipped into his sandals. "There goes your last birthday present, then."

"Last?" I smiled, interested. "What happened to the first one?"

Engen blushed. "I talked myself out of giving it to you, so I kinda...buried it."

"So *that's* why you had dirt underneath your fingernails and your jeans were filthy yesterday," I said. "Here I thought you were burying bodies without me again."

"Nope." He smirked. "I learned my lesson the first time."

"One gift I'm not going to use, and the other one is buried in the ground?" I recapped.

"Right."

"Are you ever going to tell me what it is?" I asked, intrigued.

He closed one eye, thoughtful. "Maybe."

"Fascinating." I reached into my back pocket and pulled out a pamphlet for Lakeside Adventure Park. On the cover were pictures of people on rope courses, climbing walls, and zip lines. "Here's your gift."

He took the pamphlet and inhaled sharply. "When are we doing this?"

"Monday." I smiled at his exuberance. "I ordered a car for an early pick up, but you don't *have* to take me."

Engen pulled me to him in a hug. "Of course I want to go with you!"

"Thank God, because this place sounds marvelous, and I already agreed to work Sunday in order to have Monday off."

"You're working your birthday so you can have mine off?"

"I had to go by your time off. Buv's mom isn't as lenient as Lev."

He leafed through the pamphlet. "This is incredible; you're incredible."

"I'm also gonna kick your butt at Foosball."

After Foosball and dinner, we made our way to the community center where the dance was being held. It was pitch dark, but the roaring fire provided enough light, seeing as how it was taller than Engen.

Krista flapped Dee's arm up and down. "Will you dance with me?"

"Maybe later, Kris."

"I?"

"Fine," I groaned.

Engen had no choice but to let go of my hand, seeing as how Krista had grabbed my free hand and yanked me with her to the fire.

I began by simply mimicking her movements. As the drums picked up, I started doing my own thing.

"Ida?" Krista shouted a while later.

I opened my eyes. Krista was no longer next to me. I must have gotten carried away. I lifted my hair off my sweaty back and danced my way back to her.

"How great does Lev look?" Krista asked.

I dropped my hair and followed her eye line. The fire danced and cast shadows, but it wasn't able to hide Lev's eyes which were fixed on me. He was standing in a circle with four guys, holding a red plastic cup and looking exceptionally dashing in plaid shorts that sat low on the waist, and a black button-down shirt with only two of the buttons in the middle fastened. Three girls were huddled near him, and one of them was Baba. Lev lifted his glass to me in a toasting gesture.

I put my hands to my face in embarrassment, looked away, and saw Engen watching me. I shivered. Lev's gaze had been filled with soft adoration; Engen's with intense desire.

"How long has Lev been watching?" I squeaked at Krista.

"Since the moment we got here. I thought you were showing off those sexy hips because you knew," Krista said, amused by my lack of attention to the world around me.

"Good evening," a deep, slightly accented voice said from behind me.

My eyes widened at Krista.

"See-ya," she said.

I tried to swallow, but my throat was bone dry. I swiveled around.

"You move nicely." Lev took a sip from his cup.

"What are you drinking?" I asked.

"Cherry Coke." He tilted the glass toward me. "Want some?"

"Please." I took the glass and drank thirstily. He watched me with an endearing smile; the firelight danced beautifully in his eyes. Before I knew it, the contents were gone. "I'm sorry."

"No worries." He took the empty cup, folded it, and put it in his side leg pocket. "You're so lovely."

I looked down at the ground. "Thanks."

He took my chin between two fingers and lifted my head up so I was looking at him again. "Will you dance with me?"

"I thought, after this afternoon, that you were with Matilda."

"Matilda's moving out of her soon-to-be ex-husband's house. She couldn't lift the furniture by herself, so she asked for my help." Lev bumped his hip against mine. "Will you honor me with a dance?"

I took a step closer to him and held my hands level with his. He must have thought I was going to chicken out, because he seized my hands, placing my left hand on the bare patch of skin over his heart and my right hand on his left bicep.

He circled his arms low around my waist. "Is this okay?"

"Mm-huh," I answered, looking over to where Lev had been when Krista pointed him out. His friends were watching us, along with one not-so-happy Baba. "I didn't know you had friends your own age."

Lev threw his head back and laughed. I gave an insecure sweep of the crowd for a glimpse of Engen's face to settle me. It didn't work, because now Engen was observing me with a tragic expression, as if he had just realized that what he considered a constant, could indeed disappear; how he and I both must have looked when we learned that we would never hear Janelle laugh again.

Lev, sensing my discomfort, abruptly stopped laughing. My hands were sweating like crazy against him. It helped that his hands were shaking, telling me he was nervous, too.

I tilted my head toward his neck. He smelled of aftershave and Monopoly money. "Can I ask you something?"

He pressed his lips against my temple. "Anything."

"When you set the stakes for our bet, did you have something in mind if you'd won? Which you didn't," I reminded him.

"Yes, but I don't want to tell you just yet."

"I can respect that," I said, feeling the drumbeats vibrating through his chest.

"I know. You're the exception to the rule." Lev ran a hand up my back and under my hair. "It's one of the reasons I'm so wild about you."

My heart felt full. "I need to find something to drink."

He gave a nervous laugh. "I feel like we've taken a step back. Please just tell me what you're feeling."

"Thirst."

He blinked and waited for a proper response.

"I like you, okay? But it's going to be over before we know it, so what's the point of starting anything?"

"What's the point of ignoring it?" He ran a thumb along my

cheekbones. "A wise man once said, 'Don't throw something away unless you know it's garbage.'"

"*You* say that to the kids all the time."

"Do I?" He smirked. "Need a soda?"

On the way to the drink stand, we passed Lev's buddies who were whistling and making lewd gestures.

"Sorry," Lev apologized as we got in line. "My friends consider any minute that goes by without humiliating somebody, a wasted one."

We gave our drink orders to Telly, Krista's supervisor. "How do you know those guys?" I asked.

His arm shot up next to my face as he pointed them out. "Eze lives near me; Muna, I met in high school; Kado, I knew in the orphanage, and the one on the right is my cousin-brother, Wtalo."

"Akiki's son?"

"No." Lev gaped at me, astounded. "How did you know Akiki was my uncle?"

"He told me. Did you not want me to know?"

"There isn't anything in my life I want to keep secret from you."

Lev led us to a more secluded place to sit. I sat cross-legged, and he sat with his legs stretched in front of him. He reached over and ran his pointer finger along the exposed part of my waist.

I slowly lowered the cup. "Why do you always touch me?"

"Because you're Ida Denmark."

"And...?" I prompted.

"I've yearned for you for twelve years. You were a dream that had no way of coming true." His eyes lit up with amazement and he spread his arms wide. "Yet here you are. If you came face-to-face with your dream, could you resist touching it?"

I turned away from him and watched the dancers. I breathed in the smell of the bonfire and imagined Janelle was running toward me. Lev was right, there would be no way I could resist flying into her arms.

"When did you move here from Canada?" I asked.

"When I was five." Lev plucked a blade of grass and twirled it between his fingers. "My parents worked for the Secretariat branch of the U.N. They died when our apartment building caught fire. I was seven."

"Your mom told me. I'm so sorry that happened." I was mesmerized with watching his hands. "She also mentioned that you got physically hurt in the fire."

"My right shoulder blade is scarred."

I could tell that he wanted to drop the subject, so I stood, announcing, "I need to find a restroom."

"The VC will probably be your best bet." Lev stood, too. Something behind me caused him to groan.

I turned, and saw that Engen's eyes were locked on me as he rushed over to us.

"Why did you disappear?" Engen asked me.

"I needed a drink," I responded.

"You don't owe him an explanation," Lev insisted.

"You don't know anything about us," Engen countered.

"I'm beginning to realize that," Lev agreed.

Lev headed back in the direction of his friends, only to be accosted along the way by Baba and her clan who had been hovering like vultures.

I huffed off toward the VC. "Honestly Engen, what is happening with you?"

"I don't like being separated from you." Engen picked up the pace so he was in stride with me. "Just because you're getting used to this place doesn't mean I am!"

"Even if I were, what would be wrong with that?" A strange cramping in my stomach occurred just then.

"I know Lev has feelings for you. Promise me you won't return them." Engen held the door to the VC open and waited for Bianca to pass us.

She smiled flirtatiously. "Thanks, handsome."

Engen didn't acknowledge her. "Don't give Lev a reason to tie you to this place."

"What's so wrong with me feeling something besides emptiness for a change?" I asked.

Engen's shoulders sagged. "Why him?"

"He makes me feel special and like I'm important to him."

Engen's face contorted, giving me the impression that he was experiencing stomach cramps as well. "In other words, he's doing what I didn't?"

"Engen Scott, that is *not* what I was implying." My hand flew to my stomach. "Look, I can't get into the ins and outs of us right now."

"Fine. I'll back off."

All of a sudden I felt leaking between my legs, so I excused myself. Once inside the restroom, I pulled my jeans down and saw blood on my underwear. The realization that the baby may have perished didn't make me as happy as I once thought it would.

PICTURES AND BEADS

"We had to do a sonogram anyway," Dr. Milton said, after I apologized for making him come in on a Saturday afternoon. "Lay back and lift your shirt."

I did as he instructed. He squirted some warm goo on my belly and placed the wand on top. Within seconds I heard a whooshing noise coming from the ultrasound machine.

I put my hand to my forehead in relief. "That's the heartbeat, isn't it?"

"Yes, and a strong one." He moved one hand over the machine, clicking buttons, while the other hand operated the wand. "I'm just taking some photos for further review, but looking at your placenta, I'd say you have a small subchorionic hemorrhage. It should be nothing to concern yourself with, just give yourself extra time in the morning so you can walk slower, no heavy lifting, and no strenuous activity of any kind."

"Copy that."

"I printed a few pictures of your daughter for you." Dr. Milton silently slipped the photos into an envelope for me. "I'll call you if I find anything else."

Daughter. I took my envelope and walked past Engen, who was sitting in the waiting room. I heard him slap the magazine he'd been reading onto the tabletop before following me outside.

"Is the baby okay?" Engen asked.

I handed him the envelope that read "Baby Denmark" on the front. He ran his finger under the seal and pulled out the photos.

"It's a girl," I whispered.

"The sweetest baby girl ever!" Engen flipped through the photos. "If all is well, why were you bleeding?"

"There's a tear in the wall of the placenta."

"What does that mean?"

My lower lip quivered. "It means I won't be going to Lakeside Adventure with you."

"Who cares? My best friend is having a girl!" he shouted, as we took the scenic route back to the apartment on this uncharacteristically overcast day.

A screen door swung open and banged closed. I glanced over and saw Lev jump down the three steps of the front stoop. He was carrying a big manila envelope in his hand. I was in such a funk that it hadn't occurred to me that we were in his neighborhood.

Engen put the ultrasound photos back in the envelope, and stuffed it in the back pocket of my jeans just as Lev noticed us. His face erupted in a smile. Apparently, I was forgiven for last night.

"Morning, Lev," I greeted. "Visiting your mom?"

"Just grabbing my mail. It still gets delivered here half the time." Some sort of realization dawned across his face, and he hid the bulky envelope behind his back.

"Young man!"

The three of us turned as one to watch Dr. Milton's miniature frame jog toward us, his unbuttoned lab coat billowing behind him.

"You forgot your wallet, son."

Engen took his wallet. "Thanks, doc."

"While we appreciate American money, my nurse wanted me to ask, did you mean to give her this particular bill?" Dr. Milton squinted at the note in question. "It has writing on it. 'Save for--'"

"No!" Engen's eyes widened, and he swapped out the five-dollar bill he was being handed and gave a new one to my doctor.

I held my breath, but thankfully Dr. Milton turned and jogged back to the clinic without acknowledging me.

Lev eyes were concerned. "Are you okay?"

"I'm excellent." I tapped Engen on the chest with the back of my hand. "This one needed the doctor. He threw his back out."

Lev pointed with his chin at Engen. "Then why's he rubbing

his shoulder?"

Engen cleared his throat, letting me know that he'd handle it. "My shoulder hurts, too. I'm falling apart."

"Where are you heading now, Lev?" I asked.

"The orphanage. I'm taking the older kids to make beads."

"Why?" Engen wondered.

"Volunteers make the beads, and H.O.P.E. makes them into necklaces to sell for charity," Lev explained. "Do you guys want to come with?"

"I shouldn't go because of my *back*." Engen leaned over so that he was two inches away from my face when he spat that last word at me.

"Ida?" Lev asked.

I wiped Engen's DNA off my face. "Totally."

Lev's face shone with enthusiasm. "Great, we'll walk together. I just need to drop something off at my place."

When the coast was clear, I rounded on Engen. "Do you think you can make it *back* to the apartment by yourself?"

"You and I agreed that if anything like this were to happen, we'd say it was my or your *shoulder*." Engen tapped his right shoulder with his left hand.

"I forgot, okay?"

"Yeah, again. You forgot at the airport and told Krista and Dee that you had a hernia of all things!" He lightly slapped the palm of his hand to my forehead. "And what kills me is that it was your idea."

"This time was your fault," I accused. "Who leaves their wallet at a doctor's office?"

"I was making a donation." He patted my shoulder. "From now on remember it's *shoulder*."

I hauled my arm back and punched him in the shoulder.

"Dammit, that freaking stings like a--"

"Great punch," Lev cheered.

"Don't be surprised if all your stuff is in the hallway when you get home," Engen threatened, and lumbered off by himself.

Lev turned to me, eyes masked. "I didn't know coed rooming

was allowed."

"Special circumstances. The boy/girl ratio was off this year."

Lev appeared to be deep in thought. "Weird."

"Weirder still, we share the same bedroom."

Lev breathed deeply as if he were trying to make peace with his inner self, and then took my hand. "I was going to wait until tomorrow for this, but come here."

I took his hand and he led me to his house. We walked up the three steps. Lev unlocked his front door, pushed it open, and I immediately smelled fresh pineapple. His house was immaculate. I shouldn't have been surprised, considering he ran a spotless orphanage.

"Have a seat," Lev invited, motioning to his couch.

I sat, and he sat next to me.

"This is gorgeous," I commented, referring to the bright orange, red, and yellow blanket that adorned the back of the sofa.

"My first client made it for me," Lev said.

The manila envelope I saw him with earlier was sitting on the coffee table. He picked it up and handed it to me.

Curiosity piqued, I reached inside and pulled out a book. I glanced confusedly at Lev and then back at the cover. I knew this children's series, because Paul was a fan. P.I. Polly was a child detective and the reason I started calling him Pauley. I removed the rubber band around the book, and a bunch of papers fell onto my lap. I saw the word "conphidental" written in red marker. Paul's missing children reports! I rifled through the papers and noticed that there were photos of Paul among them. I put the papers and pictures on my lap, and opened the P.I. Polly book. In the margins were Paul's notes: early guesses of who the culprit was, and tips for spotting clues.

"I know it isn't until tomorrow, but Happy Birthday," Lev whispered.

I fought back tears as I held out the photos of Paul. "How did you *know*?"

"It's in the way you stare at a kid Paul's age with a faraway look in your eyes. He's also the only one you ever completely color in when you draw. You miss your brother so much and it's all my--" Lev stopped speaking and reached over and caressed my cheek. "Anyway, I called Ransom and asked him to send me some things."

"Thank you." As precious as these gifts were to me, I let them fall to the floor as I flung myself at Lev and hugged him. "Because this gift is so wonderful, that soccer bet is off. You no longer have to do what I say."

"I want to do what you say." Lev's hand found the back of my head. "Don't you get it by now?"

I pulled out of the embrace so I could see his face. "What?"

Lev kissed me. Shocked, I sucked in my breath through my nose. I started to open my mouth, but he pulled away with a frustrated sigh. "The bead making starts soon, and we still have to pick up the kids."

"Is it okay if I leave my gift here? I don't want to risk losing a single thing."

He gave me a second kiss. "Of course."

Lev took my hand, and I followed him out. We walked the whole way to the orphanage without letting each other go. I couldn't take my eyes off him as he rounded up the kids. *Kids.* I slipped my hand in my back pocket and found nothing. Feeling helpless, I scanned the ground behind me.

The ultrasound photos had either disappeared into thin air, or they were sitting on Lev's couch.

I felt queasy, yet I managed to make it through the next two hours without letting my anxiety over the missing photos show. Lev was an expert at making beads, and seeing how skilled he was with his hands did little to calm me.

When we brought the kids back, Lev noticed the soccer ball was left out on the field, so we scrimmaged for a bit. When it was time for dinner, Lev accompanied me to the VC. Engen wasn't pleased to see Lev there. He was even more upset when I told him I'd promised to help Matilda get the kids ready for bed. He watched Lev and me walk back to the orphanage as though he were never going to see me again.

An hour later, Lev wasn't ready to leave work, so we kissed goodnight. Knowing that he worried about me, I was surprised that he didn't insist on walking me home.

On my walk to the apartment, I was lost in thoughts of when would be a good time to tell Lev I was pregnant, when I heard a clacking sound. A man was leaning against a lamppost knocking two big rocks together and leering at me creepily. It was the same guy who'd followed me and Dee to the VC a few weeks back. My heart began to race. The clacking was getting louder, which meant the guy was getting closer. It was terribly unnerving having my back to him. I mentally tried to prepare myself for a fight by remembering everything I'd been taught in regard to fending off attackers. Then...

"Don't even think about it," I heard a gruff male voice warn.

Not another one! A few random thoughts flew through my mind: the irony that I could be on a missing person flier hanging up in Paul's bedroom, maybe the construction workers had left some tools in the building next door that could be used as weapons, the baby.

The rocks clacked together and was followed by, "I've had my eye on this one."

"I've had my eye on her for far longer," said the gruff voice.

The baby. That reason alone was enough. No plotting to fight back. I broke into a run, and reached into my pocket for my phone.

"Call Engen," I managed to squeak into my phone before strong arms seized me from behind and lifted me off the ground, causing it to drop.

"Don't worry, it's me." Lev carried me past the front door and set me down when we got to the back of the building.

Even though his scent seemed to change daily, I'd know it anywhere.

Lev reached into my back pocket and pulled out my key card. He buzzed us in, and quickly closed the door. I'd never used this entrance before. There was a small office, a janitor's closet, and a staircase.

"I didn't know you could make your voice sound so intimidating," I said, my now calmer mind placing Lev's voice as the man who had said he'd had his eye on me for far longer. "That was the same guy who--"

I heard banging on the level above me.

"IDA!" Engen bellowed, petrified.

"Down here!"

I buried my head into Lev's neck and heard the pounding of footsteps.

"Get away from her!" Engen yelled. I opened my eyes and tilted my head to look over Lev's shoulder in time to see a wild-eyed, forehead-furled Engen jump the entire flight of stairs. It dawned on me that he must assume I was in danger from Lev.

"No!" I spun Lev so his back was against the wall, and whipped back around with my hands extended in front of me, giving a brief description to Engen, "There was a guy outside, my height with a wiry build. He was holding two large rocks."

Engen didn't hesitate. He launched the door open and asked, "Right or left?"

"Right, but don't go."

He went. I started to follow after him. Lev grabbed my hand. I looked at him and then at the door, feeling torn. Engen and I always had each other's backs.

"He'll be fine," Lev assured.

I thought of Dan's bloody face the day Engen found out I was pregnant. I thought about the three guys at the hockey game that he'd totaled by himself. I wrapped my arms around my middle. The look in Engen's eyes had frightened me more than the rock guy had. If Lev ever were to hurt me, God help him if Engen found out. I faced Lev, shaken at the thought, and found an odd expression on his face.

"I called Engen a split second before I knew it was you," I explained.

"You did the right thing. If anything were to happen, Engen

would never stop searching for you. Something tells me the feeling is mutual."

It definitely was.

"Would *you* stop searching for me?" I asked flirtatiously.

"Not a chance." Lev caressed my cheek with his thumb. "I'll walk you upstairs."

When we got to my door, my hand moved to my tummy. I wanted Lev to know that he was responsible for saving two lives, but I couldn't say those words, not yet; I was too preoccupied with the feeling of relief I had for the baby.

I heard footsteps and turned to see Engen walking toward us, dejected.

"Did you find him?" Lev asked.

Engen shook his head, panting, and tossed me my phone. I caught it with my right hand. Before I could express my gratitude to Engen for retrieving it, he lifted me with his left arm, and I felt his heart pounding fast against my chest. His right arm he extended to Lev for a handshake.

The male bonding was great, but meanwhile I was hanging four inches from the ground. "I'm tired of being picked up, it's degrading."

Engen set me down and whispered, "See you inside."

"I better get back to the orphanage," Lev said.

I hit the heel of my hand against my forehead. "I left my gift at your house."

"I'll bring it to work tomorrow." He gave me a kiss. "Goodnight."

I went inside and closed and locked the door behind me. Engen was sitting on the edge of the white loveseat with his head in his hands. I plunked down next to him, then slid my fingers up his neck and into his hair to massage the back of his head. He gave a light moan of approval.

"How did you know I was in trouble?" I asked, curiously.

"You called me. You don't do that anymore." He rubbed his eyes. "My God, I've never known fear like that before."

"I wasn't worried about getting hurt or that I'd never see

you or my family again. I was only worried for *her*. It was the strangest sensation." I stared at the sun-shaped rug that Dee had bought at the market to brighten up our apartment. "Whether I wanted her or not wasn't the issue, the issue was that no one had the right to harm her."

"And they never will," Engen vowed.

"Four months from now we'll be home and the baby will be Dan's problem." I stood and wiggled my fingers in front of Engen. "Have you been missing home?"

He took my hands, but didn't use any of my weight to help him stand. "Nope. My home is wherever you are."

"Gross." I heard enough of that mushy talk from Lev; I couldn't abide it from Engen, too.

"Gross?" Engen repeated playfully and made a grab for my waist.

"No, don't pick--"

Too late. Engen had me in his arms and was carrying me to our bedroom.

BECOMING JANELLE

I knocked on Lev's open office door. "Thanks again for making the kids sing 'Happy Birthday' to me. When's your birthday so I can return the favor?" I asked sweetly.

He stood up and strode over to me. "The day in which I age is the 22nd of August. The day I became alive was the 2nd of June, the day you got here."

A laugh sputtered out before I could stop it.

"Hey, you said you'd never laugh at me."

"You asked for that." My focus turned to his earlobe. "Did you used to have your ear pierced?"

His hand flew to his right earlobe. "Yeah, when I was thirteen."

"Do you have any pictures?" I asked with a smile.

"My mom might, but please don't ask to see them. I used to be so pimply and awkward."

I kissed his Adam's apple. "If you saw a picture of me when I was thirteen, you wouldn't recognize me."

"I bet I would."

"Gramps sent you pictures over the years?" I guessed.

"Yes, but I wouldn't need those. I'd know you in any form."

"How?"

He clicked his tongue in thought. "When you read a note, can you tell who wrote it without looking at the signature?"

An image of Janelle's journal popped into my mind. "Sure."

"It's kind of like that. I'd know your handwriting anywhere." Lev cleared his throat. "Can I make you dinner tonight?"

"I already have plans."

"Oh," he said, deflated.

"Another night?"

"Sure."

I gave him a quick kiss and left. Janelle's journal was floating around in my mind, and I had to get some fresh air. I decided to shoot some hoops while I waited for Engen, and reflected on how Janelle and I used to pretend to be each other. It was a way for her and me to deal with certain situations. Looking back, they were mostly mundane reasons like Janelle wanting to swipe a beer from her Dad's billiard hall. She'd ask herself if it would be something that I'd condone, find the answer to be no, and forego the beer.

When we were twelve, our parents proposed an actual switch. I'd spend a weekend at Janelle's house, and she'd spend that same weekend at mine. I think our parents were hoping that it would put the desire to be the other out of our minds, but I viewed it as a way to enhance the feeling of being her.

During the weekend of the "switch," I was going through her sock drawer looking for the pink fluffy ones, when I noticed a journal and had the notion of writing an entry as her. I located a pen and opened the green book.

The first page read: "Property of Mrs. Morelli."

My heart had plummeted to the floor. I flipped through the pages, and stopped at the most recent entry dated four days ago.

"Dan asked Ida out today and she refused him," Janelle had written. "Sometimes I wonder if she knows I'm crushing on him and whether that's the reason she steers clear of him. If not, then I don't know what her deal is. Who wouldn't want to be Dan's girlfriend?"

My eyes scanned more pages for my name:

"I was Ida again in my dream last night. Dan asked me to go with him to the dance. Just once, I'd like to dream that I'm me when Dan asks me out."

Why hadn't Janelle ever told me that she liked Dan? Then again, I never told her that sometimes being with Engen made my insides squirm. I flipped ahead a few more pages.

"I saw Dan pushing Paul on a swing today. He's so good with kids. I wonder if he wants his own? I can't think of anything better than sharing a child with Dan."

I closed the journal, set it back in the sock drawer, and covered it up. This was so messed up! Was Dan the real reason she pretended to be me? I hoped Janelle thought I had more going for me than being liked by a guy.

Even after she died, I didn't quit playing.

Thankfully, I was brought back to the present by a warm, familiar tingle in my skull which alerted me whenever Engen was near.

"Nice shot, Denmark!"

I turned to look at my friend. "Good enough to play in the big game, coach?"

His lips tugged upward. "Which big game?"

I did a between-the-legs dribble. "The one against that team, from that random school."

"Oh *that* big game." He closed one eye, pretending to consider it. "You're not ready, kid. Better luck next season."

"Aw, shucks." I rolled the basketball into the open garage door, and joined Engen. "You sort of made my day," I shared.

"Yeah?" Engen put his arm around my waist and kissed my temple. "You sort of made my life."

"Happy Birthday!" Paul greeted me later that night on the phone. "What did you do to celebrate, huh?"

I was sitting cross-legged on the sun-shaped rug, playing with a loose string. "I worked, Engen took me out for dinner and milkshakes, and then we met up with Dee to go see the play at the community center that Krista co-directed."

"Ish, fun, boring."

Engen had thought the play was boring, too. He made it through ten minutes before he was on his phone. Dee was sitting between me and Engen, so I couldn't tell exactly what he was watching, but whatever it was had caused him to gasp. I turned my head to look at him and saw that he was watching me with wide, haunted eyes. His hand covered his mouth.

"What's wrong?" I mouthed.

Engen shook his head. When he excused himself to go the bathroom, he never came back. Dee showed me a message he'd sent, letting her know that he'd gone back to the apartment. Dee then said she was going to go check on him, and left also. Confused, I checked my phone for a message elaborating on why he'd left, but there wasn't one.

"Is Dan still spending time with you?" I asked, returning my attention to Paul.

Paul scooped up the harmonica from his dresser. "Si, senorita. That means 'yes, young man.'"

"If you thought senorita meant 'young man,' why did you say it to *me*?"

"Anywho, did Mom only marry Dad because she needed free legal advice?" Paul asked, and then blew a few notes into his harmonica.

"He wasn't a lawyer when she married him."

"Does Liver want to be a lawyer?"

"I have no clue what that means," I said bluntly.

"Liver Osen, the person you said you made the girly beads with in your last message."

I rolled over on the rug, laughing. "His name is Lev Rosen, and I think he wants to continue to work with kids, for some odd reason."

I let Paul prattle on for a few more minutes before saying goodnight. Halfway to my bedroom I heard Engen say softly, "...really taking its toll on me."

"I can tell," Dee said consolingly. "What, initially, changed you two?"

"I slept with a girl who wasn't Ida," Engen confessed. "It was the worst decision I ever made."

"You need some time apart from her in order to process the fact that maybe that happened for a reason," Dee prescribed. "I'll ask her to switch bedrooms with me."

I opened the door. Dee and Engen were sitting side by side on

Engen's bed. Her hand was on his knee, and his head was buried in his hands. His head snapped up at the sound of the door. I grabbed my pillow and pajamas without looking at his face.

Heart still racing with anger, I opened the nightstand drawer, pulled out a fresh pair of earplugs, and threw them at Dee. "He snores," I said, and walked out of the door.

Engen's bed squeaked. "Ida, we need--"

"You're giving yourself time to emotionally process this, *remember*?" Dee cut in.

There were a million thoughts running through my head as I made my way back to the living room. I tossed my pillow, followed by my body, onto the purple loveseat. The last thing I wanted to do was analyze how I was feeling, so I fell asleep.

I woke up a few hours later to the sound of light snoring. Engen was laying on the floor in front of my loveseat. I crawled onto the floor, curled up next to him, and took in his peaceful face. He had a crease in his hair from wearing a ball cap all day. The sun had caused freckles to pop up on his nose, forehead, and the tops of his shoulders. He was indescribably beautiful.

"Happy Birthday," I whispered, and traced his perfect full lips with two fingers.

His snoring faltered. Worried about getting caught, I closed my eyes.

I awoke the next morning to the sound of honking. The ride to Lakeside Adventure! I sprang up from the floor and ran to the window, peering over the air conditioning unit in time to see an old tan Buick pull away, leaving a cloud of dust behind it. My heart dropped. Good thing I'd wished Engen a happy birthday last night.

I wandered into our bedroom and got dressed for the day in short jean shorts with the inside pocket material that hung down to touch my thighs, and a gray tank top. I stuffed some money in my pocket and decided to go out to get some coffee from the local doughnut stand.

The door to the apartment opened, and Engen walked in. He was whistling and carrying a cup holder with two large coffees, along with a white bag I recognized from the nearby Total station.

"You're in a good mood," I said, shocked yet pleased to see him.

"Waking up with you in my arms has that effect on me."

My cheeks flushed. "Your ride left without you."

"It was supposed to." Engen set the tray and the bag down on the coffee table. "I sent Dee and Krista."

"Why?"

"You and I always spend our birthdays together." Engen took a coffee out of the cup holder, handed it to me, and then knelt down on the floor in front of me. "I wasn't going to let this little troublemaker ruin that."

As usual, the baby responded to Engen's voice by kicking me. He tenderly set his lips on my belly, over my shirt. I ran my fingers through Engen's soft, brown hair. I felt thankful for the pregnancy for giving me this tender moment. Considering it was still an unwanted pregnancy, the feeling didn't last long.

"You're wearing my favorite outfit on you." Engen wrapped his arms around me.

"And I love you in that t-shirt," I said, complimenting his black, vintage Rolling Stones shirt. "Are you still mad at me?"

"I was never mad at you. I was upset over a certain situation. I'm better today," he said when he saw my concerned face.

"Do you want to discuss it?"

"Very badly," Engen said. "But all things considered, you're going to want me to keep it to myself for now."

Since he knew me better than anyone, I accepted that answer. "I just want to put out there that if you're tired of me--"

"Not by a long shot," he countered adamantly as he stood.

I handed him my coffee cup, went over to the table, and took the other cup out of the holder.

Engen narrowed his eyes. "What was wrong with the one I gave you?"

"You're forgetting that I'm older, wiser, and know you don't want me to have caffeine." I winked.

"Oh yeah?" Even though Engen was now stuck with the decaf, his eyes were full of desire as he reached behind me, slipping a hand up the back of my shorts so he could caress my butt cheek. "Did you know I was going to do that?"

"Yep."

His smile was heart-melting. "How?"

"Because it drives you wild when I wink at you. Now let's eat, because I just got an idea where to take you today."

Mabira Forest Reserve was by far the best place I'd seen. It was home to 312 different species of trees. I didn't know there were that many. There were butterflies and primates as well, but those didn't interest us. Engen and I were here for the bird walk. The reserve had 68 kilometers of trails, many that were dedicated to the birds alone. We spotted 45 of the 300 types, including the Purple Throated Cuckoo, Nahans, Francolin, and our agreed-upon favorite, the Shining Blue Kingfisher.

We also both agreed that the Reserve made us feel grateful for coming to Africa.

The girls got home around seven. They'd had a wonderful, although tiring time. Soon after their return, Marco stopped by to take Engen out drinking.

We girls were taking advantage of Engen being gone by playing "Do, date, or diss." Using our phones, we called up our high school yearbooks, and Krista found a way to set it up so the photos of the boys would play continuously.

It was a nice glimpse into each others' lives because most photos sparked a story. The rule was there could only be one do, date, or diss for each photo. I ended up with a lot of do's and disses because I wasn't as into the game as they were.

We'd finished Dee's yearbook and were almost halfway through mine. We were getting toward the end of the "L's" but in anticipation of seeing Engen Malone's photo, Krista was calling out "do" to each guy, so no one beat her. After Krista won the right to "do" Engen, I was so thankful this game was fake...until Daniel Morelli's face showed up to slap me back to reality.

"Do!" Krista and Dee yelled at the same time.

They started to fight over Morelli.

"Did," I mumbled.

Thad Morton came up with no one calling anything. Krista turned the image back to Dan.

"Do," Dee said victoriously, eyes on me.

"Date," Krista relented, eyes on me.

"Did," I repeated, eyes on Dan's image.

It went from hearing a pin drop to an eruption of squeals.

Krista's jaw dropped. "*That's* the guy who sent you those beautiful dresses for your birthday? He's so hot."

"Have you told Dan about Lev?" Dee asked.

I shook my head. "Dan knows I don't want to be with him."

"But you *were* with him," Dee said.

"I don't owe Dan any explanations," I responded testily. "Let's get back to the game."

Dee shrugged. "Suit yourself."

MAKING A DATE

"Ida?" Lev asked, and leaned against the orphanage's kitchen counter.

"Hmm?" I was pretty engrossed in stirring the cookie batter and didn't look up.

Ever since I turned him down for dinner on my birthday, things had shifted between us. We still had our after-work basketball games with comfortable conversation, minus the extra touching. As much as I liked Lev, it had actually been fine. I preferred it when he wasn't trying to impress me all the time.

"Would you like to come to Lake Victoria with me tomorrow?" Lev asked. "If you don't already have plans, that is."

"Plans?" I echoed foolishly.

"I spent this past week upset at you for choosing your friends over me, when the truth is you would've been blowing them off if you'd come to my place." Lev took a deep breath. "So, do you have plans on Sunday?"

"No." I then remembered I was supposed to be taking it easy. "What happens at Lake Victoria?"

He ran his finger over the length of the counter and stopped beside me. "There's fishing, sailing, and even a portion of water blocked off for swimming that's treated against bilharzia."

I smiled. A parasitic disease had never sounded so inviting.

"Did you bring a bathing suit?" he asked, eying the cookie batter.

My throat went dry. "No."

"Maybe Krista or Dorian have one you could borrow?"

"Maybe." Pregnant me in swimwear didn't sound fantastic. "Actually, I--"

"We don't have to go swimming, if that's what has you worried."

"That's not it," I choked.

"Is it the idea of spending all day alone with me?"

"Hardly."

"Then I'll meet you at your apartment tomorrow morning at eight a.m."

I gave him a quick kiss on the lips. I knew better than to try for more. Kissing Engen had been open mouth and lots of tongue from the beginning. Lev was so chaste.

Lev sighed. "Tomorrow can't come fast enough."

"There she is."

Lev and I separated at the voice, turned, and saw Megan holding Asya's hand.

"Asya wanted Ida." Megan let go of Asya's hand and she ran to me.

I knelt to Asya's level. "Hi, sweetheart."

"Pretty Ida." Asya put her tiny hands on my cheeks.

"Why can't tomorrow come fast enough, Lev?" Megan asked.

Lev told Megan about our trip to the lake tomorrow.

"Bye-bye," Asya said.

Her adoption was pending, and as far as I knew, she was unaware of that fact.

"I'm not leaving," I assured her.

Asya hugged me and whispered in my ear, "Pretty girl inside."

My breath caught. Did she mean I was pretty on the inside, or that my baby was pretty? I returned Asya's hug, but my attention was on Lev and Megan's conversation.

"Do you recommend I visit the lake, also?" Megan hedged.

"Uh, sure," Lev said.

Asya touched my belly, and started to sing. I focused on her singing softly against my shoulder. It distracted me from the upsetting fact that Lev had just agreed to Megan's request to accompany us to the lake.

During a&c, Afi spilled paint on my shoe, but I didn't bat an eyelash. There are some things in life that you just have to let go, and what it boiled down to was I'd be spending an otherwise

Lev-free day with Lev.

When I got back to the apartment, I went to the purple loveseat, stretched out, and folded my hands behind my head. I stared up at the ceiling, smiling stupidly.

The door opened, and then closed. It reopened a second later. I looked over to see Krista standing stock-still in the doorway.

"Hey," I greeted. "Did you just come in and then leave?"

"Yeah." Krista dropped her backpack. "I thought I was in the wrong apartment."

I laughed. "Didn't you see me?"

"I didn't recognize you with that goofy grin on your face." Krista closed the door and stood in front of my feet, looking offended. "What's going on with your shoe?"

"Afi spilled green paint on it," I said dreamily.

Krista took her sandals off and set them on the welcome mat. "Remind me to send flowers."

"Where to?"

"The poor kid's funeral."

"Oh, I didn't kill her," I said casually. "Hey, can I borrow a bathing suit?"

Krista grabbed a bottle of water from our mini fridge. "Sure. Why?"

I kept my back against the arm of the loveseat and drew my legs into my body. "I'm going to Lake Victoria with Lev and Megan tomorrow."

She eyed me, calculating. "Do you still hate it here?"

"I dislike it, yes."

"What do you dislike the most?"

"The way the rec room has smelled like egg salad for the last two days." *Megan,* I added silently to myself.

Krista drained the water and opened a second bottle. "Engen's going to be pissed when he hears you're spending your day off with Lev."

"Engen likes Lev now."

Krista spit her water out. "They may act amiable in front of you, but in reality they wanna kill each other."

"That isn't true."

"Really? Do you like Engen's girlfriend?"

"*Ex*-girlfriend, and no."

"You see my point then. I'm going to go change," Krista announced.

A moment later her music started, and Engen walked through the front door.

"You seem giddy." Engen noted after we exchanged 'hellos.'

I explained the outing I had planned with Lev. Engen sat down, and I made a tent with my legs over his lap.

"I heard it gets crowded at the lake." He hugged my legs to his chest. "Do you think you'll be able to handle it?"

"I have to. I don't want to make a fool of myself."

"It's unavoidable." He sighed heavily.

"Sucky day with Buv?" I guessed.

"His mom made a pass at me today."

"Want me to rough her up?"

"Naw." Engen set his chin on my knee. "So, was there an 'I love you' said when Lev asked you out?"

I rolled my eyes. "He doesn't *love* me."

"Of course he does. You're incredible, fun to hang out with, and utterly gorgeous. You don't make things complicated. You could care less about gossip and shoes." He looked down at my paint-splattered shoe and cringed. "Maybe you could care a bit more about shoes. I love discussing movies and books with you. You always have my back, you have killer legs, and don't get me started on your tits, because--"

I lifted my legs and pushed him until he stumbled off the couch.

"Did I mention you aren't a sissy?" he asked from the floor.

"I had no idea you noticed those things."

"Seriously?" Engen asked in disbelief.

I felt my face grow hot. "I know we used to kiss and fool around--"

"Fool around, huh?" Engen nodded toward our bedroom. "Care to refresh my memory?"

I chewed on my thumbnail. "Aside from a good time, I never presumed it meant anything to you."

"Well it did, and you should've known that it did."

"Should I have known when you selected Brittany? The polar opposite of me?"

Engen's expression was skeptical. "You and I were involved *years* before Brittany came into the picture, but you had your super-secret reason why we couldn't be together."

"I asked you to trust that my reason was meaningful, but you couldn't do that."

"Because since when did you keep secrets from me?"

"*That* should've been your hint to trust me."

"And this is your way of getting back at me, is it?" He re-adjusted his ball cap. "Fine. Go have your fake romance, and let me know when you get a clue."

"It might be awhile," I warned.

"I'm prepared to wait."

"That's a first," I said softly.

"You know that I regret sleeping with Brittany." Engen's chin quivered. "I'm still thoroughly disgusted over that night."

"Me, too." I exhaled a shaky breath.

"Ask him if he likes Lev!" Krista shouted from her bedroom.

"Oh, yeah," I remembered. "You like Lev now, right?"

Engen cupped his hand around his ear. "I'm sorry, what?"

"You shook Lev's hand the night of that stalker incident. Doesn't that mean you approve of him?"

Engen set his hand on my thigh. "I cannot stomach a single thing about that guy."

"Told ya!" Krista yelled triumphantly.

LAKE VICTORIA

I stood in front of Dee's little oval mirror wearing Krista's black bikini with silver sequins. I had the mirror positioned so I could see my stomach. There was a bump, but nothing anyone should notice unless they were really concentrating. My hips had widened out. The weight looked good on me. The only thing I wasn't comfortable with was my ever-growing breasts.

I heard a knock on the door. With a jolt of excitement, I pulled a light blue, airy sundress over my head. "Coming!"

Engen jumped up from the loveseat and made a beeline for the door. His hand covered the doorknob, and his tongue passed between his lips. "I can see your underwear through your dress."

"It's a bikini." I scowled.

"Well, it looks like underwear." He gave a low whistle. "What did he do to deserve you?"

There was another light knock.

I frowned. "Let him in."

"Seriously, why does he get the pleasure of your company?"

"You need me to list the reasons right now?" I hissed.

"You're killing me," Engen groaned, looking at my chest.

I put a hand on my hip and cut my eyes to the door.

Engen made a big show of twisting the knob. Finally, the door opened to reveal Lev wearing knee-length navy board shorts, and a light blue t-shirt almost the same shade as my dress.

Lev took me in. "Wow. You look incredibly h--" he eyed Engen, "healthy."

"And you're incredibly hot," I responded.

Lev didn't seem to hear me, though. He was concentrating on my feet, with delight written all over his face.

"Look, Lev," Engen said in an all-kidding-aside voice.

Lev was too busy stealing a whiff of my hair as I brushed past him into the hallway to respond.

"Dude?" Engen tried again.

Lev snapped to. "Yeah?"

"If the beach is packed--"

"See you later, Engen," I sang.

As soon as the apartment door closed, Lev's mouth covered my throat in kisses. We both jumped when we heard pounding from inside the apartment followed by cursing. Engen was going to destroy the place. I was prepared to go back in, cancel the date, anything to take his pain away. As if sensing abandonment, Lev hugged me tightly to him.

"You look severely hot," he stated.

"You mean healthy," I corrected.

"I mean mind-bogglingly sexy."

"I was going for healthy."

Lev chuckled, then gave a reluctant sigh and went to knock on Megan's door. With one last glance at my door, I walked over to join Lev.

Megan answered the door with a Kleenex held to her nose. "I'b sick."

"Gee, I'm sorry to hear that," Lev said, not sounding the least bit sorry. "Get some rest."

Megan pushed the door closed.

"Megan's sick," I said flatly, to cover my elation.

Lev ran a hand through his hair. "Thank God."

Since two people couldn't walk side-by-side down the narrow hallway, Lev motioned for me to go first. *He's just being a gentleman*, I told myself, *he didn't do it so he could look at your ass.* I checked over my shoulder. He was looking at my ass. When we got to the exit, Lev sidled around me to hold the door open. As I walked by him, the smell of his aftershave met my nostrils.

"The matatu will drive by over there." Lev nodded to the right, looking bashful. "When I was licking my wounds over you not spending your birthday with me, I genuinely missed you."

"It was a pretty sucky time," I agreed.

"I'm kind of a novice when it comes to relationships," he admitted. "I asked another girl to join us on our date. The idea of sharing me must've been devastating for you."

I bent over in laughter. As I choked back my last giggle, I noticed Lev watching me with a smile in his eyes. "What?" I asked.

"I love hearing you laugh."

A matatu slowed at the curb, and we quickly hopped in. The conductor told me it was five thousand shillings. Lev told him we'd only pay three. The conductor agreed when he realized Lev wasn't some unknowing tourist. There were only two seats left, one next to an old man holding a cage with a chicken in it, the other was in front of him next to an attractive young lady. I chose the seat next to the old man, and Lev sat with his back facing the lady.

He leaned in until our foreheads touched. "You like to examine me."

"Maybe a tad. Hey," I whispered, and nodded at the woman next to him, "you should ask her to join us."

Lev leaned forward to meet my lips in a kiss. He then turned around so all I saw was the back of his head. While Lev engaged the young woman in a conversation spoken in Lugandan, I closed my eyes and became preoccupied with listening to the sound of his voice. The man next to me reeked, but if I concentrated hard enough I could smell Lev's aftershave.

The next thing I knew, the old man beside me was poking me in the arm.

"Stage!" he yelled.

The matatu slowed at my seatmate's command.

I let him out and sat back down, this time next to the window. I expected Lev to occupy the now empty space, but he stayed where he was, conversing with his seatmate in hushed tones.

Lev's body lurched as the conductor stepped on the gas. I chewed on a strand of hair and watched the way his jaw moved. When he formed certain words, I liked to watch his tongue scrape his top teeth on the way back into his mouth. I saw an adorable mole bob up and down with the movement of his Adam's apple. I liked that even though this woman was prettier than me, Lev didn't look at her in the same way. He didn't analyze her expressions and his eyes didn't smile like they did when talking to me.

When the matatu stopped, Lev stood and said goodbye to the woman next to him. When we disembarked, he took my hand and we walked toward the shore.

"How do you know that woman?" I asked.

"I can't tell you that."

"I thought there was nothing in your life you wanted to keep secret from me," I reminded him.

"It's not my secret, it's hers."

I thought of the gigantic secret I was keeping from him and squeezed his hand in understanding.

Lev swept his free hand in front of him. "What do you think?"

I took in the world's largest tropical lake. The small waves were rolling in, and with the sun shining on the water, it was truly a beautiful sight. There was lake as far as the eye could see, and already full of swimmers, boats, and men fishing on oversized canoes. The beach was also bursting with activity. Parents were setting up blankets and large umbrellas, and slathering sunscreen on children. There were naked toddlers playing in the sand, and men constructing volleyball nets. Women were carrying large bowls of bananas on their heads, encouraging the beach-goers to purchase them.

"It's gorgeous," I said. "What are we going to do first?"

"A boat ride?" he suggested.

"Sounds excellent."

Lev paid our way onto the boat. We found a spot by the railing and leaned against it. He rested his hand on top of mine, and I smiled. The boat pulled away from the dock, and the crew members started to sing. Soon all the passengers aside from Lev and me were singing. I wondered if Lev longed to join in, but when I glanced at him, he was looking at me with a peaceful expression on his face.

When we got off the boat, Lev ran into a few guys he knew from high school hanging out on the beach. After he introduced me, I slipped away, removed my dress, and headed for the water.

I swam out waist-deep and watched Lev's pleasant expression turn panic-stricken when he saw my discarded dress in a heap on the sand, but no me nearby. He bid a quick farewell to his friends, shaded his eyes with his hand, and scanned the water. He smiled when he saw me, peeled off his shirt in one cool movement, and dove into the water.

When Lev got to me, I put my arms around his neck. His wet skin felt glorious against mine. I found his burn scar on the back of his shoulder, and lightly ran my fingers over it. He circled an arm around my waist and pressed his wet lips to mine. I opened my mouth, and when his tongue slid inside it I was instantly consumed with pleasure.

Once we'd taken our fill of the lake, we found a sandy hill. I was laying on my front, propped up on my elbows. Lev was on his side, his head in his hand, gently running his fingertips along the curve of my spine. He filled me in on the history of the lake. Many people relied on it for food, water, and employment. Due to the increase in dams, climate change, and evaporation, the lake had heavily shrunk in size. The fishing docks were extended super far off the original shoreline now, because the fish stuck to deeper water.

"I've been dying to ask you something all day," Lev said after the lesson. He gently ran his hand down the length of my leg and pinched my ankle bracelet. "Have you always worn this around your ankle?"

"Yeah. Gramps gave it to me with a note that read, 'to: You, from: Africa," I shared. "He told me it was a necklace, but since my relationship with Gramps has always been weird, I looped it twice and made it into an ankle bracelet. That way he didn't know just how often I wore it."

"The girl's neck I used as a model was a malnourished six-year old, so it probably wouldn't have fit your neck, anyway," Lev said.

"You made this?" I asked, aghast.

"For you, yes. I made this for myself." Pleased, he lifted his wrist.

"I noticed yours my first day," I said. It was just too surreal to know that I'd been wearing something his hands had made, that we'd been connected all this time. "Why would you make this for me?"

"Because the first time Ransom showed me a photo of you, I somehow knew that it could only be you for me." He stood and extended his hands. I took them in mine, and he lifted me to my feet. "The girl who'd climb to the top of a willow tree and sit there for hours. The girl who claimed to hate Swahili, yet spoke it in her sleep. The girl who fixed my truck and beat me at football."

With one hand on the small of my back and the other resting on my hip, he kissed me. It started out soft and tender, almost as if the young boy inside of him was experiencing his first kiss. Then it grew more amorous. A hand traveled up and over the clasp of my bikini top and into my hair, where it became tangled in the wet mess. I laughed the whole time he unwound the strands from his fingers. The situation was ridiculous, and he was being way too cautious not to hurt me.

"I don't do this often," he apologized, after his hand was freed. "It's been at least three years since I kissed a girl that I liked. I've been too busy!" he added, seeing the disbelief on my face.

"Then you have a lot of making up to do."

He beamed and went back to work on my lips. Eventually, we couldn't ignore our rumbling stomachs, so we went in search of food. I slipped my sundress on over the sandy bikini. Lev opted to keep his shirt off, and I didn't argue.

We walked to a cafe not too far off the shoreline. We sat at an outdoor table with our iced teas and grilled Tilapia, and talked for hours. Lev divulged his childhood struggles of life in the orphanage and how he'd worried he would remain there forever. He had finally been adopted at the age of ten by Omo and Nolan Rosen, and went to live with them at the home Omo now shared with Akiki. Lev spoke of their divorce and losing Nolan to America. He went on to tell me that even though he enjoyed his job immensely, he planned on attending Makerere University in Kampala. He wanted to get a degree in Child Development, and hoped to work as a youth counselor one day.

I wished I could have said that I was planning on attending a university, but I was the girl who didn't want to do anything. That's when it hit me hard: jealousy. I was flat out jealous of all the girls going to college. Jealous of their books, course schedules, and assuredness. Jealous of the girls who'd get to sit near Lev in class. How many of those girls would get to find out how blue his eyes pierced when he was worried? How many would figure out that despite the use of cologne or aftershave, Lev always smelled like some variation of crayons, paste, or play-doh?

My throat closed as I stared at the condensation sweating down the edge of my glass. If Janelle were alive and sitting here with us, she would be able to contribute to the college talk by telling Lev which schools she was interested in attending.

"What are you thinking about?" Lev pulled his shirt on.

Murdering your future girlfriends. I went with a more rational answer, "Janelle."

"Who's Janelle?"

"The curly-haired girl from my drawings." I lifted my necklace out from under my dress. "She used to wear one of these charms. She died in a motorcycle accident six months ago. She was smart and creative. Now the world will never know what she was capable of." I felt a stinging sensation in my nose. Lev moved his chair closer and pulled me into a hug. "One thing she never got to create was a relationship with this guy she liked, Dan."

A sob escaped my throat. Thinking of Dan and what I'd done with him caused a feeling of anguish in my gut. Lev held me and asked me questions pertaining to Janelle until it was time to go. We were lucky enough to share a seat on the matatu this time.

Once we were outside my building, I wrapped my arms

around his waist. I breathed in the smell of the lake and sand that clung to his cheek. Our intimate moment was interrupted by Lev's ringing phone, which he had just turned on two minutes ago, when we'd disembarked the matatu.

Lev gave a sigh of frustration and reached into his pocket. He answered his phone with a curt, "Hold on."

I could hear the desperation in the caller's voice as she said, "Lev, don't--"

He pressed the phone against his chest to muffle her voice. "Thank you for the most perfect day of my life, Ida."

I swallowed my curiosity at why he seemed to want to take this girl's phone call in private, and said, "Bye."

He waited until I was inside before he returned to the caller.

GONE

Even though I'd had a tough phone conversation this morning with Dan where I had broken the news that I was getting involved with Lev, I still practically skipped into the orphanage.

"Good morning, kids!" I called, while not breaking stride. "Hey, Stuart. You look frazzled."

"We have three appointments right after breakfast."

I gave him the A-OK hand signal. "You and Becky will be great."

"That's just it, Becky's...okay, you're just gonna keep walking."

I waved over my shoulder and continued toward Lev's office. I had no idea what Stu was saying; I just knew I was going to burst if I didn't see—

"Becky?"

Becky turned from the filing cabinet. "Yes, hon?"

I stood frozen in the doorway. "Um, I forgot what the art project was today."

"Oh, that's easy." Becky nodded to the cork board. "I was afraid by your expression that there was a problem. I sure hope nothing goes wrong this week."

I exhaled slowly and wondered what the kids were going to do with something as mundane as paper mâché skills. "This *week*?"

"Lev called late last night to say that he's going to cover for Chris, the leader of an orphanage in Bulenga. Good thing we're capable of operating without him."

"Yeah, good thing."

"I was hoping you'd take the kids out for their football game after a&c."

"Consider it done."

Becky beamed. Who could smile in a place that didn't include Lev? I trudged my way to the kitchen. Was that actually my problem? Did the fact that my insides were burning have anything to do with Lev's absence? I hoped not. My arms shook as I put the apron over my head. My fingers fumbled with the ties. I gave up and tossed the apron to the floor. One week without Lev's dancing eyes or warm touch. Shouldn't be a problem.

I reached into the sack of oatmeal mix and started scooping it into a giant bowl. Most of the oatmeal ended up on the floor. Why didn't Lev tell me he was going away? I tossed the scooper to the ground, picked up the bag, and turned the contents into the bowl. The baby moved inside of me, and I rolled my eyes. I added water to the mix, went to stir it, and dropped my spoon yet again.

"I hear a lot of banging coming from back here," Megan said, entering the kitchen. "Are you alright?"

"Yes. Thank you," I said dismissively.

If it hadn't been for Megan canceling yesterday, I wouldn't know what it was like to have Lev's tongue down my throat. Half of me wanted to shake her until her teeth fell out. The other half wanted to make her the godmother of my child.

Megan started to pour juice into cups. "It's going to be a long week for you."

I never wanted to hear the word 'week' again. "Aren't you ill?" I asked.

"Nope," she said with a wink. "I just enjoy making people uncomfortable. It worked like a charm on you two."

I paused in my stirring. "How did you know that Lev and I wanted a chance to be together…alone?"

Wow, that was an awkward sentence to hear myself say.

Megan shrugged. "He never tried to hide it, and you tried too hard."

I began to ladle the oatmeal into twenty wooden bowls. "Stuart said there were clients coming today, shouldn't you be getting the kids ready?"

"They already are. Lev stopped by the apartment last night--"

Splat.

"What?" Megan siphoned the answer from my brain. "Oh, he didn't tell you he was leaving."

I tasted sour milk in my mouth. My blood felt thick as sludge.

Megan put her arm around me, and I didn't bother to shrug it off.

My bad mood was affecting my workday. The kids complained that their oatmeal tasted horrible, a&c was a mess, and I didn't join the soccer game. I simply observed while trying to get ahold of Dan. He didn't pick up, so I decided to call Paul instead.

An orange and black cat face answered on the first ring. "Meow?"

Paul's face appeared. "Why for art thou ringing me at this hour, Herr Sister?"

"What just happened?" I asked.

"Putt happened. I got him from Dan who got him from Mrs. K. as a tip for delivering groceries. It's like I got tipped for doing nothing."

"Is Morelli there?"

"It's four in the morning."

I slammed the palm of my hand into my head. "Sorry. I'm not myself today."

"Ohh, who are you? El chupacabra?"

"Sure." My brother kept strange hours, so it wasn't shocking that he was awake. "Having your four a.m. Hot Pocket?"

"I am indeedy." Paul held up the remaining chunk as proof. "Oh, FYI, Dad came home from work early yesterday and saw your sister reading some girly novel when she was supposed to be in some boring engineering lecture!"

"Adora, stop teasing the girls!" I yelled, and went back to Paul. "Why isn't she going to class?"

"Like you, she doesn't know what she wants to do with her life," he disclosed, and took a bite of food.

"How is it that *you're* so driven?"

"Got me." He shrugged. "*Both* of my sisters are terrified of their lost-ness."

"My lost-ness doesn't scare me anymore," I realized.

Paul stopped mid-chew. "What scares you now?"

"My found-ness."

We were able to get in a few more minutes of conversation before I had to let Paul go so I could intervene with Adroa, who would not let up on the girls.

◆ ◆ ◆

Asya's adoption had gone through to some movie director who lived in England, so I drove her to Entebbe airport Saturday after lunch. I cried when she assured me that we'd meet again, and I wept the whole way back. I didn't know if it was the pregnancy amping up my emotions or if I was truly going to miss her.

I dropped the orange truck off and went inside to check Lev's office to make sure he hadn't done something crazy like return from Bulenga. He hadn't. I said farewell to my coworkers, walked home, and went straight to bed. Maybe Lev would decide to stay away for another week. I suppose I would know if I actually answered any of his phone calls or listened to one of his eight messages.

Later that evening, I was sitting on the love seat with my legs on Engen's lap. He'd offered a foot massage and there was no way I was turning that down. Krista and Dee were getting ready to go to the VC for a movie night. Engen and Marco were going out drinking, and I was so lost in bliss at the idea of being alone that I barely registered the knock.

"I'll get it!" Krista yelled, and opened the door. "Ida, it's for you. If you don't want it, I'll take it."

My head snapped up. Without a word, I withdrew my feet from Engen's lap. I didn't dare take my eyes off the dirty, sweaty guy standing in the doorway for fear he'd disappear. I walked swiftly toward him. Krista jumped out of my way.

Lev dropped his knapsack and raised his hands in a surrender pose. "Let me explain."

With one hand, I pushed him out into the hallway. He staggered back the two feet and smacked into the opposite wall. His tired eyes were surprised as I closed the apartment door behind me. Ignoring his pleas for forgiveness, I threw myself into his arms and kissed him. Our lips had barely touched when I forced his mouth open with mine. His stubble scratched my face. Our tongues collided, and a struggle ensued as we vied for entry into the other's mouth.

He broke the kiss and sighed. "I stood outside your building for twenty minutes trying to figure out how to tell you goodbye. Megan saw me, so I told her I was there to ask her to go into work early. Please forgive my cowardice."

"You were just doing your job." I lifted the bottom of his shirt and rested my fingertips on the ridges of his abs. I no longer wanted to be alone tonight. "Do you want to go somewhere else?"

"I'll go anywhere you want," Lev answered.

"Bulenga?"

"Maybe not there."

I opened the apartment door, grabbed my shoes, and yelled, "See you guys!"

As soon as we got to Lev's house, he excused himself to go take a much needed shower. His matatu had broken down, and the conductor said another one would come to get them in a couple hours, but he couldn't wait that long to see me, so he ran the rest of the way to my apartment.

While he bathed, I took the liberty of poking around his house for the ultrasound pictures. After ten minutes of unsuccessful searching, I knocked on the bathroom door. I could hear the smile in his voice when he invited me in. I opened the door and practically fell over. Lev was standing in front of the mirror applying shaving cream along his jaw line. A white towel hung low around his hips.

I sat on the sink in front of him, and enjoyed watching the way his ab muscles scrunched when he maneuvered around me to swirl his foamy razor in the sink water.

"If I have to go away again, will you promise to answer my calls?" Lev blurted out.

"No. I see this past week as practice for the inevitable future," I told him. I wasn't looking forward to being away from him, but one of us needed to be practical.

Lev's eyes turned sad. "My adoptive father wanted my mom and me to move to America with him, but I refused, so she divorced him. Even though I *would* be willing to move to America to be with you, I can't leave her."

"A couple months isn't long enough for us to be discussing the idea of relocating."

"I don't want to lose you." Lev hugged me to his damp, tan chest. "I still don't know everything about you."

The most important thing he needed to know, I couldn't bring myself to tell him. Lev seemed to hold me in such high regard, how would he perceive me once he found out I was pregnant?

Lev walked me back to my apartment in time for curfew. I had the next day off, and after promising to spend it with him, I floated to bed.

Once I had laid down, Engen asked, "Are you in love with Lev?"

I rested my hands atop my belly to feel the baby's reaction to the sound of Engen's voice, as I searched his intoxicated eyes.

"Are you?" he repeated.

My breath hitched at how worried he sounded, as if his entire life depended on my answer. Did that mean he actually might...no. I shut down that line of thinking. His past actions had made it quite clear that he didn't want me anymore.

I gazed at the troubled set of his jaw. "How could you think--"

"--that it's any of your business?" Krista said loudly from the doorway.

I sat up and pulled the lamp string on the nightstand, flooding the room with light. "Did we wake you?"

"Dee and I were never asleep." Krista flipped aside my mosquito netting and sat on the edge of my bed.

"This guy only stopped pacing five minutes ago," Dee shared as she entered the room, moved aside Engen's mosquito netting, and sat on the end of his bed.

"Engen has the right to worry," I said, drawing my knees up to my chin. "I was sent to Africa because--"

"We know," Dee interrupted.

I glanced at Engen questionably, but he shook his head no.

"Engen didn't spill. These walls are paper thin and you two talk about it constantly," Dee offered.

"What we don't know is how far along you are."

"A little over five months," I answered.

"You're like a blade of grass, though," Krista commented, with a note of jealousy in her voice.

"It's Dan's baby," Dee proclaimed, and hung her head. "I can't imagine what you're going through."

I stretched my legs out. "I've come to terms with it."

"Who else knows?" Dee asked.

"Just us and Akiki, right?" Engen asked me.

"And Megan and her psychic priest friend," I added.

"Well, yeah, that went without saying," Engen said and shot me a wink.

My eyelids fluttered. Judging by the jolt that just went to my stomach, him winking at me drove me wild, too.

"When are you going to tell Lev?" Krista asked.

I tore my eyes from Engen. "Soon."

"Well that's that." Krista clapped her hand on my shoulder. "I'll say goodbye to Smiley Ida now."

"Lev's not the reason for my smile." I twisted my hair into a bun and pulled the binder from my wrist to hold it up. "It's the kids. I enjoy the work I do with them."

Krista snorted. "And Engen's madly in love with me."

Engen cut his eyes to mine and shifted uncomfortably. "I'm

definitely not."

Dee and Krista laughed uproariously.

With a scrunched face, Engen nudged Dee with his foot until she fell, taking the mosquito netting with her. Dee giggled like crazy as Engen stood, picked her up, and carried her into her bedroom. I heard the bed squeak as he plunked her down on it. When he came back in, Krista stood and eagerly raised her arms. Engen tossed her over his shoulder like she was a bag of oranges. I could still hear the girls cackling after Engen returned.

He walked up to me and bent to give me a kiss goodnight. However, instead of the usual cheek kiss, he set his lips directly on mine. Every cell I possessed erupted.

It'd been ten months since our lips touched, but I remembered their feel like it was yesterday. He took my bottom lip and massaged it between his. He'd been drinking rum and Coke tonight, but his apple-cinnamon taste that I loved was present as well.

My heart was racing, and I could tell his was, too. His eyelashes flickered against my cheek, and he staggered back, panting. He quickly put my mosquito netting back in place. I felt a blush rise to my cheeks, eyes on his bare, lower back, while he rehung his mosquito netting.

"You know, Ida, kissing you was all I wanted to do with my life, and here it's been *ten* months. You still taste like Christmas morning." As if he couldn't believe how we had gotten to this point in our relationship, he stated incredulously, "Just last year we went to the Science Museum, paid sixty bucks each to get in for that History of Auto Mechanics exhibit, and then spent *four* hours making out on the balcony. We missed the entire show."

I kept my mouth closed. Reminiscing on happier times was too painful. The only way I'd managed to get through that last heartbreak was by mentally constructing a filter around my heart to only let feelings of friendship for him out. Dwelling on this kiss would mean that it'd meant something, and my pride wasn't ready to allow that to happen again.

MY REASON?

The next day, Lev picked me up in the orphanage's truck and took me to Kampala. I couldn't imagine a more bustling or hectic city. I almost got run over three times by boda-bodas. I'd never seen bigger potholes in my life, and that was saying something coming from a lifelong resident of Minnesota.

We ate Chinese food for lunch, and the baby loved the chow mein as much as I did. After lunch, we went to a bowling alley/karaoke place. Lev wanted to make a bet that whoever lost at bowling had to get up and sing a song of the other's choosing. I accepted and lost by fifty-three pins, therefore, I had to sing the corny love song he picked out. I was terrible, but he clapped and laughed until tears streamed down his face.

The city was entirely overrun with people, and I was going to ask Lev if we could leave when he suggested we sit down and get some ice cream. Turned out he wanted to ask me how Engen and I got to be such good buddies. I did my best to convey it, but how do you explain why your soul mate is your soul mate? Lev said there were girls he interacted with, but none he'd consider a friend. He didn't believe that a man and woman could enjoy the other's company unless there was something romantic between them.

I vowed never to tell Lev my history with Engen after that comment.

On my first date with Lev it had been busy at Lake Victoria, but it hadn't bothered me because I had Lev to focus on. Now that I was feeling irked at him over the whole boy-girl-being-friends thing, the frantic activity of the city made me feel like I was suffocating. I took a deep breath and focused on Janelle. I told myself that she would have liked this busy city with the vendors shouting prices, the narrow, busy streets, and the boda-bodas weaving in and out of traffic at alarming breakneck speeds.

It didn't work. The attack had started.

Lev removed his sunglasses to reveal concerned eyes. "Are you hyperventilating?"

"I can't...be here." I used the table for support as I stood, then I walked toward the parked truck.

Lev caught up with me easily, but didn't say a word. It seemed like hours, but I was finally seated in the truck. By my breathing you'd have thought it was a ten-mile hike.

Lev turned on the air conditioning and rubbed circles into my back. "Were you having a panic attack back there?"

"I was." I tried to swallow and catch my breath at the same time. "I sometimes get...anxious being in crowds."

"I'm sorry. I didn't know."

"I'm getting...better." I set my hand on his leg and didn't speak again until I had it under control. "I'll understand if you don't want anything to do with me."

Lev took my chin and lifted it. "I am so in love with you. That isn't going to change just because you get uncomfortable being in crowds. In fact, it's kind of nice; we can have more alone time."

"That's a good way to--wait," I did a double take, "you're in love with me?"

"Oh yeah. I'm in this for the long haul." Lev blew out his lips as though a big weight had been lifted off his shoulders. "If there's anything you need to get off your chest, feel free."

"I'm pregnant!" my mind screamed. I chickened out and went with, "I don't want our day to be over. Can we go to your place?"

Lev did as I requested and took us to his house to play video games. When eleven-thirty rolled around, he drove me to my building. I was quiet as I entered the apartment, but it didn't matter because you-know-who was awake.

"It's late," Engen greeted me with a yawn. He was sitting on the purple loveseat, reading my pregnancy book.

"I had an attack in Kampala today."

Engen turned a page. "Let me guess, too overrun with people?"

I believed the attack had been caused by Lev and me discussing Engen, but I was reluctant to tell him that.

"I explained my problem to Lev and he was fine with it," I continued. "He said he'd love me no matter what."

Engen blinked. "Did you say it back?"

"No." I sat down on the white loveseat across from him. "Have you ever said it to a girl?"

"No," he said remorsefully.

"Have you ever felt it?" I held my breath.

Engen got up and replanted himself next to me. He placed a hand on top of my exposed knee. "Absolutely I do."

There was a sinking feeling in my stomach. "What does it feel like?"

"At the moment, it feels hopeless." His other hand stroked my cheek. "You don't have the slightest idea how it feels to be in love?"

I made the mistake of looking into his eyes. "Not that I recall."

Engen's eyes changed from shocked to injured in a matter of seconds. He removed his hands from my body. "Will you do me a favor?"

I gave him a faint smile. "Do you even have to ask?"

"Could you not talk to me about Lev anymore?"

My smile vanished.

"It's just that--"

"I get it." I stood up and faked a yawn. "Night."

Engen entered the room just as I was making my bed.

"Don't be mad," he said.

"Jesus, it's like living with a married couple," Krista said from her bedroom.

Engen shut our door. He removed his shirt, came up behind me, and put an arm around my middle. I leaned back against his chest.

He pressed his lips to the side of my neck. "Do you remember--"

"Yes," I breathed.

His lips smiled against my skin. "You didn't let me finish."

"If it was about us, then I remember."

"Well, that's not true."

One of his hands moved down my body and lifted my dress so it could rest on top of my thigh. My whole body felt like it was vibrating.

"You don't love him," Engen deduced, his lips moving lower down my neck.

I could barely concentrate over his intoxicating scent. "Why don't I?"

"Because he's your Brittany." He slipped my dress strap off my shoulder and kissed where it had been. "Please give me another chance," he whispered.

Last fall, Engen and I had been very close to finally having sex when we got into an argument. He had left me and went straight to Brittany's house even after I begged him not to. The next day, I found out from her that they'd had sex. He wasn't my boyfriend, yet my shattered heart was betrayed. It took a good two months before I was able to be with him in the same room without my stomach turning. My guard dropped right after Janelle died and I found myself wanting him again. Due to his guilt over her passing, he completely shut me out, resulting in another heartbreak.

"What's on your mind?" Engen asked, since I hadn't responded.

It wasn't a filter I needed around my heart, it was a brick wall.

"You can tell me, Ida. I'll tell you what I'm thinking."

I swallowed hard, already aware what he was thinking about. "What you did--"

"Was unforgivable?" Engen guessed.

"No."

"Then what?"

In truth, it was his ability to walk away when things went

sour that worried me. However, since I wasn't sure I was even processing this conversation correctly, I kept my mouth shut.

Engen let me go. "It's Lev, isn't it?"

Without waiting for an answer, he grabbed his pillow off his bed and left to go sleep on a loveseat. Not wanting to chase after him and not wanting to be without him, I crawled into his bed.

Dee entered a few moments later. "I've never met two people who need each other more," she said, and sat down on the edge of my bed. "Why were you arguing?"

"He told me I don't love Lev. How can he know that, when *I* don't know that?" I whispered.

"He's just hoping that you don't." Dee reached out and patted my arm. "Do you want me to stay with you tonight?"

"Sure."

She sprawled out on my bed and fell asleep almost immediately. For some reason, this fight with Engen got the wheels in my head turning, and my thoughts kept me awake for a long time.

TAKE IT BACK

I found Lev in his office the next morning, engrossed in his work. I walked to the corner of his desk and sat on top of it, facing him.

"I was up all night thinking about you," I announced.

Lev didn't look up from his paperwork.

I hadn't expected him to act all lovey-dovey around me in the workplace, but I did expect at least *some* sort of reaction. "What did I do wrong?"

He finally looked at me. "It's nothing you can undo."

Something irrevocable could only mean one thing, he must have found the ultrasound pictures! He knew I was pregnant! I turned around and walked out of his office toward the kitchen. It was one thing for me to be ashamed of the pregnancy, but I couldn't stand for Lev to be.

I pushed the kitchen door open, aware that he was following me. I grabbed the apron and hung it over my neck just as the door swung open.

"If it's going to be a problem for you, I can be transferred," I suggested.

"It's not going to go away by being apart," Lev said calmly.

I put my hand possessively on my stomach. "Too bad taking it back isn't an option, huh?"

"I'm not asking for it back. It belongs solely to you and always will." Lev stood in front of me. "It's freaking me out that you don't feel the same."

"Hold on. What exactly is the 'it' you're referring to?" I asked.

"My love." He drew me to his chest. "The fact that you permanently possess it, but won't return it."

I set my hand on top of Lev's wrist, pleased that he trusted me enough to speak his mind. Lev was a hard worker with a kind soul. He cared about me, made me happy, and made me feel like I was not only special, but of use.

"Just because I'm not there *yet*," I said, "doesn't mean I *can't* see myself falling for you."

Lev pressed me against the counter. He had just filled my mouth with his when I felt a sharp poke from inside my belly.

Lev pulled his face away from mine in shock. "What was that?"

I gently pushed him back and took a deep breath. "Can I really tell you anything?"

"I insist."

"I'm almost six months pregnant."

Lev wagged his finger at me. "There's that classic sense of humor."

"You know the Ida that Gramps told you about. You know me now, here in Africa. You didn't know me right after Janelle died. You couldn't have known me because I didn't even know myself." I scratched my head. "And that me did a very stupid thing."

Lev glanced out the window, powerless. "Why would you keep this from me?"

"I treated this pregnancy as a need-to-know matter, and I didn't think you needed to know until recently," I admitted.

He ran both hands through his hair. "Why did you apply for the program?"

"My parents made me apply *because* I'm pregnant."

"That's why you were on the 'turn down' list," he murmured. "If I knew you were pregnant I never would've brought you here."

My face crumpled. "What do you mean *you* never would've brought me here?"

"Akiki was stuck in a meeting in Kampala the day the pass list was due." Lev sunk onto a stool. "Since his secretary was out sick, he asked me to run to his office and e-mail the pass list to YAHN. While I was boxing up the files of turn downs, I saw your--"

"No. No-no." I leaned against the counter.

"I had to make sure, so I opened your file to look at your picture. I didn't care why you were rejected, all that mattered was that it was *you*." Lev rubbed his hands against the sides of his khaki shorts. "So...I altered the 'approved' list. I omitted William Baker who was assigned to me, and added you."

So that's why the ratio of boys to girls was off. I pulled the apron over my head and threw it on the counter.

"You're the reason I'm here?" I asked, still processing this disturbing news.

"You don't understand, I *had* to meet you."

I didn't attempt to hold back the fury in my voice, "I left my brother, my parents, my--"

"Your lover."

"My best friend's grave!" I shouted in irritation. "I don't have a lover. I have a friend who I turned into a one-time mistake. I didn't...it wasn't...I'm not going to discuss *that* with you."

Lev's face turned red. "The less I know concerning your sex life the better."

"I'll keep that in mind!"

I left before he could say another word.

◆ ◆ ◆

As soon as my feet touched the sand, I kicked my shoes off and walked straight into Lake Victoria. I waded out and felt tiny fish darting around my legs. When I was knee deep, I dove underwater.

Lev was the reason I ended up here. It was too impossible to fathom. Who falls in love with a person by listening to an old man's stories? Who brings a person to Africa to satisfy their own selfish curiosities? I may not have had a whole lot going on at home, but that didn't mean I wanted to come here.

I swam out as far as I could before reaching the blue wall

that protected the treated pool of water from crocodiles and disease. I stared up at the sky as I floated, and thought about Janelle. I didn't want to be me right now, so this would be the perfect opportunity for her to take over. I focused on Janelle, and the fact that I hadn't been alone in long while and how extraordinary it felt. *"No, it doesn't feel good,"* a voice inside my head countered. *"Being an only child, I'm alone quite a bit, thank you very much."* My head became clouded. Recognizing what was happening to me, I headed for land. Janelle was afraid of water, after all.

When I got to the shore, I scouted out a place to rest, and that's when I saw the blonde head. Lev was sitting on the sand, his arms wrapped around his legs. His face was the embodiment of misery. I wanted to be disappointed that he had followed me, but my heart reached out to him when I saw my shoes lying next to him. *"Ahh, he is too sweet for words,"* I thought. That's when I knew the change had happened: Janelle was operating my mind. Janelle loved the feel of the wet cotton clinging to her body. I wanted to ignore Lev, but Janelle didn't. She'd never been in his presence before, and was immediately attracted to him. I found myself sitting down in front of him, gazing out at the water.

"You should've had more faith in my ability to handle it." Lev's voice was crushed.

"I wasn't in a hurry to advertise my failure." I pinched the bridge of my nose. "Why didn't you tell me that you were the reason I was here?"

"I didn't want you to know that you hadn't been accepted on your own." He reached out to touch my back, right behind my heart.

Janelle found what he'd done to be quite charming. She thought it was stupid to waste precious life on fighting. I was determined to let her calm and level spirit get me through this.

Lev sighed forlornly. "Who's the father?"

I leaned into his hand, still on my back. "His name is Dan Morelli." My heart gave a small stagger at his name, telling me that Janelle was still present.

"Dan Morelli didn't deserve you."

It was strangely endearing that Lev thought he was doing me a favor by bringing me here. Africa was his home and he loved his home. He couldn't understand why any person wouldn't want to be here.

Feeling proud of herself for helping me forgive Lev, Janelle took her leave. The tension knots in my stomach returned, but began to unravel a bit because I was bursting with pride at how much Janelle had enjoyed Lev's company.

Lev's fingertips traveled up my spine as he stood. He walked around so he was standing in front of me, and knelt down.

"Did you get in trouble for tampering with YAHN business?" I asked, half-hoping the answer was "yes."

"Akiki yelled at me like you wouldn't believe." Lev gave a sly smile. "But he got over it."

I rested both hands on my belly. "*This* honestly doesn't make you stop loving me?" I asked.

"How can I stop when I haven't thoroughly started?"

PICTURE THIS

"What's wrong, honey?" Lev lifted his head up to look at my face. "You don't seem into this anymore."

Lev was lying on top of me, on his couch. We'd had our lips attached for the last hour.

"I have this craving that I can't shake," I answered.

"You know my feelings, but if you truly need me..."

Earlier this week, when we were getting hot and heavy, Lev had pulled away. When I asked him why, he answered, "I couldn't handle losing you after knowing what it was like to make love to you."

On the one hand, I thought it was stupid considering he was the one who had pushed for this relationship. On the other, I had to take into consideration that he'd never had sex before, and his values deserved respect.

"I meant a hunger craving." I rested my hand on the back of his head. "Strawberry bagels slathered with plain cream cheese and banana slices."

"You hate cream cheese."

"I still want it."

Lev lifted himself as if he was going to do a push-up, and carefully positioned himself so he was sitting by my feet. When he bent over to pick up my shirt, I leaned over and ran my hand along the leathery burn scar on his shoulder. I was obsessed with it. He tossed me my shirt, and I put it on.

"Are we going somewhere?" I asked.

He fished his shirt out from under the couch. "We're going to find you what you crave."

Lev put his arms through his t-shirt holes, then stood and pulled the shirt over his head and the rest of the way down. The way his muscles worked to perform this simple task entranced me.

He patted the back of his jeans. "I don't have my wallet."

Lev got on his hands and knees and peered under the sofa. He resurfaced after a few moments with dust bunnies in his hair and a wallet in his hand. His arm went back under to retrieve more items. Of all the crap that was there, including a notebook, chip bags, and video game cases, the only thing that interested me was a white envelope. I knelt down and turned it over just as Lev emerged.

"Baby Denmark?" he read off the envelope.

I peered at him cautiously. "An ultrasound was the real reason Engen and I were at the doctor's office the day after the dance."

Lev ran his hand through his hair. "Can I look?"

I smiled in relief and handed it over.

Lev carefully opened the envelope and studied each photo. "These are wonderful." He sorted through the pictures again. He awoke from his reverie in order to drop an A-bomb on me. "I've been meaning to tell you, I'm leaving in a few weeks for a YAHN meeting in Kampala."

I wandered into Lev's kitchen. "How long will you be gone?"

"Two days."

I returned with an apple. "That isn't so awful."

Lev took in my face. "That's a Ransom look."

"I look like an old man?"

"You're displeased." He smiled widely. "You're going to miss me."

"I wish I'd known your family so I could search your face for the traits you share with them." I took a bite. "Do you look more like your mom or your dad?"

"You tell me."

Lev opened his wallet, pulled out a worn photo, and held it out to me. I wiped my juicy hand on my jeans and took the picture. I examined the people who'd created Lev and immediately felt a connection to them.

"You're the perfect combination of them both," I surmised. "They had the kindest souls; you can tell by their eyes."

"They would've loved you," he said confidently, and patted my knee. "Let's go get you that bagel."

I handed Lev his photo and remembered the conversation I had with Omo a few months back while I was walking her to the nursing home. She mentioned that Lev's parents hadn't had a proper funeral. Then it came to me. I would need to enlist some help, but I was pretty sure I had the perfect birthday gift for Lev.

Lev's good friend, Eze, carved figurines out of wood and sold them to local souvenir shops. Elephants, he informed me, were his top seller, but that didn't mean his talent was limited to figurines.

The shed Eze worked out of was a veritable mess, littered with wood chips, chainsaws, cutting knives, and stumps of wood. I'd sketched Eze a drawing of a simple memorial cross inserted into a rectangular base. He'd taken the liberty of carving the cross ahead of time, along with the base to set the cross in. He also had the stencils in place and the wood clamped to the table when I arrived. Eze had some spare wood set aside for me to practice on. Thanks to my background in mechanics, I quickly got the hang of it. We got Lev's parents' names completed that day. I went back one week later to work on the base that would hold his parents' last name. It was rewarding when I got to fit the completed cross into the base.

With things staying busy at the orphanage, and assorted events at the VC, August 22nd arrived before I knew it. Lev had to work until five on his birthday, so I had time to clean up and change. I grabbed my short orange dress, brush, and cosmetics bag, and headed to the restroom.

As I was leaving the apartment, I heard Krista say, "Dee, grab your makeup bag. I'll get my curling iron."

I rolled my eyes. If those two got their hands on me, I would be unrecognizable.

"Girls, Ida didn't ask for your help," I heard Engen say.

"But she *really* needs it," Krista said.

"Underestimating Ida Denmark would be a huge mistake," Engen warned.

I smiled and continued to the bathroom. Thanks to Engen, I was able to get ready in peace. I returned to the apartment fifteen minutes later, wearing subtle eye makeup and hair done in a French braid.

Engen took one look at me and his jaw dropped. "You're the prettiest girl on the planet."

I stared into his earnest gray eyes. "Thanks."

"What was wrong with your jeans and J.D. Salinger t-shirt?"

I looked down at my dress. "You said I was pretty."

He set his hand on my cheek. "Nothing you can do, jeans or short dresses, hair up or down, will make it any easier for me to breathe around you."

Engen refused to let me go unaccompanied, so he walked with me to Eze's to pick up the cross. On the way, Engen announced that he was no longer going to allow Lev to drive a wedge between us. He insisted that things go back to normal, thus I could talk freely about Lev if Engen could openly hate him. It was a deal. We hugged and he left me at Lev's to set up the cross. I positioned it in his backyard, tied a red bow around it, and then went out front to wait on the stoop.

When Lev came up the front walk, I covered his eyes and led him straight to his backyard. I stopped in front of the marker and removed my hands. It took his eyes a moment to focus on the cross.

"Surprise."

Lev fell to his knees and ran his hand over the carved letters on the smooth wood. He looked over at me, mystified, like he was seeing me for the first time. "Did you carve this?"

"Most of it. Eze inscribed the heart. He also carved the cross, so technically this present is from both of us," I admitted.

With one hand on the cross, Lev continued to stare at me, his lips slightly parted.

"The heart on the bottom signifies you. Did you know that 'Lev' is the Hebrew word for 'heart'?" I rambled.

"No." He looked back at the marker, a mixture of touched and disbelief.

"Do you like it?" I asked tentatively.

"I love it." He stood up. "How did you know my surname used to be Faustin?"

"I asked Gramps. He also told me that your father was born in Russia."

Lev inspected the callouses on my hands from carving. "There's no going back from this relationship. Do you feel that way also?"

My thoughts uncontrollably shifted to Engen. *Please give me another chance.* His request had replayed in my mind more times than I cared to admit.

Lev's eyes were expectantly penetrating mine for an answer.

"Lev, I--"

I was cut off by a knock at the front door, followed by an obnoxious, "Yoo-hoo, Levy!"

Lev cursed, entered the back door, and stormed through the house. I followed behind him.

"What do you want?" he asked angrily, as he opened the front door.

I made my way into the living room and was immediately sickened by the sight of Baba standing in front of Lev, wearing a see-through red negligee. A jacket lay at her feet.

"Let's pick up where we left off on your last birthday," Baba purred.

Lev ran a hand through his hair, frazzled. "I told you that was a mistake."

"I heard that her belly swells with a different man's child," Baba said as she ran her hands over her slim hips. "This body would be all yours."

"If you care about me, you'll respect that I'm with Ida." Lev closed and locked the door behind him. He looked at me, discomposed, and said, "I'm sorry for that."

I moved into the kitchen. "What happened on your last birthday?"

"According to some friends, I got drunk and made out with her."

I placed a hand on the back of a kitchen chair. "At the lake you said it'd been *three years* since you kissed a girl."

"What I said was it'd been three years since I kissed a girl that I *liked*. I don't count the ones I can't remember due to intoxication." Lev took two steps toward me. "Does this change us?"

"No. If the evidence wasn't growing inside of my body, I wouldn't count Dan."

"That's why I can only love you. You make sense of me." Lev placed his hand on my waist. "I suppose Baba interrupting us is going to be the thing you hate most today?"

Engen had been kind enough to share with Lev that Krista and I played that game every night.

"Second. The VC running out of ketchup is the first."

"I have some in the cupboard."

On that note, my stomach growled and we got to work on cooking some burgers.

I had lied when I told Lev the Baba incident wasn't the thing I hated the most. I was so fazed by it that I felt compelled to discuss the situation with the girls after I left his house.

"He did make out with her," Dee reasoned. "Baba was right to think he was interested in her."

"Those things always mean more to one person than they do the other," I whispered, careful to not disturb Engen.

"For sure," agreed Engen, poking his head out of our bedroom. "All in favor of Ida ditching Lev because he's an untrustworthy dick, raise your hand."

Apparently, we weren't as quiet as I thought.

Engen entered the living room, sat next to me on the love-seat, and set his hand on my thigh.

"Hey, I have the right to a fair trial," I told him.

"Plead your cases," Dee ordered.

"I don't want Ida to get hurt," Engen said simply. "Lev's shady history with girls clearly upsets her, so best just to ditch him."

I stood, clasped my hands behind my back, and paced in front of Dee and Krista, both seated on the floor. "December first is ever looming over our heads, reminding us that we'll soon be separated. That's why we bickered over Baba. It had nothing to do with Lev's history."

"Lev is an easy and safe cop-out." Engen's hands made a steeple. "Ida can overlook *Lev's* past because in just a few months she's outta here for good."

"I believe, Engen, that you're speaking out of jealousy," Dee accused, and squinted at him. "I could enter into evidence what I overheard you telling Marco."

"No need," I said, after seeing how uncomfortable Engen was becoming.

"I say Ida should forgive Lev for that tramp showing up at his house today," Krista declared.

"I second that," Dee concurred.

"Thank you, ladies," I said, and shook hands with Dee and Krista. A feeling of absence set in a split second before I heard the door close. Engen had taken off.

"You should go after him," Dee said to me.

"He wouldn't like that."

"He'd go after you."

I faced Dee. "No, he wouldn't."

I don't know what she thought she knew about me and Engen, but whatever it was, it wasn't the half of it.

I got up and looked out the window to see the new apartment building. It was still missing doors, panes of glass for the windows, and furniture. Krista had recently flirted with one of the construction workers, and he'd said there was three weeks left of work on the building. Three more weeks until it would be ready to house more teens like us. They'd grow and change as people, just as we had. A few would get to work at New Beginnings. They would get to cook for those sweet children and laugh with them during art projects and soccer games. Ruminating over who would be my job replacement was enough to give me a migraine.

The migraine lasted until Engen entered our bedroom at 11:58. I closed my eyes and pretended like I was asleep. I heard him peel his t-shirt off, and got a whiff of his apple-cinnamon scent. I could feel his eyes on me as he pulled aside the mosquito netting attached to my bed. He knelt down, swept the hair away from my face, and brushed his lips against mine.

"You just stopped breathing," Engen said. "That's one of the many things I miss about kissing you, taking your breath away."

Engen smelled faintly of beer. He must've been at the local bar. He lightly touched the corner of my mouth, and then moved his fingertips down my neck, arm and waist, stopping to rest on top of my thigh.

"One night I'd been hanging out with Marco, Dee, and some other volunteers," Engen started. "Marco had been saying how hot you are, and I agreed. I started to brag about our past. That prompted him to make a lot of sexual innuendos regarding us sharing a room." Engen set his nose on my shoulder and inhaled deeply. "Instead of laughing them off, I should've been denying them. It gave those who overheard me the wrong impression."

I turned onto my side so my back was facing him. The movement caused my small nightgown to ride up a bit, which Engen took full advantage of.

"Talk to me." Engen's hand rubbed circles into my left butt

cheek as his mouth nibbled on my shoulder blade.

Considering how far we had gone with each other's bodies, there was no point in chastising him.

After a few moments of silence, Engen got up. I heard him remove his sweatpants, aware that his eyes were still glued to my back. His bed creaked when he sat down on it. It didn't creak again, indicating he hadn't laid down yet.

"I would do anything for you, and you won't even talk to me." Engen exhaled and whispered, "I've never needed anyone more than I need you."

I thought back to Janelle's funeral. I remembered sitting in the pew, kneading my arms and legs to make sure it was actually me. Since Janelle and I used to mentally swap places, maybe she had imagined she was me in the moment she was dying. What if she was able to achieve the ultimate "switch" and it was really me trapped inside that casket? I swiveled my head to the side to watch Engen, who was sitting directly across the aisle from me. The tears were flowing freely down his cheeks. If anyone knew the truth, it'd be Engen. I looked over at him, and seconds later he met my stare.

"Am I me?" I mouthed.

He appraised me. I thought maybe he hadn't understood my question, when at last he nodded. We stayed with our eyes locked on each other until Brittany nudged him with her shoulder. It took three nudges before he tore his gaze away from mine. My hands shook and I faced forward. Brittany had no business being here. She was of zero use to Engen. In fact, he'd yelled at her five minutes before the funeral started. My parents were an okay source of comfort to me, but I required Engen so completely that I thought my heart would rupture.

Engen didn't want me to be me. That much became clear when he wouldn't stand next to me at Janelle's gravesite. I watched him as he exhaled his frozen breath and threw a yellow rose on top of her casket. He looked so handsome in his suit and tie. My eyes traveled away from Engen and landed on Dan who'd been staring at me in anguish. I tilted my head to the side and evaluated him. Janelle had wanted to date Dan, wanted his children. There must have been something to him that I'd missed. My eyes flickered back to Engen in time to see his narrowed eyes glance from Dan to me. Engen's right eye twitched before he whirled around. My insides twisted when he left with Brittany without even saying goodbye.

"She was ours! This happened to us both!" I wanted to yell after him. How could he not see that? How could he not need me during this time?

Dan slowly made his way over to me, spreading his arms wide. I accepted the offer, and was glad I had because he had held me so tenderly. I would have given anything to be able to trade spots with Janelle so she could know what it felt like in his arms.

And just like that, I knew what I had to do.

The sounds of yelling from outside caused my eyes to fly open to reveal the bedroom wall in Mukono. I had gone from needing Engen so forcefully the day of Janelle's funeral, and hating how he'd ignored me, to ignoring him now.

I sat up and swung my legs over the side of the bed. Engen was still sitting up looking at me. I stared into his wet eyes, and my heart collapsed. I opened my arms. He didn't hesitate as he came over to my bed, wrapped his arms around my waist, and laid his head over my heart. I ran my hand through the hair at his neck.

Engen sighed in contentment. "Please touch me forever."

"It's great that you're able to confide in Dee," I said. "But, I want us to be able to discuss whatever is on your mind, especially if you're upset at something I've done."

"Something you've done." Engen ran a finger down my cheek. "I'd love to have this conversation with you, but I've been drinking. Another time?"

"Another time," I echoed, and continued to hold him.

LESSONS

Lev called me when he got home from his meeting, to make plans for the evening. He also passed along two items he learned at the meeting he'd attended that morning: Number one, New York and Illinois joined YAHN, and number two, after the next cycle of volunteers, they were reducing the term from six to two months. Due to the popularity of the program, they wanted to be able to put more volunteers through.

I then told Lev about the message Dan had left me, stating an ultimatum: he was not taking the baby unless I came with her. I didn't respond to Dan yet, because I needed to clear my head and review the facts: I agreed to give birth to the baby under the urgings of Dan, who made me believe he genuinely wanted her. Once I had the baby, the plan was to turn her over to Dan to raise. However, Dan had only said he wanted the baby because he was operating under the hope that once I had her, I would suddenly realize that I loved him and wanted us to be a family. How could he be so selfish? I admit that I had grown to care for the well-being of the baby, but that didn't mean I was ready to be a mom, did it?

Anyway, Lev thought it was great news that Dan wanted out of the baby's life; however, I was still reeling. And to top it all off, I was now facing a new problem. Krista and I had been staring at the contraptions in front of us with open mouths for two whole minutes.

"Where are we right now?" Krista asked.

"According to the sign, we're in a computer lab."

Krista continued to gape. "Would you be so kind as to check the sign again?"

I peeked at the sign on the door behind me. "Computer Lab," I confirmed.

We weren't expecting the latest in technology, but we also weren't expecting *this*.

"These monitors are like half an inch thick and those keypad things are plugged into them for some God-awful reason." Krista turned to me. "I guess we need that sleepy lady's help after all."

We turned around and headed back to the help desk.

"I think we were a bit hasty when we declined your help earlier," I glanced at her name tag, "Pamela."

"How are we going to listen to, and dictate our assignments with those dinosaurs in there?" Krista asked.

"You'll read and type them," Pamela replied groggily.

"We'll do *what*?" Krista screeched.

Pamela stood, and we followed her snail-like pace into the computer lab. "You didn't turn them on?"

"Power up," I told my monitor.

Krista said, "Activate."

Nothing happened. We looked at Pamela, the Master of Ancient Tech.

She smiled. "That never gets old. Push the button on the tower."

"That thing," Krista pointed at the tower and then at the monitor, "is part of this, too?"

"What did you think it was?" Pamela yawned at our apparent stupidity.

"A garbage can?" Krista guessed.

Pamela leaned over and pressed buttons on top of our towers. "I bet your garbage cans talk to you just like your computers do, huh?"

"Naturally," Krista said.

"You can program them not to," I pointed out.

"But why would you?" Krista asked.

"Right," I agreed.

Pamela took pity on us and helped us retrieve our lessons. She showed us some "simple" commands on the keypad and left us to fend for ourselves.

An hour later, we heard a male voice say, "No need to get up,

Pamela."

"Hello, Lev," responded a perky female voice.

Krista and I feigned shock. "Did Pammy just complete a sentence without nodding off?"

Krista laughed. "Lev has the power to wake the dead."

Lev leaned down to kiss my cheek. The brim of his cap blocked my view of the monitor. "Almost finished?"

"Just completed the first lesson." I swiveled my head to see Lev. "I've never seen you in a cap before. You look very cute."

Lev smiled. "Consider it part of my permanent attire from now on. How's it going, Krista?"

She watched him dotingly. "Fine."

"That's good." Lev sat down in the chair next to me. "You said it would only take you an hour to complete your lessons."

I gestured toward the computer. "That was before I knew what I was up against."

"Most volunteers download their assignments onto their phones," Lev informed me.

Krista beat her head against the desk top. "Why didn't we do that, again?"

"Because you were too creeped out by your teachers to give them your number, and I was too lazy," I reminded her.

"My fingers are *killing* me." Krista stood and gathered her things. "Have a good night, you two."

"Goodnight." I groaned when I saw how many pages of history I had to read. "Let's go, too. Your cousin's get-together already started."

He took in an eyeful of my tan legs. "You're the boss."

Fifteen minutes later, I was longing for my homework. I looked apprehensively at Lev as we walked into a house where the musical style of Kidandali was literally shaking the foundation. My ears rang as I silently gave myself a pep talk.

"There he is!" A loud voice exclaimed.

I recognized the owner of the voice from the night of the bonfire as Lev's cousin, Wtalo.

Lev took my hand. I followed closely, and Lev yelled introductions over the music, "Next to Wtalo is his girlfriend, Na-mono. There's Baba's eight year-old sister, Randy, and you already know Baba."

I gripped his arm tighter as dancing couples closed in on us.

"Hey," Lev greeted Wtalo with a handshake. "I'd like you to meet--"

"Ida," Wtalo supplied. He took my hand and brought it to his lips.

"Hi, Wtalo," I said.

"You turned my cousin into putty." Wtalo's face told me this was not a good thing to have done.

Lev grabbed my hand away from his cousin's lips. "Don't touch her or look at her...especially like that."

Namono laughed. "The word possessive just came to mind."

While all of this was taking place, Baba gazed longingly at Lev. She played with one of the gold hoops in her ear, showing off her long, red fingernails. "You still calling this one your girlfriend, Levy?"

"Am I still calling you my girlfriend?" Lev shouted over the music, playfully.

Lev and I had hung out and made out, but that didn't automatically make me his girlfriend. "No, actually."

Lev knit his eyebrows together. "I'm not?"

Suddenly Lev's buddy, Muna, grabbed my arm and twirled me onto the dance floor. It felt awkward having a man besides Lev or Engen hold me close. Before I knew it, Lev had squished himself between me and Muna and shoved my grinning captor away.

Lev set his hands on my shoulders. "How am I not your boyfriend?"

"Because you never asked me to be your girlfriend."

"Do I have to spell it out for you?" he shouted over the music.

"Y-E-S," I spelled out.

Lev smiled as he repositioned his cap. "It's a good thing I don't have a girlfriend, or she might get jealous if I danced with another woman," he threatened.

"Good thing."

Lev turned around and walked off in the direction of Baba.

I was too shocked to look away as he continued toward my nemesis. He said something to Baba, but when he turned around it was her sister he was leading. I bit my lip to keep from smiling. Lev brought Randy into the group of dancers, and together they moved around like a couple of crazy people.

When the song changed, I heard what sounded like cheering coming from old TV speakers. Curious, I made my way through the crowd and down a narrow hallway. I peered into a room and saw a young boy of around twelve playing a video game. He looked like a mini Wtalo.

I knocked on the half-closed door. "Is that Mauer 2.0?"

"Yeah." The boy didn't look up. "Can't get past the seventh inning."

"I can show you a trick."

"Go on, then." The boy nodded to a controller on his bed.

I signed in and selected a player.

When we made it past the seventh inning, the boy turned to me and smiled widely. "Thanks!"

I heard clapping and shifted my eyes to see Lev leaning against the doorway. "Hey, Benny, can I have Ida back?"

"I suppose," Benny said, then excused himself so he could use the bathroom.

Lev rubbed Benny's head as he squeezed past him, and then said to me, "Remind me to add 'gamer' to the list of reasons why you're the only girl for me."

"Earlier you wanted me to believe you were going to dance with Baba." I searched his eyes. "Why is it so important for you to make me jealous?"

"So that you'll be too afraid to leave." He closed his eyes against my cheek. "You have no idea how terrifying it is to be a man in love. To have found the one girl you can see yourself committing to forever, and then constantly worrying about losing her; it's stressful."

I grabbed the collar of his shirt. "I'll be your girlfriend."

He stared at me, almost like he couldn't believe his luck.

"Thank you."

"Remind me why you didn't come home last night," Engen chastised, as soon as Lev and I walked through the door the next morning.

"The party ran late, and I didn't want to wake you guys up."

"Remind me why you aren't wearing a shirt," Lev muttered.

Engen sneered at Lev as though he was violating the sanctity of our apartment. Eyes back on me, he asked, "Why didn't you call me?"

"If you need to blame someone, blame me," Lev demanded.

Engen's glare grew more withering with each word Lev spoke.

"Want a drink while you wait?" I asked Lev.

"Wait for what?" Engen asked intrusively.

"For me. We're going out."

Engen flinched. "Why did you bother coming back?"

"To shower and--"

"Whoa," Lev broke in. "You don't answer to him."

"She'll answer because she wants to, so butt out." Engen regarded me expectantly.

Lev took a step toward Engen. "Where do you get off speaking to us like this?"

Engen stood. "'*Us*?' You honestly think *you* and her qualify as an 'us?'"

"What we are is none of your business," Lev said.

I kept an eye on Lev's movement. He was getting too close to Engen for my liking.

"If it concerns Ida, it concerns me," Engen said.

Lev cracked his neck and continued toward Engen.

"Enough!" I positioned myself between the guys. Facing Lev, I added, "Back up."

"Ida?" Lev asked, hurt.

I not only knew what Engen was capable of, but I was angry at Lev for thinking he could challenge my friend. "Walk away from this."

"Fine," Lev acquiesced. "I'll pick you up in an hour."

Lev tried to kiss me, but I shook my head. He gave Engen an accusatory glare and left.

"I'm sorry I overreacted." Engen followed me to our room. "But, I was hoping to take you to the Ssezibwa Falls today."

"That does sound fun," I said with a hint of regret while picking out a clean outfit. "Bianca digs you. Ask her." I moved into the hallway so I didn't have to see if he was entertaining the idea.

Engen took my hips and swiveled me back around. "Your company and another girl's company aren't interchangeable."

"I already made plans."

"Remember when you were going to go with Lev to pick up the supplies, when I showed up?" Engen's hands moved up to knead my waist. "You said even if we didn't have plans and I just asked you out of the blue to come with me, that you'd still have chosen me over him?"

I tried to push my breath out, but it felt trapped. "I remember."

"We're still the same people, aren't we?"

He was right. It wasn't hard to put myself in his position, either. I'd hate it if he found a girlfriend here and I rarely saw him. It'd be doubly annoying if the only reason I'd applied for the program was to be with him, like he'd done for me.

"I miss hanging out, just the two of us," Engen murmured. "Things have shifted, and we need to do something to get back on track."

"I agree. Consider my plans canceled."

"Thank you." He narrowed his eyes. "You honestly didn't want me to ask Bianca, did you?"

"No," I admitted.

"Good." He took in my undergarment selection and smiled. "Why is everything you own sexy as hell?"

The answer was Janelle. She was into lingerie and made sure I was, too.

I concentrated on Engen's chin, feeling ashamed. Whenever I thought of Janelle lately, I was forced to see my shortcomings. Engen tightened his grip on me and looked at my face as though he was memorizing every detail. My knees were weak. I set a hand against his bare chest and felt his heart, pounding like mad.

"You're shaking," he noted.

I gazed up at him. "I'm freezing."

"It's 800 degrees in here."

He leaned down just as I stood on my tiptoes, so our faces were seemingly an inch apart. "I would've guessed 790...tops," I teased.

Engen smiled and pressed his forehead to mine. "I love you, Ida."

I sucked in my breath. I'd waited a long time to hear these words from him. I'd been tempted to tell him many times, but I was unable to say it to his face, so two years ago I'd taken Engen's phone and made him a video. In it, I'd confessed that I was in love with him. He'd never acknowledged it, so either he never saw the video, or he didn't feel the same way and was afraid to tell me. The fact that he chose to tell me now that I was involved with Lev made me infuriated, unless, of course, he had meant he loved me as a friend.

I couldn't do this. My emotions were all over the place and I needed to not dwell on this drama.

I cleared my throat. "I have to get ready."

In the shower, I thought of Janelle. If she were alive, she would have been disappointed in me for that scene with Engen. As the lukewarm water washed over me, I got lost in thoughts of the past...

The opportunity to fulfill Janelle's wish to be with Dan came two weeks after her funeral while my family was taking Marilyn out to dinner for her nineteenth birthday. I'd told them I was staying home to study for a Mechanics test, and there was no dispute considering I was mopey and no fun to be around. I called Dan and asked him to come over, that I needed his help studying. He was in his car before we'd disconnected. I'd put on an outfit that used to belong to Janelle: a short black skirt and a sheer black top with a black bra underneath. I caught my reflection in the hallway mirror and called myself a creep. Any qualms I'd had with this plan flew out of the window as soon as Dan's presence was announced by Paige, our electronic security system.

"Let him in, Paige."

When Dan saw me, he said, "Wow."

"These were Janelle's clothes." I needed to make that clear. "Should we go up to my room?"

"Is that where you want to study for the test?"

This is the test, I thought, as I clumsily ran my hands up and down his chest. "Actually, the couch looks kind of cozy."

"What's going on?" Dan inquired. "You never touch me."

"Don't you want this?"

Dan allowed me to bring him over to the couch. He sat down and his face flushed as I lifted my skirt and sat with his thighs between mine. "What exactly are you offering?" he asked.

Should I warn him that he wasn't actually going to be having sex with *me*? No, he wouldn't understand that I was going to let Janelle take over my body so *she* could experience having sex with him.

"I'm offering me," I said simply.

"I wasn't expecting this. I don't have anything for protection," Dan said, even though I could see the excitement in his eyes. "Do you?"

"I just assumed you would."

"Should I go buy some?" he asked.

"No," I said exuberantly. "If you leave, it'll ruin the moment."

That being determined, Dan slid his hand between our bodies and unbuttoned his jeans. "Have you done this before?"

"No."

"You and Engen never did it?" he asked in disbelief.

"He's with Brittany."

"Something tells me he'd be willing to make an exception for you."

With Engen on my mind I was ready to do this, but I felt too much like me, and that defeated the purpose. I put my arms around Dan's neck and lowered my head to his shoulder. Dan wanted to do this, there was no question, but me, I wasn't any better than Engen, who also used his first time with a person he didn't love.

I pushed those thoughts aside, concentrated on the feel of Dan's athletic body, and waited for Janelle to take over. Dan's mouth explored my neck. That's when it happened. I lifted his shirt off and hid my face in his neck. He smelled good, not of anything in particular, just guy-like.

"I want to see your face during this," Dan stated.

I could allow that. As long as I knew who I was doing this for, nothing else mattered...

The water shut off in my shower and caused me to snap back to the present. I dried off and saw that my phone was blinking. It was a message from Lev. He said that he'd made the mistake of stopping at the orphanage after he left, found it in complete disarray, and could we go to the lake tomorrow night instead?

Perfect. I hadn't been looking forward to telling him my reason for canceling, anyway.

While I showered, Engen had put together a backpack with sunscreen, bug spray, protein bars, and a sheet from his bed for a picnic. He also borrowed a cooler from Marco, so we headed to the Total station for ice, drinks, and sandwiches, and then hopped in a cab. When the driver, Mikey, found out we were going to Ssezibwa Falls, he launched into a story about the two rivers that I couldn't understand due not only to his heavy accent, but to the noisy traffic around us.

The falls were beautiful, and Engen was funny and charming. Most important of all, he was happy. We had a great day, so great that I dreamed of him that night. I must have said his name out loud because when I opened my eyes, he was staring at me with a smile on his face.

"What was it about?" he wondered.

"The night I worked late at my dad's office and you brought me dinner that ended up getting cold before we got around to it."

"Holy shit." Engen bit his pillow. "That was a glorious day."

"I think about the days that followed," I said sadly.

Janelle had discovered that Engen and I had been hanging out without her, so in jealousy she made sure to keep me busy the rest of the weekend, claiming we needed 'girl time.' Engen had taken my silence as a personal insult, and went back to Brittany.

"You *would* choose to remember the dark times." Engen was silent for a beat. "We had a ton of incredible moments, but for the most part all we did was deny each other each other. Why couldn't we ever figure us out as a couple?"

Janelle had been the primary reason, but I didn't feel like selling her out.

"I craved your company night and day," he persisted. "Why didn't you try?"

"I was scared." I turned onto my back. "What if it didn't work out and I lost you? I'd rather be torn to pieces by a pack of rabid wolves than be without your friendship."

"Would never happen," Engen whispered. "The wolves would have to get through me first."

"And then for some reason, I couldn't get past--"

"I know, I know. That was almost a year ago, though." Engen groaned. "I've changed. Plus, you got back at me by screwing Dan."

"Dan was for *Janelle*. It had nothing to do with you."

"It was excruciating, and I haven't been able to let it go." Engen sat up in bed. "I know how it felt and still feels for you, when you found out that I slept with Brittany."

"No, you don't know," I said through clenched teeth.

"Yes, I do." Engen stood up. "In fact, it's a thousand times worse for me."

"How dare you?" I flew to my feet. "I literally *begged* you not to go to her."

"You're pregnant with another guy's baby!" Engen took my shoulders. "Your body is changing and growing a life because of him. You can't imagine what that does to me."

"To *you*?" I pushed him back.

I opened the door to our bedroom, gave Engen one last look of disbelief, then turned and headed out to sleep on one of the loveseats.

GETTING CLOSER

Lev held the door to the nursing home open for me. He was volunteering for a few hours tonight and asked me to come along. I'd walked Omo here before, but had never gone inside. The right side of the room held four circular tables, and to the left there was a sitting area with a TV showing the evening news. An old man in a blue terrycloth robe was settled in a reclining chair, a second elderly man snoozed on a couch, and an old woman was playing chess with herself.

"Lev, it's good to see you, my boy!" A voice boomed.

"Mr. Prince, how's the foot treating you?"

Mr. Prince leaned forward in his recliner. "My bunions are red. I think they are infected."

Lev winced. "That doesn't sound good."

Mr. Prince winked at Lev. "Keep Jacobi away from her, or he won't let her out of his sight."

"Noted." Lev turned to me and whispered, "You look sort of pale."

"I don't want to meet Jacobi," I hissed.

We proceeded across the lobby. "Jacobi is blind."

I put my hand to my throat. "Oh, thank God."

Lev tried to look at me scoldingly, but couldn't pull it off. "That's not very nice."

Thankfully, Jacobi was napping, so we moved to the lady playing chess with herself.

"Hello, Mrs. M. Who's winning?" Lev asked.

"Oluchi, but I'm two moves away from taking her last bishop," Mrs. M. cackled. She abruptly stopped, and her head snapped up to assess me. "It's you. The girl who is so hard to read. Or maybe it's the baby clouding you. When are you due?"

"November something," I answered.

"Seventeenth," Lev supplied.

"Soon, your belly will be the size of a cantaloupe," Mrs. M. informed me.

"Can't wait," I replied dryly.

Mrs. M. turned to Lev. "She's not yours."

"No." Lev met my gaze. "I wish she were, though."

My heart dissolved when I saw the pained look on his face.

Lev started to walk away, probably expecting me to follow, but Mrs. M. had taken me by the hand. "I've been waiting for you."

"Me?" I asked. "Why?"

"Because Lev is a special young man. Looking into his future, we saw that the source of his happiness resided with you." Mrs. M. let go of my hand, took the bishop, and pointed it at me. "What are you going to do about *him*?"

"Lev? I haven't--"

"No. The young man whose aura is all over you. His aura mixed with yours is overpowering. He isn't going to give you up so easily." Mrs. M.'s hand flew to her temple. "At this point, I don't foresee a path you can travel that will spare suffering for either one."

"I cause suffering?"

"Let him go, your lifelong partner. Separate to unite. Only then will you truly know."

"Know what?" I asked, allowing myself to hope for one minute that this was real and Mrs. M. would tell me something useful.

"Your blinders make you unpredictable." She closed her eyes, putting an end to the conversation.

I scurried to catch up to Lev. "Does Mrs. M. think she's psychic?"

"She *is* psychic. So is Oluchi, her daughter."

Lev pushed the door marked 'staff' open. It led into a decent-sized kitchen. The door swung shut, and I watched Mrs. M. out of the circular window. She had her thumb in a nostril, scratching enthusiastically.

"Are you su--" I didn't get to finish because Lev spun me around, kissing me purposefully.

"We have to leave right now," he stated.

"Actually, we have to feed diced peaches to old people," I reminded him.

"I want to take the next step with you," he said, breathing heavily.

"You were so unsure before," I said as he nibbled my bottom lip. "What changed your mind?"

"It just hit me, seeing these old people, that life is short. There's no reason not to." Lev pulled back so he could see my face. "Did *you* change your mind?"

It was hard to say, because I'd been feeling off all day. I think it had to do with the fact that I couldn't forgive Engen for his jerk comments last night, as if he actually thought this pregnancy was harder on him than me. I'd been with Dan for Janelle's sake. Engen had been with Brittany to be an asshole.

"I thought it was off the table," I answered honestly. "So I haven't considered it lately."

"When I found out you were pregnant, you briefly spoke of your time with...that guy." Lev sounded like he was using his dying breath to utter those two words. "You said, 'I didn't, it wasn't,' then you stopped."

"I didn't feel a thing, it wasn't even me," I recalled. I explained to him how Janelle and I used to pretend to be each other, how her greatest wish was to have a life and kids with Dan, and how I had to do it for her, *as* her, so she could be one step closer to completing the things she'd wanted to do in her life. "I did a naive thing, and look what happened - she wanted his kid, and now I'm having it."

"You imagined you were your friend, and used *your* body so *she* could have sex with a guy she liked?" Lev asked slowly, processing it.

"It seemed like the right thing to do for Janelle...at the time."

"Promise me two things." Lev kissed my cheek. "One: you

won't let Janelle use your body to fulfill any additional unre-quited loves she may have had, and two: you let me make love to *the* Ida Denmark...when she's ready." He offered me his hand. "Deal?"

I took his hand. "Deal."

◆ ◆ ◆

The next morning, I opened the door to the apartment and stuck my head in. Krista was lounging on the white love seat, painting her nails. "Are you alone?" I whispered.

"Yeah. Dee and Engen are eating breakfast at the VC." Krista nodded at my key card on the coffee table. "I scanned it before curfew."

I pocketed the card. "I appreciate that."

"It's fine. I like not having to share Engen with you," Krista said matter of factly. She took my left hand, set it on her right knee, and started painting my nails a pretty violet.

I couldn't help but feel sorry for her. Considering I had insider knowledge to Engen's head, I knew that he didn't trust Krista, therefore rarely spoke to her.

Krista must've sensed that we were in need of a subject change because she asked, "How was last night?"

The door opened, and Dee walked in. She lowered her eyes as she walked past me. Engen stood in the doorway and stared at me. He side-nodded toward the hallway and then headed off.

Krista capped the polish. "We'll finish later."

I flashed her a "Gee, thanks" smile and then took off after Engen, who hadn't bothered to wait for me. I walked around the building to where the bonfire pit was.

Engen was pacing in front of the lawn chairs. "Where were you last night?"

I briefly considered lying, but I'd already lied to him once, when I told him I didn't know what it felt like to be in love, and I didn't want to do it again. "Lev and I volunteered at the nursing home and then we went back to his house."

"Why won't you focus on my eyes?" Engen asked.

I walked over to him. "It's not what you're thinking."

He circled an arm around my waist. "Good, because the closer you get to him, the further away you feel to me."

"We're going to lose touch when you go away for college, you realize."

He narrowed his eyes. "Why do you think I'm going away?"

"Last week during our bonfire I went inside to get us more drinks, and when I came back I heard you talking to your mom on the phone." I squeezed his biceps. "South Dakota State University will be lucky to have you."

"You're right, they *would* be lucky to have me," Engen agreed cockily. "But that doesn't mean I'm accepting. I have to see how things are with us first."

"You're never going to base a life decision like college on me, got that?" I said sternly.

"I'd kill for you. It only stands to reason I'd base a decision like college on you."

I set a hand on his chest. "Promise that you'll take me out of the equation when you make a final choice."

"I can never make that promise because I'm always thinking about you one way or another."

"I'll take myself out of the equation, then," I threatened.

"That's right, you want to buy a house in the country and disappear." He kissed my nose. "Doesn't scare me. I'll find you."

"Then I'll have to think of something worse," I said thoughtfully.

"You're always going to be in my life. You're never going to shake me."

"I don't want to shake you. I just want you to get the most out of life." I ran my fingernails against the back of his neck. "Which is why I talked Lev into bringing you on the whitewater rafting trip with him and his buddies at the end of the month."

"Wait...what?" Engen asked, eyes bulging.

"It's a two-day trip."

"Two days!" Engen shouted, and then got control of his voice. "Are you crazy? Two days with Lev?"

"He's not too thrilled either," I admitted. "I had to agree to give him my firstborn."

Engen's eyes turned fierce. "Don't joke like that."

"Why not?"

"Think of the potential your baby holds. You'd give that up?" He swallowed deeply. "She could change the world."

I shook my head at the sincerity in his last comment. "You definitely need a guys' weekend."

BEFORE I LOST YOU

It was our fourth month in Mukono, and Engen and I were laying on our beds, doing homework (I got all that straightened out. No more ancient computers for me). I was in the middle of translating French when I felt Engen's eyes on me.

"What's shaking, Malone?" I asked, still looking at my phone.

"Watching you is my favorite thing to do," he answered.

"Is your assignment on how to be a creeper? 'Cause if it is, you're going to get an A-plus."

"I can tell you're studying French, because your head is bobbing side to side, and your fingers look like you're holding a cigarette."

"Looking back, I should've taken German like you did, in preparation for our trip," I said regretfully.

Engen was named after the village in Germany where his parents met. When we were thirteen, we'd vowed to vacation there together for our twenty-first birthdays.

"That would've been wise," he said.

"Which explains why I didn't do it, right?"

He laughed, then cleared his throat. "You never asked me why I left the play the night of your birthday."

"Oh, the night you and Dee were in here discussing the possibility of trading rooms?"

"That was not *my* idea."

"Whatever." I waved my hand through the air. "I figured you'd tell me why you left the play, if you wanted to."

"I'd been looking at old videos--"

He was interrupted when Dee yelled, "Engen, Krista's home for roughly three minutes, so come tell us your idea!"

"In a sec!" Engen shouted.

"Now or never, hot stuff," Krista replied.

Engen sighed, then heaved himself off the bed. I followed him out to the living room.

"I want us to take the Kampala City Tour," he announced and sat down on the purple loveseat. "Do we all have next Sunday off?"

"Yes, but--" I started.

Engen held up his hand. "Don't say you're hanging out with Lev, or I'll lose it."

I sat next to him. "I was going to say it would probably be boring for Lev."

"He isn't invited," Engen said with a note of finality.

Krista walked behind Engen, kissed his cheek, and then joined Dee on the floor.

"What happens on a city tour?" I wondered, giving the lipstick marks on his cheek a repulsed look.

"We'll visit churches, the Kasubi Tombs, the Uganda Museum, and a crafts market," Engen listed, and raised his hand. "Who's in on this Lev-free city tour?"

Dee raised her hand. Krista's followed. Engen grabbed my wrist and raised my arm high in the air.

"I'll go," I assented.

Engen held me close to his side. "I'll make a reservation."

"I can't take you seriously with that mark on your face." I spit on my gray shirt sleeve and rubbed the lipstick off his cheek.

"Appreciate that, bud." Engen positioned his body so he was facing me, and leaned into my ear. "Gray is my favorite color on you."

Remembering the last time he had told me that, I whispered in response, "I've always been fond of gray."

"Always?"

"Always." I pulled my head back so I could look into his gray eyes. "And the long sleeves reminded me of fall."

"Our favorite time of year." Engen lifted my hand and kissed the inside of my wrist. "Think of all we're missing out on."   "

The apple orchard, hayrides, haunted houses."

"Remember the hayride at that pumpkin patch?" Engen

chuckled. "The same tractor driver every year with his dumb jokes?"

"So great. Also--"

"Yeah, yeah, you have history," Krista said. "Back to the tour, I say steamy Lev gets to come with."

Engen narrowed his eyes at Krista. "I want to spend some time with Ida without that guy shoving his tongue down her throat every ten seconds. It's disturbing enough *knowing* he's having impure thoughts about her when I'm not around. I don't want to *witness* him having them."

"Ida's forced to hang out with you and Krista, and she's constantly having impure thoughts about you," Dee said.

"No, I get it," I told the group. "In ninth grade I saw Engen kissing Brittany, and I wanted to hurl."

"You had your first panic attack that night," Engen recalled. "You missed three days of school."

"I don't remember that." Or much from that first few weeks of high school.

Dee and Krista were staring at us with curious expressions on their faces.

"Panic attacks can be debilitating," Engen explained.

"You know what else is debilitating? Seeing the guy you adore kiss a random girl," Dee said.

Engen took his arm back, steepled his fingers, and leaned forward, thoughtful.

"How did Engen react to the news that Dan had impregnated you?" Krista asked me.

"He wasn't even talking to me then," I said uncomfortably.

"So you just let it go?" Dee interrogated Engen.

"I gave him two black eyes and a fractured jaw before Ida broke it up," Engen replied vengefully.

Dee shook her head. "I feel sorry for the poor souls who try and get between you two."

"I gotta get going." Krista then said aside to Dee, "Let me know if I miss anything."

Engen pressed his joined fingers to his mouth. "Ida didn't care a thing for Dan, so when he bragged to me that he'd slept with her, I just assumed the worst."

"Why weren't you speaking to her?" Dee asked.

"At the start of high school, Ida brought up the idea of going away after graduation." Engen stood and walked into the kitchen. "It didn't seem like it was a reality at the time, but I knew once Janelle died there was nothing I could say to make her stay, so I decided to cut her off. Get a jump on my meaningless existence without her."

I walked over to him and put my arms around him, hoping to absorb his anguish.

"It was hell not talking to you after her death," Engen continued, loosely wrapping his arms low around my waist, "but at least I could still watch you twirl your long hair around your finger during class, and I could still listen to your voice at the lunch table when you told stories about Paul. When you said you were coming here for *six* months, I snapped. I couldn't lose you before I lost you."

"You'd never lose me. Even though I do actually have to go." I had a date with Lev, but right now didn't feel like the time to advertise it.

"Please come back tonight," Engen pleaded. "I need to talk to you."

Engen got his wish two hours later, much to Lev's dismay.

"Don't make me leave you." Lev held the back of my neck, set his lips against my cheek, and inhaled deeply.

He and I were outside my apartment door, saying goodbye. We'd just shared an evening picnic at the park by the community center. It had been fun, but it ran sort of late and fatigue was taking over.

"Engen wants to talk..." I stopped mid-sentence. Something was off. Engen must not--

"He's gone," Dee proclaimed, confirming my suspicion. She made her way down the hallway toward us from the restroom. "Buv's mom went into labor, and the oldest sibling took her to the hospital. Eze came by to drive Engen over to watch the kids."

Suddenly I felt empty and desperate to go help Engen.

Dee entered the apartment, and Lev followed after her, but I stayed rooted to the hallway floor.

"You coming?" Lev asked.

I shook my head.

"I'll give you a ride to Buv's," Lev stated, dejectedly.

I was taken aback. "Seriously?"

"Quick, before I change my mind," Lev said, with a ghost of a smile.

I grabbed a change of clothes from my room and then joined Lev, who had gone to wait in the truck.

"I forgot to tell you," Lev said after I fastened my seat belt, "me and the orphanage leader from Bulenga, Chris, signed up to have a booth at a music festival to raise money for our orphanages. I leave Friday morning, and the concert goes through Sunday."

I rolled my window down. So that's why he was cool with taking me to Engen; he felt guilty for the short notice.

"I received two free tickets for the Sunday show," Lev informed me, "and I'd like you to come."

"That's the day of the Kampala city tour," I reminded him.

"Can't you skip it?"

I breathed in the night air. "Engen already booked the tickets. He's extremely excited for it."

"Of course, since he gets to spend all day with the most remarkable person on the planet...my girlfriend."

"What about you?" I asked, noting and disliking his jealous tone. "Can't you send Becky to the concert?"

Lev took my hand. "Chris agreed to pay half the fee for the booth," he said. "I don't think she'll go if I don't, and then I'd have to pay the entire fee myself."

I narrowed my eyes. "Why wouldn't she go without you?"

"She sort of likes me."

I cracked my knuckles. "You're going to be spending three nights in a hotel--"

"Separate rooms--"

"With a girl who's crushing on you? Speaking as your girl-friend, that sounds like a poor arrangement."

"You'll finally be closer to knowing what it's like for me when you go home to Engen," he bit back.

I rested my hand on Lev's thigh. "You know how I feel about you."

"And I don't even want to know what he's *feeling* while in a bed two feet from my sexy, beautiful-smelling girlfriend," Lev insinuated. He braked in front of Buv's circular mud hut, then put the truck in park.

"Are we good?" I asked, feeling like an awful girlfriend.

"Yes." He gave me a kiss goodbye.

I walked up to Buv's house and heard mass chaos inside. I gave the door a loud knock. Engen opened it, looking haggard, a young boy was attached to his leg. When Engen saw me, his face broke into a relieved smile. I turned to give Lev a wave, and he waved back and drove off.

Engen pulled me inside the hut and into a tight embrace. "How did you know I needed you?"

"Don't you always?"

"Yes," he breathed, oblivious to the fact that a shoe just sailed by our heads.

"It's me and you through this ordeal, right?"

"Me and you," he repeated, breaking the hug. "And four kids under the age of twelve."

"Small potatoes. I'm used to twenty."

He waved his arm, indicating the madness. "They're all yours."

"Hey, kids!" I shouted. They all stopped and turned to look at me. "I have a bag of gummy bears and five thousand shillings for the kid who falls asleep first."

The kids gasped in absolute delight, probably envisioning the liter of milk and loaf of bread they could buy with that money, and scattered. They each had their own beaten-up mat-tress with a different colored shower curtain attached to a rope that was tied to the stick rafters, closing them off in their "rooms."

"Nicely done," Engen complimented, and nodded to Buv in the corner. "What's your suggestion for him?"

We ended up making a fort out of chairs and bed sheets. We tried to coax Buv in, but after ten minutes of watching us wave our arms, he went to his mattress to sleep.

"I was drowning until you showed up," Engen declared.

"You would've thought of something," I said confidently.

"How did you know I was stuck here?"

"Dee told me," I replied. I peeked out of the fort and shook my head in astonishment. "I can't believe there's going to be another kid here soon."

Engen nodded in agreement. "There must've been a complication, because Zoya planned on having the baby at home. She isn't going to be able to afford the hospital bill."

"We could have a fundraiser for her," I suggested. "They have a music room at the community center. For a donation, you could give drum lessons. Krista could do nails, and Dee would be thrilled to do makeup. I'll ask Megan to read palms, and I could give reading lessons." I was getting excited. "We could involve all the volunteers in the apartment building."

"Marco's dad owns a pizza joint. Maybe he could ship us some ingredients and we could sell pizza by the slice," Engen said. "This could be fun, but if we want to raise a substantial amount of money, we should ask our families and classmates back home to donate."

"We should see if Dee's dad could donate items to sell," I remarked. Mr. Tran was a clothing designer and he was bound to have extra pieces laying around. "I'll...well maybe you should ask Krista to get permission to use the community center while Dee and I work on advertising."

Engen's eyes sparkled with delight. "You're adorable and impressive, and I'm going to be enamored with you until the day that I die."

I felt my face flush, but told myself not to get too worked up over that comment. It didn't stop my heart from dancing or my hands from shaking, though.

I was leaning against a tree with my arms crossed, moodily watching Engen and Buvama attempt to kill each other. The fight had started inside Buv's hut and worked its way out into the broiling heat. I had pointed out, what seemed like three hours ago, that Buv didn't need to wear a shirt to go on a walk, but Engen wanted him to wear one, hence the arguing.

I watched Engen and thought about how planning this fundraiser together for Zoya had left no time to miss Lev. And, since things were going better with the pregnancy, we'd decided to tackle Lakeside Adventure Park. It was fun and challenging, with archery, obstacle and ropes courses. We opted for the high ropes course. Physically spent, we left afterward and went to dinner at a French restaurant called l'Epicurien. Engen had managed to book us an outdoor table in one of the private gazebos in the gardens. Just remembering that decadent menu caused me to lick my lips.

"You daydreaming about me, or the food last night?" Engen asked.

"The food. It was unbelievable, and the restaurant itself was so rom..." I trailed off.

I had Engen's undivided attention at this point.

"Were you going to say 'romantic?'" he inquired with a raised eyebrow.

"No, rom...an. As in Roman-inspired. That's what the décor was," I rambled.

"Oh, sure, that makes sense," he said, placating me.

I took out my phone and typed a quick response to the message Paul had sent yesterday.

"How's the surfer?" Engen asked, eyes squinted.

"Assuming you mean Lev, it's not him." I smirked. "But since you asked, he's with a girl who has the hots for him, so I'm guessing he's doing A-OK."

Engen smiled, coyly. "And you're with a guy who has the hots for..."

"Roman décor?" I guessed.

"Oh, I got it bad. The columns, the sculptures...don't get me started on the rugs."

I laughed. "Also, Lev's probably getting hit on left and right..."

Engen let go of Buv and lazily drifted over to me with a flirtatious smile on his face. "Did I mention you're looking fine as hell in that low-cut dress?"

I lifted the bottom of his white tank top so I could set my hands on his hard, tight skin. "You're looking pretty great yourself."

He tugged back the material at my chest, peeked down it, and moaned. "Wanna go back to my place after this?" he teased.

"What do you have against my place?"

"Your roommates are kinda psychotic." He kissed my nose and returned to his chore. "There, you've officially been hit on, beautiful."

Buv suddenly screamed. His yell was disconcerting, because it was for no apparent reason. Engen returned to his task of trying to stuff Buv into a shirt.

"A little help here, Ida," Engen pleaded.

Buv dropped to the ground and gaped quietly up at the sky. Poor kid had the largest, misshapen teeth I'd ever seen.

I knelt down in front of him. "What's wrong?"

Buv pointed to the sky and then to his bright red shirt still clutched in Engen's hand, then pointed back to the sky.

"Try a blue shirt," I told Engen, who took off into Buv's house.

Buv flapped his hands. "Like blue."

"If you knew the words, why didn't you just tell Engen?"

Buv put his hands to his head and shook it back and forth.

"It's not easy to express things in words, is it?" I said, thinking of the many unsaid words I had for Engen.

Engen returned from Buv's hut with a light blue shirt. Buv stood and raised his long arms above his head, and Engen put the shirt on him easily.

Buv threw his arms around Engen's waist. "Words hard."

Astounded, Engen patted Buv's back. Physical contact initiated by Buv was a rare occurrence. When they were done, I threw myself in Engen's arms.

Engen made a startled noise in the back of his throat. "What's this?"

"Words hard," I whispered into his neck.

"I love you, too," he breathed into my hair. "*So* much that I can't get my head around it, much less expect you to ever."

"I would rather have *her* than his whore of a mother," said a sinister voice from behind me.

I craned my neck to see a man shift his preying eyes from Buv to me. The stranger was portly with dark, weathered skin, and a graying mustache.

"Well, that's never gonna happen," Engen informed him. "Also, Zoya just had a baby, so she isn't accepting clients right now."

Buv flapped his hands and squawked like a bird at the man.

"She is yours, tall man?" The stranger opened his wallet. "I'm willing to pay heavily to have her for my side dish."

"*Side dish?*" Engen repeated, and looked back at me. "Do you want to handle this, or shall I?"

"I am all over this," I said and stepped forward.

FUNDRAISER

"How was the concert?" I asked Lev in between kisses.

We'd met up at Lake Victoria after my shift on Monday. I'd taken a matatu, and he'd come right from the concert with the orange pick-up.

"It was fine," Lev sighed into my mouth. "How was the city tour yesterday?"

"Also fine," I replied. My hands traveled down his back where I found something tucked into his back jeans pocket. "What's this?"

He reached back and when his hand reemerged, it was to give me a wrinkled, bright green t-shirt that said "Bayimba International Festival of Music and Arts".

"Thank you." I put it on over my tank top, and sat down on the blanket that Lev had laid out on the sand next to a fire pit. It was supposed to be a cool evening, so Lev was going to build a bonfire.

"I also got this," Lev said, and unfolded another article of clothing exactly like the shirt he'd gotten me, only it was in the form of a onesie.

I took the tiny outfit. "You bought something for the baby?"

His soft eyes took in mine. "Even if you aren't planning on keeping her, she needs clothes."

I peered at him over my daughter's first and only outfit. "You think I should, don't you?"

"It's your decision." He repositioned his cap loosely on top of his head. "If you do decide to give her up, I'd like to adopt her."

"You want to adopt my unborn baby?" I asked in astonishment. "You, personally, would raise her?"

Lev nodded his head. "I can't stand that there would be a part of you that would be out there roaming around without either of us knowing her."

I admired the sun setting behind the water, and imagined Lev walking with my daughter on this very beach. I pictured her giggling as he tossed her in the air and caught her before she hit the water. I suddenly felt left out. I was afraid of a future where Lev got to spend every day with my baby and I wasn't involved.

I stood up and walked down to the water's edge. I stroked my belly, and tried to picture what it was like for this baby, living within a horrendous person like me. I never talked to her, sang to her, or did any of those things that I thought loving parents did. Lev adopting her was the opportunity of a lifetime, and yet...

Lev wrapped his arms around me and laced his fingers through mine, resting on my baby bump. "Please tell me what you're thinking."

How could I tell him that now that he'd expressed interest in taking her, I'd awoken to the thought of keeping her?

"I never pictured the baby growing up so far away," I said honestly.

Lev turned me around. "If you keep her, I'll be thrilled. I just wanted you to know that I'm interested in being a parent to her."

I smiled. "I feel relieved to know you're an option."

"I hope you'll always consider me an option."

Lev and I didn't get a chance to discuss his offer further, because he was leaving again. This time it was for his, and thanks to my interfering, a reluctant Engen's rafting trip.

Lev was sitting on the purple loveseat in my apartment living room, waiting impatiently. His legs were crossed and his foot was bobbing up and down like crazy. He consulted his watch for the fifth time. "You might have to cancel your girls' night."

"I'll go check on him," I volunteered, and headed to our bedroom.

Engen was sitting on my bed, hugging my pillow. He watched me enter our room, looking pained. "Me and Lev together for two days isn't a good idea," he informed me. "Do you want me stuck in an African prison? Would that give you joy?"

"Little bit," I joked. He threw my pillow at me. I deflected it and it sailed onto his bed. "Rafting sounded like something you'd like to try."

"Normally it would be, but I cannot convey to you how badly I want Lev to drop off the face of the planet."

"Fine," I said, shaking at Engen's uneasiness. "I'll tell him to go ahead without you."

"Don't." Engen sighed deeply. "You want me to do this, I'll do this."

"It isn't that I *want* you to, I just thought you'd enjoy the physical challenge."

Engen stood, grabbed his duffel bag, and followed me out to the living room. "Don't forget to take Buvama for his walk tomorrow," he told me. "If any of Zoya's clients hit on you again, beat them senseless."

Lev stood and walked over to me. "Who was hitting on you?"

"Some creep that hangs out at Buv's house," I responded, flippantly.

"She handled herself beautifully," Engen said, not liking Lev's accusatory tone.

"*You* should've been the one handling it," Lev blamed in a raised voice. "Not her."

"Ida Denmark thrives at taking care of herself," Engen advised Lev.

Enough of this. I opened the apartment door and engaged in some eye communication with Engen. He took the hint and exited. I lightly closed the door and went over to Lev.

"I'll see you tomorrow night," he said.

"You mean Sunday night."

"I just cut the trip short." Lev gave me a crooked smile.

"Promise me that if he's," I side-nodded at the door, "having fun, you'll stay."

Many emotions crossed over Lev's face, and not all of them were particularly happy. "You don't want me to come home early?"

"I think Engen needs this," I justified.

"I think I'm looking at what he needs," Lev muttered.

"Hardly," I dismissed.

I opened the door and met Engen's eyes, which were full of lust.

Engen pulled me to him in a hug and whispered in my ear, "Just to clarify, Lev *was* looking at what I need."

My stomach did a flip as Engen patted my baby bump and said, "Be good to your mama, little beauty."

I waved until the guys were out of sight, then headed back into the apartment. I flopped down on the purple loveseat and waited for Dee and Krista to get back with the snacks from the Total station a block away. There was a knock on the door a moment later. Megan entered, carrying a plastic bag.

"Am I too early?" Megan asked.

"Nope." I motioned for her to come in.

She sat down on the white love seat. Krista and Dee entered the apartment next and held up plastic bags bursting with potato chips, cookies, and soda.

"Aren't Bianca, Eve, and Maddie coming?" Krista inquired after Megan's roommates.

"Yeah. They're trying to get the guys in the building to come, too," Megan informed in her monotone voice.

"Men aren't allowed at this baby shower," Dee said, scandalized.

"You guys are throwing me a shower?" I asked.

Dee shook her head at my apparent idiocy. "Duh, the baby needs things."

Krista began pulling items out of a bag. "Didn't you worry about diapers, formula, or accessorizing?"

My eyes shifted downward in embarrassment at how unconcerned I'd been with this pregnancy.

Megan raised her eyebrows at me. "I believe 'Thank you, my intelligent friends' are the words you're searching for."

I tore open a bag of chips. "Thank you, ladies."

While I wasn't one hundred percent sold on the idea of being a mom yet, I could admit that the shower gifts had gotten me a little excited for the baby's arrival. After the shower, Krista, Dee and I gave ourselves a salsa dance lesson. The three of us had started out in the living room, spilled out into the hallway, and ended up in the bedrooms. I already felt close to Krista and Dee, but couldn't help thinking that we would have been even closer if we had planned more girls' nights.

Engen returned two nights later from his rafting trip. He ended up having a great time with the guys, which pleased me to the core. Plus, he didn't murder Lev, which I considered a bonus.

The week flew by and before I knew it, the day of the fund-raiser had arrived. Dee's father came through for us by not only sending two thousand dollars toward Zoya's hospital bill, but he express mailed a bunch of clothing for Zoya's fundraiser. He sent denim shorts and skirts, along with casual dresses and sandals that would appeal to the ten to sixteen-year age range for the girls. For the boys, he sent button-down short-sleeve shirts, and jeans.

Marco's dad had shipped a ton of ingredients from their pizza restaurant. Marco received permission to cook the pizzas in the VC, and Stuart and Sheldon volunteered to cart the cooked pizzas from the VC to the community center to sell it. I told Paul that I was going to be giving reading lessons, so he and the rest of my family cleaned out their bookshelves and shipped close to one hundred of their used books for me to give away to each "customer."

Lev was bringing the kids from the orphanage, plus he contacted the orphanage leaders nearby to let them know about the event. I was surprised Lev was taking the time to do this. As the newly named Best Man in Wtalo and Namono's recently announced engagement, Lev had offered to host a party in a few weeks. He'd been busy running around and making lists since the news broke. When I asked Lev why he was freaking out, he told me that the wedding was in mid-January, which was only a couple of months away.

I had quizzed the kids prior to today about what they would most likely spend their money on. The older girls were into the idea of getting their nails done and sifting through the clothes, so Bianca had agreed to help Krista with nails, and Eve was enlisted to man the clothing table. The younger girls and boys were into the reading lessons, so Megan would be on standby in case I was busy and she wasn't with palm reading. The older boys seemed only interested in two things: Engen's drum lessons and Marco's pizza.

Engen gave the lessons in groups of five. Ralf, one of Marco's roommates, was on hand to translate Engen's instructions in case there were any non-English speaking customers. I was stationed outside and away from the noise so that my customers could hear their lessons. We'd been open and steadily busy for two hours until there was finally a lull. I was going to lay down, when Engen sauntered up to me and handed me a plate with a slice of sausage pizza on it.

"You're my savior," I said graciously, eying the plump, juicy sausage chunks. "Did you eat?"

Engen sat next to me on the blanket. "No. The pizza is backed up, and this is the only slice I could snag. Sheldon will deliver mine soon."

"You take it." I offered him the plate. "You're in there being all physical and stuff. I'm just sitting here."

He pushed it back. "Eat, Denmark."

I set the plate on the blanket and said, decidedly, "I'll wait for you, Malone."

"I just heard your stomach grumble," Engen laughed.

"That was yours," I countered.

He squinted at me. "Was it, though?"

"Okay, it was mine. Wanna split it?"

"Deal."

Engen tore the slice in half and we devoured our portions within seconds. Engen stretched out and laid his head on my lap. He gazed up at me as I absently worked my hand between the buttons of his shirt and ran my fingers over his bare chest.

"I sure do like you, Engen Scott," I sighed.

"Yeah?" he asked, like the thought had never occurred to him. "How much?"

"More than the kids like Marco's pizza," I answered.

"That's quite a bit."

"You're rocking some seriously sexy facial hair, by the way," I commented.

"So are you."

I burst out laughing. "Thanks for noticing."

Engen reached up and twirled a loose strand of my hair around his finger. "Will you read to me?"

I held out the tin collection plate and shook it. Engen reached into his pocket and plunked some money into the dish as I grabbed an old paperback with a worn cover.

"Can you read with one hand?" Engen pressed a hand on top of the one I had on his chest. "I want this one to stay right where it is."

"That'll be extra."

He gladly tossed more coins in.

I cleared my throat and began, "Based on the way he was clumsily unhooking her bra, she figured it had to be his first time. When she asked him to confirm that, he responded in a shaky voice, 'I've been with girls, but this is my first time making love to a woman.'"

"Smooth," Engen remarked.

"Well, this woman doesn't want to make love. This woman wants it..." I paused mid-sentence and looked Engen dead in the eye and said, "rough and hard."

Engen gulped.

I bit back my smile and continued, "Her nipples were hard and aching as she unzipped his pants. He suckled--"

"Hold on a second," Engen broke in. "You're teaching kids how to read *this*?"

"Just the women," I clarified. "I'll stop if--"

"No!" Engen sat straight up. "I mean, please go on."

My lips twitched as I reopened the book. "He suckled her plump breasts and she reached for his--" I abruptly stopped. "This is pure trash."

"It's poetry." Engen rubbed the back of my hand against my cheek. "I paid you to read."

"Okay," I relented. "She whispered sultrily in his ear, 'I'm going to...'"

"What? Going to what?" Engen demanded.

I coughed back a laugh and said, "I have customers."

Engen whipped his head around to see two girls around six years old, smiling toothy grins at us.

He dug into his pocket and handed the girls some money. "The reading blanket is closed until further notice."

The girls excitedly skipped into the community center. I rolled onto the blanket and clutched my stomach, laughing.

"Where's that book?" Engen asked, his hand frantically searching the ground.

I reached underneath my back and showed him the busted cover of a P.I. Polly book that had belonged to Paul.

"You made it up?" he asked.

I nodded.

"Excuse me, Engen, I have your pizza," Sheldon said.

"Thanks," Engen mumbled.

He took the slice, pepperoni this time, again ripped it in two, and gave the larger half to me.

"Oh, and you have a line for drum lessons," Sheldon informed Engen before departing.

Engen shoved some pizza in his mouth. "Made-up or not, you're finishing that story tonight."

"I can't," I chuckled. "I'm helping Lev plan an engage--"

There was no point in continuing, for Engen sprung to his feet at the mention of Lev's name and hurried off.

"Damn it," I muttered. I didn't get a lot of time to dwell on my sickness over his discomfort, because the kids from the orphanage had arrived and were forming a line in front of Lev, who had begun passing out coins. Once they had their money, they ran past me into the community center.

"Hello, lovely." Lev sat down next to me. "Since my girlfriend took Stuart and Megan away, Wtalo and Kado agreed to help keep an eye on the children."

"Thank you for bringing the kids," I said.

"Anything for my heart." Lev leaned over and kissed me.

"I want a YAHN girl to kiss me," I heard Kado say, followed by a sigh.

"American girls may be hot, but one thing is certain," Wtalo responded with contempt, "when their time is up, they go home...and they never come back."

Lev had told me the tragic story of Wtalo's first love, Casey. She had been out here with YAHN four years ago, and when Casey left, she took his heart with her. Wtalo tried to keep in touch, but the only phone call Casey answered was the one when she decided to tell him he had only been a fling.

Lev's kissing faltered and his lips lost some firmness. His hand found mine and held it tightly. I knew he was dreading the inevitable day when I would leave.

The constant pressure I underwent from Lev over where to live was almost too much. I missed my family, however, this place *had* managed to get under my skin. I would miss things about it that had nothing to do with Lev, like my work at the orphanage, and how there was no day-to-day sense of urgency. The people were calm and laid-back, and that was exactly what I needed. And then there was this fundraiser. I would never have thought to be involved in something like this five months ago. My way of thinking had changed for the better. I now felt like setting goals for myself, for finding a purpose, as opposed to hiding away.

The time had flown by. It was bizarre to think my YAHN replacement was already being trained in.

THE KINDEST GIFT

Lev and I spent a grueling week preparing for Wtalo and Na-mono's engagement party. I'd barely seen or spoken to Engen since the fundraiser, so I wasn't surprised when he frostily de-clined my invitation to attend the gathering. Krista elected to stay back as well. When I asked her why she'd pass up a party, she told me she was going to make a move on Engen. Dee, who was coming with, wished her luck.

Since Lev was the host, Muna was coming to pick us up in his boda-boda. Muna promised Lev he'd go easy on us, unlike his customers whom he loved to terrorize.

"Did I tell you Rocky was spying on Lev and me at the orphan-age earlier this week?" I asked Dee while we were waiting.

"I overheard you telling Krista. What's his deal?"

"Lev's worried that I fit his victim profile or something. I'm more upset that I brought that psycho's attention to the or-phanage."

Dee shivered. "That is scary."

"Lev called the police and gave them a heads up. I doubt they can do anything, though."

Muna pulled up just then, putting an end to our conversa-tion.

As soon as I got to Lev's house, I was thankful that Dee was with me. Aside from Omo, Dee and I were the only girls there without exposed midriffs. I scanned the room and saw that my boyfriend was currently getting a shoulder massage from the owner of the barest, flattest belly of them all. Baba.

I looked down at my plain, white cotton dress with my pro-truding belly. Why any guy could be attracted to *this* was beyond me.

Dee squeezed my hand reassuringly. "You look beautiful."

"Thanks, so do you."

We slalomed our way through the crowd, to the kitchen, to say hello to Omo.

"Lev ran to my house to get more plates; he should be back soon," Omo greeted, while chopping watermelon.

"He's here," I told her. "He's just...busy."

I shouldn't be jealous, considering I'd gotten my fair share of foot rubs from Engen. It just burned me to see that tramp's hands on my favorite part of Lev's body, his scar.

Something in my tone made Omo look up. She spotted her son and didn't look too pleased. "That Baba has never been able to keep her hands off him. She has told Lev that as soon as he enrolls in Mak to let her know, so she can take all the same courses."

"Stalker," Dee and I said in unison.

"Baba associates with some terrible boys; a few of them have been in prison," Omo shared. "Lev is one of the only decent influences in her life. It is no wonder she clings to him."

"Maybe you should go break that up," Dee said, and nodded behind her.

Figuring she was right, I went over, sat next to Lev, and slid my hand up and down his thigh. With eyes still closed, he exhaled. "Finally. I was worried."

"You're the most relaxed, yet troubled guy I've ever seen."

Lev took the hint. "Thank you, Baba," he excused her.

"Anytime, lover," Baba said sweetly. She glowered at me, then vanished.

"Lover?" I asked with raised eyebrows. "What exactly did I interrupt?"

"A harmless back rub." Lev rested his hands on my bare shoulders. "Do you know how hard it is to run an orphanage, plan a party, and spend as much time with your girlfriend as possible before she flies a million miles away? It's been stressful."

There was that word again: stressful. I might feel bad for him if he was the one eight-plus months pregnant and working in a foreign country.

"Allow me to remove some stress from your life," I said.

I stood and made my way through the masses and out the door. I determinedly walked across the street and let myself into Omo's house. I plopped down on her couch, and my eye caught on an open envelope that had "Lev Rosen" written on it in gold, looped writing. I picked it up. Omo was always getting Lev's mail. I pulled out a decorative card inviting Lev and a guest to the 5th annual dinner and award ceremony for YAHN. Based on the invitation, the event seemed fancy, therefore I had two weeks to find a nice maternity dress.

My phone rang. I dug it out of my purse. "Answer," I said, and Engen's image appeared. "What's up?"

"Are you coming home tonight?" Engen asked.

I put the invitation back where I found it. "Why, were you and Krista planning on pushing our beds together?"

"Get real," he scoffed. "I want to discuss something with you."

"Use protection; teen pregnancy isn't just a myth."

Engen sighed, annoyed. "That's quite the rager you're at."

"I got upset and left the party."

Engen frowned. "Wanna talk about it?"

"Nope."

"Well, maybe this will bring you joy; we're going on a two-day safari. We leave Friday night. Ask Lev for the weekend off."

"Will do. Wait! *This* Friday night?"

"Yep. Everyone else already has the time off."

"Everyone?" I asked suspiciously.

"Krista and Dee. Krista planned it."

I put my hand to my head, hoping my assumption was wrong. "Could you look in the nightstand for me?"

Engen leaned over and pulled the drawer open. "What am I looking for?"

"An envelope." I saw Engen pick it up. "Is the seal broken?"

"Yeah. Why, what's in it?" he asked.

Damn her! Krista had seen the concert tickets for Engen and me for this Friday night, and so she went and made different arrangements for him. What a conniving witch.

"Nothing," I said, feeling ill. I heard footsteps outside Omo's front door. "I just realized that I can't go on safari this weekend. Thanks for thinking of me at the last minute, though. Done."

The door opened and closed. I slipped my phone back into my purse and studied Lev's confused face.

"I never meant to make you think you *needed* to spend time with me," I said.

Lev sat next to me. "That came out wrong. I don't get to spend enough time with you because of all the extra stuff."

I slid my hand under the collar of his shirt and felt his scar. "Do you think Baba could have something to do with why Rocky is following me?"

Judging by the look on Lev's face, it wasn't unlikely. "I'll do some asking around, see what I can find out regarding that theory."

"I suppose you want to get back to the party."

"I only hosted the party because I'm Best Man." Lev locked the front door. "I'd rather be alone with you."

"In that case..." I patted the seat next to me on the couch.

It was hard saying goodbye to Engen on Friday, hard because I couldn't get near him. Krista was so pushy and aggressive with him lately. I could tell he was annoyed with her, but it didn't change the fact that he'd just walked out the apartment door to go on safari with her. I swallowed the lump in my throat. Bed sounded like a great idea, so I made my way there. Just to torture myself, I opened the nightstand drawer and saw that Engen had put the envelope back.

I took the tickets out and gazed at them. I felt tears sting my eyes. I'd been looking forward to surprising Engen with this getaway. I set the tickets down on the foot of the bed and curled up on my side to mope, when I heard footsteps stop in the doorway.

"The Silver Springs Hotel proudly presents The Who, The Doors, and The Beatles cover bands for a one-night only music extravaganza," Engen read off the ticket. He came around the bed and knelt down so we were face to face, and held up the tickets. "Did you get these for us?"

"No, some other music nerd."

"Ida," he said calmly.

"They *were* for us; the show is tonight." I sniffed. "I never mentioned it because I wanted it to be a surprise."

He took off his ball cap and ruffled his hair. "If I knew about the concert, I would not have agreed to the safari."

"Hearing songs you know by heart doesn't compare to an African safari."

Engen brushed some hair off my face. "What did Lev think of this outing with me?"

"I didn't ask." I propped myself up on my elbow.

His jaw muscles tensed. "Are you bringing him now?"

"No," I said softly. "They were intended for you."

As if he internally couldn't help himself, Engen kissed me. "Did Krista know?"

I turned my face away. "I'm not sure."

Engen nodded as though that confirmed it for him. "That would explain why you aren't coming with, as well as the tension between you and her."

My phone vibrated, but I didn't reach for it.

I smiled at him. "Can we make it a point to spend some time together when you get back?"

Engen's eyes said that he clearly could not be happier with that idea, as he placed another kiss on my lips, then moved his head down to kiss my belly. "Be good for your mama, little beauty," he said.

"Stop being so cute."

Engen stood, and I experienced a brief bout of panic. I didn't want him to leave.

He turned back to look at me when he reached the doorway. "I'm sorry things happened this way."

My phone vibrated again. I waited until I heard the apartment door close, before I answered it.

"Hey, Morelli."

"Idle, were you *ignoring* my call?" he asked, hurt.

"Trying to." My head fell onto my pillow. "What's up?"

"I dropped off a car seat at your house last night. You know, for the baby?"

I inspected my fingernails. "I figured it was for the baby, seeing as how I outgrew car seats two years ago."

"I don't suppose you gave any thought to--"

"There's nothing to mull over," I interrupted. "I don't want us to be a family."

"I want nothing to do with the baby, then."

I covered my trembling mouth. "Understood."

"Amelia and I have been hanging out, and she warned me that if I wanted to continue seeing her, I needed to stay away from you and the baby."

"I won't speak unless spoken to," I assured him. "Done."

I ended the call before he had a chance to change his mind, and let out a shaky breath. Finally.

Dan would no longer have to wait for a relationship that was never going to happen, and I no longer had to fend off his advances. I was so happy, I cried, for we were both free.

FALLING APART

I was starting to get nervous. It was the day of the awards dinner, and Lev still hadn't asked me to accompany him. The bigger my belly grew, the more scatterbrained he became, it seemed. There had been a get-together for the volunteers on Friday night, so Lev had gone out with his friends. He told me he would call me when he got home, but never had.

When I got to work Saturday morning, Lev wasn't in his office. I saw a white dress shirt, black suit coat, and black slacks hanging on the peg of his office door, so I knew he must be around. After breakfast, I entered the employee restroom and was surprised to see Lev drying his hair with a towel. He was so preoccupied, he didn't hear me. I padded up to him and hugged him from behind.

Lev jumped. "Did I forget to lock the door?"

"Yep," I replied. "Late start this morning?"

"Yeah."

He swiveled around to face me. His lips hovered in front of mine, so I closed the distance and kissed him. He wasn't kissing me back, which was unlike him, so I took a few steps back.

He tossed the towel into his locker and pulled out a clean shirt. "I told you I'm up for an award tonight, right? Best Kept Orphanage for ages 3-12."

I gave a yelp of joy. "I didn't know you were *nominated.*"

Lev put the shirt on. "I didn't tell you? The ceremony is tonight."

I laid my hand over his heart. "I saw the invitation at your mom's. When do we leave?"

"Sorry?"

"The invite was for Lev Rosen plus one, so I bought a dress in

Kampala the day after the engagement party. It's silver and has a slit up the side."

Lev ran his hand through his damp hair. "My mom's coming with me."

"Oh." My heart sank with stupidity.

"You hate crowds and YAHN," Lev declared, and scratched his jaw like a gangster. "I thought I was doing you a favor."

I sat down on the toilet seat lid. "I think it's great that you're taking your mom. I feel incredibly dumb for spending all that money on a dress, that's all."

"It serves you right for going through people's mail and assuming things."

"Rosen shoots, he scores." I put my hands to my mouth and pretended like a crowd was cheering.

Lev knelt in front of me. "I missed you last night."

"I missed you, too," I replied, hoping that was the end of his frostiness. "Did you have a good time with your friends?"

"I always have fun with my friends," Lev said annoyed. "Probably not as much fun as you and Engen, but we can't all have that special bond."

"Where's all this hatred coming from?" I asked. "What changed since I last saw you?"

Lev put his lips to my clasped hands, and said, "Last night I was telling my friends how amazing you are, and how there will never be anyone else for me, and you know what? They laughed at me. They found it completely pathetic that I allowed myself to get so invested in a girl who was just going to leave me."

That was why Wtalo was so mean to me lately; he resented me for my inevitable departure from his cousin.

"All the volunteers leave," I stated.

His eyes clouded over. "When you saw that I was falling harder for you, why didn't you break it off? That would've been the decent thing to do."

"Think of all the great moments we would've missed out on," I squeaked, as I stood up and walked over to the sink.

"Our relationship is dying, but at least I'll have memories

to taunt me with what it felt like to be completely whole," Lev scoffed, then stood. "My friends also made me realize how harshly I've been neglecting them and my family for you. What have you sacrificed for me?"

I raised my hands hip level, palms out. "Why does this relationship have to involve sacrifice?"

"I'm miserable unless we're together. You altered me so drastically. How did you do that?"

"It's *your* fault, Lev, you brought me here!"

"No, it was your sorry excuse of wanting to act like that slut Janelle that got you knocked up and sent here!"

I gasped. My knees wobbled, but with the support of the sink I remained standing. Strangely enough, I no longer had to use the bathroom. I could tell by his face that he knew he'd gone too far. He made his way toward me.

"Stop. I don't want you any closer," I warned.

He sighed like I was some obnoxious kid who couldn't be reasoned with. "Look, I regret that slut comment, okay?"

I shook my head. "And I regret that I have to wait three more weeks before I put eight thousand miles between us...forever."

Lev looked like he was fighting to keep his insides within his body. "Don't say 'forever.'"

"Oh, it'll be great," I said snidely. "You'll get to go back to drunken nights spent making out with random girls." I set my bag on top of the sink and rifled through it to see if I had anything for the migraine that he'd caused.

"I don't want that. I want *you*," Lev whispered.

I popped two pills in my mouth, swallowed them dry, and glared at his reflection in the mirror. "It doesn't change the fact that I'm leaving."

Lev hung his head and exited the bathroom.

I sank to the floor and recalled a memory of Janelle and me in a lingerie store. She had been telling me how important it was to always have beautiful, matching underwear, because you never knew when a guy would ask to see it. At that moment, hadn't I called her a few choice names in my head?

And then there was me. I messed around with Engen for years, *and* I had slept with Dan. Lev was the only guy I'd been with who I called my boyfriend. Maybe Lev had hit the nail on the head with his comment after all.

To ease my mind over not attending the awards ceremony, Engen asked me to go out to dinner at a fancy restaurant in Kampala so I could wear the silver dress I'd purchased. To make it fun, Engen dressed up, too.

My back was, for the most part, exposed in this dress, and Engen couldn't keep his hands off my skin. It drove Krista crazy with jealousy, and in the half hour it took for the matatu to arrive, she commanded him five times to keep his hands to himself.

When Krista and the gang had returned from safari, she'd taken me aside, admitted to, and apologized for booking the safari to overlap with the concert. She'd blamed it on her desperate infatuation with Engen. When I told her that I forgave her, she shared with me that Engen had denied all of her advances. Even so, she still tried to tell him what to do.

I hadn't taken my phone with me to dinner, and had come back to six messages from Lev. I tried calling him back Sunday morning. He didn't pick up, so I left him a message.

Since my back was killing me and Engen had a headache, we stayed in bed most of the day and only got out of it to shower, eat lunch, and to talk with Omo when she showed up for a visit Sunday night.

"Did Lev win the award?" I asked her, after Engen excused himself to go to the living room. "He didn't say in his messages."

"Yes." Omo embraced me, and I was overjoyed to be hugged by a mom. "He won the greatest, most beautiful prize in the world. Now he feels like he has lost her."

I stared into her dark brown eyes. "He said I ruined his life."

"Lev loves you so much that even I cannot breathe on account of it. If it were not for me keeping him here, he would have had his flight to America booked the day after he knew you returned his feelings," Omo said, and adjusted her glasses.

After a few more minutes of chatting, Omo had to get to work. Due to Engen messing up my back during a dance at the restaurant last night, I couldn't handle walking with her, so Engen offered.

I was sitting on the couch, reading up on how long is too long to go without feeling your baby move before being concerned, when Engen returned. He hopped onto the back of the loveseat. I scooted forward, and he slid down the back of the couch so I was nestled between his legs.

He began to rub my shoulders. "You're the most treasured thing in the world to me, too."

"I never said anything of the sort," I replied, and set the book on the coffee table.

"We never said a lot of things, but that doesn't mean they aren't true," he whispered.

I rolled my shoulders under his strong hands. "How was the walk?"

"Enlightening. I met a resident at the nursing home."

"Ah, Mrs. M." His 'most treasured' comment made sense now. "What did she have to say?"

"That we aren't done hurting each other." Engen turned my head so he could see my face. "Have I *really* broken your heart?"

"Once or twice," I downplayed. "Have I broken yours?"

"Many times."

I let my body fall back into his chest. "I'd rather my heart be broken a billion times over, than yours once."

Engen placed a kiss on the corner of my mouth. "Mrs. M. told me you'd say that."

"Did she say anything else of interest?"

"It actually got morbid." Engen wrinkled his forehead. "She said my daughter would kill me."

A weird surge went through me. It was either the thought of him having a daughter, or the thought of him dying that caused it. Maybe it was both.

"Did she give you a time frame for when this was supposed to happen?" I asked.

"No, and I didn't ask." He wrapped his arms around me, laced his fingers together, and rested them on my belly. "The less I know pertaining to the future, the better."

On the contrary, I never wanted to know the details of the future more than I did at this moment.

The walk to the orphanage the next morning left me depleted. To top it off, I was terrified. The baby hadn't moved in twenty hours. Since I'd overheard Stu telling Megan it would be busy on Monday, I sucked it up and trudged into work. Also, I didn't want Lev to think I was afraid to see him.

I entered the kitchen and grabbed the apron off the hook. I made my way further inside and saw what could only have been Lev's award. I felt a rush of pride as I grasped the gold-plated, heart-shaped statue.

"Did you know 'Lev' is the Hebrew word for 'heart'?" somebody asked, sorrowfully.

I whirled around and saw Lev with his hands in his jeans pockets.

"Congratulations," I said, and set the award and the apron down on the counter. "If you hadn't won, I was going to bad-mouth the crap out of YAHN when I got home."

He gave a faint smile. "How come you didn't answer my calls?"

"I left my phone at the apartment, but I listened to your messages when I got back."

"You went out?"

"Yeah, Engen and I had dinner in Kampala."

"Do you forgive me?" Lev asked, jaw tight.

"There isn't room in my head to think about that fight right now," I said honestly, as I rubbed my belly. "This one hasn't been active lately."

Lev rested his hip against the counter, concerned. "You

should be at the doctor."

"I made an appointment for tomorrow." My phone buzzed. I dug it out of my pocket. "Answer. Hi, Engen."

"How's your back?" Engen said instead of 'Hello.'

I placed a hand at the lower center of my back. "Still hurts. Oh, but, on the bright side, I just felt the baby hiccup!"

"That must be a good sign. Since it's my fault your back hurts, Buv and I'll come by to help you with your work," Engen offered.

I watched Lev as he paced like a tiger in a zoo, then told Engen, "I can manage."

Engen shook his head. "We'll be there soon. I love you."

"Love you, too. Done."

Lev's face was beet red. His lips were tight and his body began to shake uncontrollably.

"Are you having a heart attack?" I asked, nervously.

"Never tell another guy that you love him in front of me again," he said, enunciating each word.

"I am so sick of you two being jealous of each other," I said wearily.

"He's just your *friend*." Lev slapped the counter with the palm of his hand. "He has no right to be jealous of me!"

I stood up and put the apron around my neck. "I'm not doing this."

"What did he do to hurt your back?" Lev asked.

"We danced at the restaurant, and he did the dipping thing all wrong," I grumbled, avoiding Lev's eyes.

"What happened after dinner last night?"

"We picked up some prostitutes and took them snorkeling in Lake Victoria."

Lev didn't bat an eyelash. "You feel guilty for something. It would explain why you never answered your phone."

"I told you, I forgot the stupid phone at the apartment," I said, irritated. "I wouldn't have talked to you anyway, seeing as how you were drunk!"

"The woman I love told me she hated me," he pronounced. "I had to do something to get those crippling words out of my head."

"Then you should've listened to the message *I* left when I called you back on Sunday morning."

Lev took his phone out of his pocket and scrolled through it. I could tell when he found my message, because his shoulders sagged; he hadn't believed that I had called. He listened to my message, and his features softened. "I must've been driving when you called. I wish you would've stopped by my house. Didn't you want to fix things?" he asked.

I busied myself getting out bowls and spoons. "Just because you left me messages doesn't mean you tried to fix things."

"I was all ready to forget our fight until Engen called, and you two proclaimed your love!"

I closed my eyes and exhaled. "This needs to be over."

"No...Ida, you're the one," Lev said, frazzled. He came up behind me and set his hands on my shoulders. "Why else would I put up with you having a guy for a best friend?"

"Whoa, did you really just say 'put up with?'" I swiveled around to face him. "Are you trying to drive me crazy?"

"It's driving *me* crazy not knowing if anything else happened between the two of you!"

"Stop!" I was angry and exhausted. "I'm done."

"Do you mean that?" he asked in a strangled tone.

"The way you've been acting, I'll breathe wrong and it'll send you off the deep end." I put my fingers to my crinkled forehead. "I'm not in the mood to keep defending myself or my friendships."

"If you feel comfortable leaving things this way, then I guess we're done," Lev said, defeated, and walked out.

Maybe sending him away was the wrong move, but the only thing I had the energy to focus on was my inactive baby.

I made it through breakfast and a&c in a daze. I was snapped out of it when I heard:

"Look for Ida!"

There was no mistaking Buv's voice.

"I know you were just looking for Ida," Engen said consolingly, as he pushed the door to the rec room open.

"My heroes have arrived," I addressed the guys.

Engen ogled the room. "Wow. This looks more like a 'wreck' room if you get my meaning. Where should Buv start?"

"With the tables."

Engen explained the task to Buv, and then came over to the sink where I was washing the paintbrushes.

Engen cupped his hand around my hip and asked me, "How're you feeling?"

"Same. Was Buvama getting into trouble out there?"

"He opened Lev's office door and demanded to know where you were," Engen replied.

"Lev rarely shuts his door. He must've had a client in there," I decided.

"He was eating lunch with that girl with the big hair."

Engen's eyes shifted. Engen not making eye contact with me only happened when he had something to hide.

"And?" I pressed.

"They were hugging."

"He took me literally," I mused.

Engen's eyes made their way back to mine. "What did you say to him?"

"'I'm done.'"

Engen picked up a messy paintbrush, and fondly touched it to my nose. "Good for you."

"I had just meant done with that particular fight," I explained.

"Don't ignore," Buvama said.

"You're right, Buv," I concurred. "I need to clear this up."

I opened the door and almost ran into Lev, who was throwing the soccer ball up in the air. Baba was watching him like he was a king.

"Lev, can we talk?" I asked.

"See you outside?" Lev asked Baba.

She gave a small wave. "Ta-ta."

I watched her saunter off down the hallway.

Lev tucked the ball under his arm. "What did you want to discuss?"

I rolled my lips in and out of my mouth. "I wanted to let you know that our conversation earlier might've been misinterpreted."

"Really? Because I got the message loud and clear."

I rested my hand on my belly and imagined I felt my baby move. *My baby*. If I was going to be a mother, I had to be strong. I didn't have to justify myself to Lev. I was tired of his attempts to make me jealous, and in turn, getting jealous at the drop of a hat.

Lev raised his eyebrows. "Does your silence mean we're done here?"

"Yes," I uttered. "At least with Baba, you won't have to act like you care about raising her kid."

Lev took a step forward. "It would be my honor to raise your child as my own."

"Levy?"

I turned my head to see Baba. Figures she wouldn't go far.

"What is it, Baba?" Lev asked.

Baba cleared her throat. "You told me that you and the little mommy here were finally done."

I glared at Lev. "You said that?"

He held up a finger. "Not exact--"

"Don't let her hurt you anymore," Baba said, and sneered at me.

"If you think *this*," I pointed to my belly while keeping my eyes on Baba, "is going to keep me from dropping you, try me."

Baba's eyes turned ferocious. "It won't stop me either."

"*I* will, though," Lev said. "Leave."

"You told me--" Baba started.

"Leave," he repeated firmly.

"You played me false," Baba said to Lev, looking humiliated, and left.

"I know we've been stressed, but *finally* done? That's exceedingly harsh," I stated.

"You don't under--"

"Save it."

I went back inside the rec room and slammed the door on his stunned face.

"Things go well?" Engen asked.

Lev kicked the door behind me and swore.

"Not so much," I responded. I moved away from the door.

"What can I do?" Engen asked.

"Nothing. I think I need my mom for this one," I whimpered.

Engen took out his phone. "Call Gretchen."

I gave my fantastic friend a grateful smile. I then sat down on one of the rec room chairs, and talked to my mom for the first time in over five months.

It may have been an excruciating day for me, but it was good for the orphanage; four kids' adoptions had gone through.

Engen had taken Buv home, and I was waiting outside for Becky to get back with the truck so I could beg for a ride to my apartment when someone sat next to me and breathed heavily.

"Hey, Megan," I greeted, recognizing the angst-filed sigh. "I didn't know you were still here."

"I'm going to spend the night. Lev needs the help," she added.

"That's nice of you."

I looked at Megan. She didn't wear as much eye makeup as she did when I first met her. Either she'd run out of it, or grown out of it.

"It doesn't seem right that our time here counts toward our grades back home," Megan declared.

"I know. How do they figure out what letter to assign to an experience like this?" I yawned.

"No clue," Megan responded. "Do you think you'll ever come back to Africa?"

"No," she answered right away. "Do you think you'll ever leave?"

That was an odd question. I was about to say so when I heard the sound that brought back frightening memories: clacking rocks. I frantically scanned the area, but didn't see Rocky, just the orphanage truck approaching.

LYING?

I was laying on my back in bed, too worried about the baby to sleep. I rolled over to face my friend, and found him staring at me. I propped up my head in my hand.

"I miss Janelle," I whispered.

"I miss us," Engen replied.

Engen's eyes were serious in the moonlight that shone through the window. When I searched them, I saw complete and utter love. It was undeniable, unconditional, and to be honest, scary.

"Janelle's happy that I found myself here," I informed him. I slid my hand under the mosquito netting and reached my hand out just as he did the same. They hung, clasped together between our beds. "What if I lose myself again?"

"Then I'll do whatever it takes to find you," Engen vowed.

I listened to the rain hitting the window and the thunder in the distance, and became morose. With Engen going away to college, he wouldn't be around to find me.

"Can I hold you?" he asked.

I stared at his strong jaw. "Sure."

Engen got out of his bed, lifted the mosquito netting on mine, and stepped over my legs. I moved as far as I could to the edge of the bed so he would fit. My tummy jutted out over the side of the mattress, but after much maneuvering, my back was to Engen's front, the top of my head nestled underneath his chin. His large hand supported my belly. My silk nightie stuck to his bare torso, and it was tough for us to find a comfortable position because his body was reacting to my closeness. I didn't want to draw attention to it, so I just tried not to move.

"Sorry," he murmured.

"No big deal," I responded.

He nuzzled his face into my hair. "You don't think it's a big deal?"

"It's probably the hugest deal I'll ever encounter."

I felt his lips smile. "Good."

I still managed to fall asleep. I don't think I'd been out for long before I heard pounding on the apartment door. Maybe it was the neighbor's door, because Engen hadn't stirred. I had just settled back into his secure hold, when our bedroom door burst open.

Engen and I bolted upright. Dee was at the door. Her eyes were wide as she tried and failed to block the view from Lev. It wasn't the terrified look on Lev's face, the state of his clothing, or that he was dripping wet that stuck out the most. At that moment, the only thing I was aware of was Engen's hand gripping the bend of my waist and how awful it must appear to Lev.

Lev's face was startled. He cleared his throat and said robotic- ally, "There was a fire at the orphanage."

I slipped out of Engen's hold and walked briskly toward Lev. "Are the kids okay? Megan?"

Lev nodded, rubbing his eyes, and sidestepped down the hall toward the living room. "The fire started in the kitchen, the fur- thest spot from their sleeping quarters," he said. "The kids are being checked over by a doctor, just to be safe."

"What can I do to help?" I asked Lev, who was still retreat- ing.

Lev glowered hatefully at the strap that had slipped off my shoulder, undoubtedly hating my skin now that he could im- agine Engen's hands on it.

"The firemen said the kids shouldn't stay there tonight," he shared. "I was hoping you could take a couple, but it's already too crowded in here."

The door leading to the hallway was still open. He backed out of it and took off running.

"Lev, wait!" I chased him out of the door into the rainy night. I smelled smoke in his wake, through the dampness in the air.

"Stop!" I urged.

I was closing in on him when I lost my footing and slipped. I shrieked as I landed hard, the left side of my stomach connecting with a jagged rock. I clutched my gravel-caked hands under my belly. I heard Lev's feet sloshing in the mud toward me. He tried to help me stand, but I shoved his hands away. I wouldn't be on this ground if it wasn't for him running away from me.

"Do you feel hurt, does the baby?" Lev asked worriedly.

"She's not doing anything, as usual," I said, and stood without his help. Lev walked with me over to the picnic table, and I sat. "You said the fire was in the kitchen," I recalled. The pains in my stomach were sharp, and it hurt to breathe. "Was it my fault?"

"No." Lev held my elbow. "I'm calling Dr. Milton."

I watched him on the phone and thought about how we'd kissed at this table back when our relationship was new and only semi-complicated.

"Dr. Milton will pick you up here," Lev informed, and sat next to me. "Why were you and Engen in bed together?"

Janelle, help me out with this one, I thought, never more in need of her guidance.

Lev shook his head, disappointed at my silence.

I needed to stall until Janelle came up with an answer for me. "He was comforting me."

"From what?" Lev asked as the rain continued to pelt down on us.

"You're going to meet so many girls at college," I dodged. "Smart, beautiful girls without babies."

"Those girls won't compare to you." Lev's eyes were full of devotion. "What are you doing to me?"

My throat was sore from holding back tears. "I'm giving you a way to forget me."

"A lobotomy couldn't make me forget you!"

I muddled through the fog in my brain and came up with a solution: I simply tell Lev the truth, and given his state of mind, he would likely interpret the worst.

"I left out the most important thing about the girls you're

going to meet," I said through clenched teeth. "They wouldn't sleep with their best friends behind your back."

Lev's eyes unwillingly closed. It was as if his eyelids were suddenly overburdened. When he reopened his eyes, tears were seeping out of them.

The apartment building's front door opened to reveal Engen. He was still shirtless, but at least he had pants on over his boxer-briefs. Engen looked at the mud on my nightgown and in my hair, and saw my hands clutching my stomach. He knelt in front of me. I studied Lev as he watched Engen tend to me and touch my legs unabashedly, checking for injuries. I didn't think Lev's eyes could pierce any bluer until I saw the mad and broken tears in them.

The pain in my stomach grew almost to the point of unbearable, and I squirmed when Engen touched a scratch on my leg.

"That hurt?" Engen asked, sympathetically.

"It hurts terribly, but it'll be the kind of pain that goes away," I paused and met Lev's eyes, "in time."

Lev stood, turned, and left in the direction of the orphanage. This time he wasn't running.

I buried my face in Engen's shoulder and wept.

Engen patted my back. "What just happened?"

My system was at a standstill. My head was painfully dizzy. "I ensured that Lev would hate me for the rest of his life," I uttered.

"Why?"

"Promise me you won't interfere," I pleaded.

My brain clouded over. *I said that out loud, didn't I? Engen knew not to interfere, right?*

"Ida? Ida, wake up!"

I was laying on my back, being shaken. Why was Engen shaking me? Rain fell in my mouth as my body was lifted into strong arms. I was on the brink of drifting away.

"Lev!" Engen bellowed. "Help us!"

The lie was for the best. Lev needed to hate me, and I needed...

VICTORIA

Aside from the ache in my stomach, the only thing I could make sense of was the fact that the baby was no longer inside of me. Almost forty weeks, and poof, she was out. *Finally done.* I didn't know how to deal with that right now. One thing at a time, and the first thing to do was open my eyes.

"It's my turn!" Dee exclaimed.

"No way," Engen hissed. "You and Krista just make her cry."

"Big surprise, Ida's baby only wants Engen," Krista said, in an all-knowing tone.

I turned my head slightly to the voices and forced my heavy eyelids open. Engen was holding a pink, fuzzy bundled blanket, staring at it dreamily. Krista and Dee were bent over, cooing.

I turned my head in the opposite direction. On the nightstand was a small white card that read "to: You, from: Africa." The card was propped against a tiny package. A new pain, an eye-popping pressure, hit me. Thinking of Lev, and what he must be going through right now, was excruciating.

"Hey, Mommy's awake," Engen said in a small voice.

Mommy? That was going to take a while to get used to.

"I'll get the doctor," Dee announced. Before she left, she gave me a kiss on the cheek. "She's beautiful."

"How're you feeling?" Engen asked me.

My hands drifted to my strangely empty stomach. "I hurt."

He nodded in understanding. "Your body's been through a lot. They needed to cut this little beauty out of you."

"She's so tiny," I noted.

"She's 5 pounds, 2 ounces," Engen informed me. "Her temp is good, she's eating, and her lungs work perfectly fine."

"Also, she's completely obsessed with Engen," Krista chimed

in.

Engen gazed at the baby. "It's a mutual infatuation."

I felt a pang of jealousy that others knew facts in connection to my baby that I didn't. "I don't remember going into labor," I said.

"Your baby was under respiratory distress," Dr. Milton said, as he entered the room. "I did an ultrasound and saw that the umbilical cord was strangling her. Engen mentioned you hadn't been feeling the baby move; the cord wrapped around her neck was the reason." He checked one of the many monitors I was hooked up to, and then continued, "You fainted before we brought you in, and since I couldn't bring you around, I put you under so you wouldn't wake up during the delivery. I'm pleased to report you're both doing well."

The doctor excused himself a few minutes later, saying he'd send in a nurse to go over the feeding options for the baby.

"Can I hold her?" I asked Engen, even though she looked like the embodiment of peace.

Engen placed my daughter in my arms. I experienced a searing pain in my stomach, and shook my head. Immediately understanding, Engen adjusted her higher up on my body and the baby wailed. She had the best mouth I'd ever seen, lips so tiny and perfect. Her cheeks were incredibly soft, her eyelids were the thinnest, sweetest things, and were squeezed shut so I didn't know what color they were. I was overwhelmed with the desire to know, but didn't ask. I wanted to discover everything about her myself.

"How much of her life have I missed?" I asked in amazement.

"Almost three hours," Engen said dotingly.

"And you were with her for those three hours?"

"Nowhere else I'd rather be," Engen responded, and watched my daughter with as much love as I felt. "What are you going to name her?"

"Victoria Janelle Scottie Denmark."

Engen swallowed a lump in his throat. "Two middle names?"

"In honor of my two best friends."

Engen turned away, wiping his eyes. I concentrated on the small package next to me to hide my own tears.

"Lev was here," Krista broke the silence. "After you passed out, Engen yelled for Lev to come back and help. He left shortly after Victoria was born."

I kissed my daughter's velvety forehead. She started to settle down.

"Did you see the way Lev regarded me?" Engen asked the girls.

"You were in bed with his girlfriend *and* you were the first person to hold his girlfriend's baby. Lev has reason to be pissed," Dee said, and proudly took Krista's hand. "Should we head out, Kris?"

"Yes." Krista yawned. "I need sleep."

"I kind of let Lev think that you and I had sex last night," I disclosed to Engen, once the girls had left.

"Why?"

I hugged my baby close to me. "Because I'm a frightened fool who saw an easy way out of a complicated situation."

Engen nodded, as if that made sense to him. "I thought you would've chosen Janelle for her first name."

"I was at Lake Victoria when I first entertained the thought of keeping her," I shared.

"She looks just like you," Engen commented, as he stroked Victoria's arm. "I was going to have to adopt her if you hadn't decided to keep her."

"Would you settle for being in our lives forever?"

"You got it," he accepted.

As I was feeding Victoria her 3 a.m. bottle, I thought back on the emotionally draining day I'd had. Stuart had stopped by for a visit in the late afternoon. He'd heard of the break-up. Apparently, Lev hadn't skimped on the details. I could tell that Stuart was wishing I would deny the allegations, but I remained silent.

After Stuart had left, Megan showed up for a chat. She, too, wanted to talk about Lev, so I shut down. Eventually, Megan had given up trying to engage me, and took Victoria outside for a change of scenery. When I watched them leave, my eye had caught sight of the scissors on my bedside table. I grasped a chunk of hair and recalled how much Janelle had admired it. I thought about how my lie to Lev could have been prevented if only Janelle hadn't abandoned me, then grabbed the scissors and chopped my hair off. Thankfully Dee had come by for a visit next and offered to fix my hack job. It was now shoulder length and the ends flipped up.

I burped Victoria, and she fell asleep on my chest. The surgery didn't give me the strength to put her back in her hospital crib, and there was no way I was waking Engen, so I settled in with her the best I could, and stared at her tiny wrist.

The package Lev had left by my bedside table was a small handmade bracelet just like the one he wore around his wrist, and I around my ankle. I had tied it around Victoria's wrist right away. It was heartwarming to think that he had made her the bracelet without my knowledge.

I glanced over at a snoring Engen and smiled tenderly. When he had called his family to proudly announce the birth of Victoria, his mom informed him that South Dakota State University wanted an answer regarding the partial football scholarship they offered him, and he still hadn't accepted. He had been biding his time, trying to get me to focus on colleges, specifically, one in Colorado that offered family housing and free daycare to students. I was flattered, but I didn't know what I wanted to do, and I wasn't going to pay the outrageous tuition to take general courses out of state when I could take them at a college near home.

As much as I wanted Engen around, I honestly didn't want him to make a huge life decision based on me and Victoria. Engen's dad had always said that going to college out of state was an experience that every young man should have. I didn't think Engen shared that belief until two years ago when I overheard him list to his brother-in-law, Doug, the quintessential college experiences he hoped to have when he was out of Minnesota. Take a guess at how many of those items involved a baby.

And just like that, my conundrum over which continent to live on was solved.

◆ ◆ ◆

"You ready to get outta here?" Engen asked after my second afternoon spent at the clinic.

"Completely." I'd been at the window with Victoria cradled in my arm, pointing at objects and telling her their names in Swahili.

Engen opened his arms for the baby. I handed her over, and his face swooned. "I don't know how I got through the day," he said. "I couldn't wait to get back to you girls."

"We missed you, too," I replied.

He gave me a kiss. "I love your haircut."

"So you've mentioned," I said with a smile, and touched Victoria's pink knitted cap, a gift from Omo. "Engen, are you going to miss this place at all?"

"No way. The bathroom is nice, but it smells like lemons in here, and I hate lemons."

I rolled my eyes. "Not the doctor's office. Mukono."

His eyes were shining as he repositioned Victoria so she was upright, resting against his shoulder. "Not really."

I set my fingertips on the nape of Victoria's neck. "It can't go back to the way it was. You must feel that, too. Can you imagine sitting at the lunch table at school and listening to gossip, or who got what phone where?"

"Yes," he answered adamantly, "because that's where our lives are."

I shook my head. "I don't want the most important things in Victoria's life to be going to the mall, or getting the latest in technology."

The reality of my words sinking in, Engen stumbled backwards, his eyes frightened. "You don't...you couldn't...you mean you want to stay?"

"Yes."

"This is crazy. You can't move here."

"What does it matter to you?" I touched Victoria's nose. "Not one college you've looked at is in Minnesota."

"But they're all in America," he countered.

"Regardless, it's going to feel like we're a world apart, so why not make it so?"

Nurse Katherine stuck her head in. "You all packed?" she asked me.

"Yes," I responded. "Thanks again for the ride."

"Of course," she said.

Engen handed me Victoria, grabbed the two paper bags by the door that were full of baby clothes, blankets, bottles, and toys—hand-me-downs from the nurses—and left.

My disagreeable mood faded when I watched the nurses cooing their goodbyes to my girl. It was hard to believe that she was mine, but her soft brown eyes and pouty bottom lip were evidence. Needless to say, I'd forgiven Dan for setting me up to keep her, and I was indeed keeping her.

We had been at the apartment all of three hours before I began to feel useless. I missed the orphanage, so Engen and I went to visit the next day. Dee agreed to watch Victoria because I didn't want her near the damage. There might still be potentially harmful gases in the air that her tiny lungs wouldn't be able to handle.

I walked more slowly than I had ever walked in my entire life, but Engen didn't complain. Once we arrived, we noticed that there didn't appear to be any damage to the outside. Lev had taken charge of getting the kitchen window replaced. The fire would have caused more damage if it hadn't been for the sprinkler system Lev installed two years before. It had taken awhile for the system to kick in, but at least it had.

Engen knelt down and picked up a rock. "How did all this happen, anyway?"

"According to Megan, the firemen found a bottle. I guess someone lit it and threw it through the window."

I pressed my nose against the new pane of glass, and peered inside. Most of the appliances were gone. The items that remained were charred, including the cupboards.

Engen pushed up from his knees and stood. He threw the rock up in the air and let it drop. It made a familiar clacking noise as it landed on top of another one, drawing my attention to the ground. My eyes widened at what I saw.

"Rocky," I blurted out. "He's responsible."

"How do you figure?" Engen asked, interested.

"Those two rocks don't fit in here."

"The orphanage doesn't have a specific landscaping motif. What do you mean they don't 'fit in?'" he challenged.

"They're too big to be amongst all this tiny gravel." I started to pace. "Rocky knows Lev and I work here. Maybe he wanted to get back at Lev for interfering with his plan to capture me that night, three months ago."

"I'm not buying into this theory," Engen said.

"Because you're a semi-decent person who doesn't contemplate revenge tactics. I should tell Lev."

"Lev is busy picking up cleaning supplies," a slow, accented voice said.

I looked over to see Akiki standing nearby with his hands clasped behind his back.

"Lev has hired a crew to start work on the kitchen restoration tomorrow," Akiki informed. "After today, he will be taking some time off of work."

I swallowed my curiosity as to why. "I think I know who started the fire," I told Akiki. I described Rocky to Akiki, and told him how I thought Baba set Rocky up to stalk me.

"I will inform my good friend in law enforcement." Akiki scratched his eyebrow. "The VC offered New Beginnings the use of their kitchen, so that is where you will report tomorrow. Will you be bringing your daughter to work with you?"

I nodded. "Yes, sir."

"Then I will see you both tomorrow morning."

Akiki gave me a respectful nod as Engen and I passed him on our way inside the orphanage. We found the kids in the rec room with Megan overseeing the a&c lesson. The kids ran to me, all speaking at once. They let me know that Stuart's oatmeal tasted bad, but his eggs were better than mine. They told me how many goals they'd scored during soccer, and that Becky was cranky.

When I noticed Engen fidgeting, I told the kids I had to go. Engen and I walked out together. I hugged his arm, suddenly very thankful for him.

"I'm worried how Krista's going to handle being away from you. She's so into you," I told him.

"And you can't imagine why, I'm sure."

"Of course I know why." I stood on my tiptoes, and kissed him on the cheek. "You're the best guy in the universe."

Engen blushed. "I thought I was only 'semi-decent.'"

"That's true," I amended. "You're either beating people up or threatening to."

"All of my violent acts are inspired by you," Engen admitted matter-of-factly.

"Thanks for never beating up Lev," I said, and then grew quiet.

"Hey, I'm sure deep down, Lev knows you didn't cheat on him. Men aren't stupid, okay?" Engen tripped on his shoelaces. "Are you ever going to tell him the truth?"

"I can't go to him," I whispered.

"Well, you can't expect him to come to you."

Basically, if I ever wanted things to be made right with Lev, I would have to come clean with him.

FEELINGS TO FORGET

The days flew by. Last night, the volunteers watched a composite video of past YAHN volunteers, and their stories on readjusting once they got home. The video displayed the person's name and where they'd been assigned. One fifteen-year old girl named Anne had stated that when she came to Mukono, she had one goal in life, to medal in the 200-meter individual medley at the next Olympics. After six months in Africa, *bam,* it no longer mattered to her. Now, not only had swimming become mundane to her, but America as well. Something about Anne's story struck a chord. I risked a glance at Engen who was sitting with the guys in the aisle seat of the row in front of me, and saw that he was looking at me as if to say, "See, proof that people's ideals can change." My attention was returned to Anne's story when I heard her say, "You, too, have changed. You won't realize how monumental the change is until you get home."

I wasn't ready to accept that our time here was up, and the goodbye dinner tonight would force me to face that. The dinner was a chance for supervisors and coworkers to say farewell, and for members of YAHN to thank us for our service. Engen didn't feel well, therefore wasn't attending, and Matilda had kindly offered to watch Victoria.

The long cafeteria table at the VC had been replaced with ten smaller tables that sat five people each. My eyes sought and found the blue eyed, blonde-haired man, striking in his black slacks and olive-green dress shirt. When Lev saw me, his eyes widened and his lips parted. So maybe my low cut, lavender sundress was a little tighter in the bust than I usually went for, but I didn't think it lascivious enough to elicit this sort of reaction. Lev make a back and forth slicing motion with his hand, low at his neck, clarifying that it was my short hair that had surprised him.

A booming voice told us to take a seat. Everyone gravitated toward tables with their coworkers. Megan, Stu, Lev, Becky, and Akiki occupied a table. Buvama and Zoya sat at a table along with Sheldon, Sheldon's home care kid, and the kid's father. The available chair at that table belonged to Engen. Even though he wasn't here, it didn't feel right to take it.

I took a seat at an empty table and gulped a tall glass of water with melting ice chunks. It was roasting in here. I grabbed the glass sitting in front of the seat next to me and chugged half of that as well. Megan and Stu were making flustered faces at Akiki for taking what, essentially, should have been my chair. Zoya asked with her eyes if I wanted the seat next to her, but I politely waved the invitation away. Considering I had planned a life of solitude for myself, I was perfectly fine being alone.

With his eyes on me, Lev poured himself a glass of wine, and drank at least two inches of it. I felt my skull tingle just as a loud sneeze caused me to jump and turn. My face broke into a wide smile when I saw Engen standing behind me, a tissue pressed to his nose.

Engen hungrily took in my face, almost as if he had just been through the longest hour of his life without seeing it. "Looks like it's just me and you."

Engen sat next to me, and set his hand on top of mine just as a man stepped up to the podium. He was a tall, thin, middle aged African man dressed in an expensive-looking suit. He introduced himself as the Vice President of the Ugandan branch of YAHN. His voice was nasally and irksome. I looked at Engen, and at the same time we began making faces and moving our mouths, mimicking the man. We leaned into each other, chortling silently, or so we thought until the man stopped his speech and gaped at our table, along with the rest of the room.

Engen waved to the man at the podium, and said, "Carry on."

As soon as the final speech ended, with the promise of dinner to closely follow, Lev walked by, shot Engen a glare, and pushed the door open with one hand. His free hand securely held onto a bottle of wine. Engen squeezed my fingers to get my attention. I looked at him and he sneezed all over me.

"Sorry," Engen said.

"It happens." I dabbed at my face with a napkin. "I thought you were feeling too sucky to come tonight."

"Turns out I feel worse without you around." He stood. "I'm going to go visit Buv. Wanna come?"

"No, you go ahead."

I watched Engen walk away, and then my gaze moved to Megan and Stu, laughing together. She caught my eye and waved me over. I shook my head. I didn't feel like I would be a good conversationalist right now. In fact, when it became obvious hat I wasn't going to be able to function as long as my nerves were so on edge, I decided to get some air. I walked out into the warm evening and wandered in the direction of the community center. I got as far as the playground before my C-section scar twinged. I thought it best to turn around and head back for dinner, when I heard the squeak of a swing.

"Your haircut makes you look older," Lev said. He stared at me. "You're so beautiful. It makes my heart hurt."

I headed for the swing set and sat, making sure to leave an empty one between us. "Thanks for setting up the crib at the apartment."

"No problem," he responded tersely. "Akiki told me that Victoria wears the bracelet I gave her. I made it before you murdered my heart."

"No two words can drive a break-up message home harder than 'Finally done.'"

"So, because of a misunderstanding, Engen has me to thank for the best night of his life," Lev said, and stumbled a bit before making it onto his feet. "Just sitting here with you makes me sick. It makes me sick because I'm *still* so in love with you."

"Don't love me anymore," I urged, feeling like I had swallowed sand. "It's a waste of your time."

"You messed me up." Lev's face contorted. "Yet, I'm going out of my mind missing you. Whatever I did to make you stray, I'm sorry."

"You were the perfect boyfriend."

"Then why? You know what," Lev held up his hands, "never mind."

He took off without a backward glance.

◆ ◆ ◆

My internal clock woke me up. I was staring at Engen's empty bed. I glanced at the alarm and saw that it was three-fifteen. Engen appointed himself the job of Victoria's 3 a.m. feeding, and they must still be at it.

I padded down the hallway and saw Engen laying on the white loveseat. Victoria was asleep on his bare chest. Engen's hand covered almost her entire body, and an empty milk bottle lay on the floor.

I leaned against the archway and watched the sweet scene with a smile on my face. My eyes traveled down to Engen's legs sticking off the arm of the couch, and my smile grew. I set a palm against my chest, which ached happily at the sight of them. Thanks to the streetlight shining through the blinds, I was able to see Engen's profile. I admired his full lips, long eyelashes, and light facial hair. All of a sudden, my legs started to shake and I felt my cheeks grow warm. The wall around my heart that I had built to keep him out started to quake, and the bricks loosened. I gave a small gasp. *Please no,* I thought, recognizing what was happening. *I can't fall in love with him again.*

Engen's eyes slowly opened. He turned his head toward me. We admired each other for a few moments. I bit the corner of my lower lip. Sweat was gathering on my chest, so I ran the hand that was still covering my heart down my front and rested it on the opposite hip. I was wearing a short, white, silk nightgown, but based on the heat in Engen's eyes, I needed to remind myself that I was indeed clothed.

"Hi," I mouthed.

His lips parted, but no words came out.

My heart hammered, causing a few bricks to fall. I pushed myself off the archway, walked over to the loveseat, and knelt down beside him. I rested my head on his shoulder and looked at my daughter. I put my hand on top of Engen's, which was on her back. He bent his fingers backward, and I intertwined them with mine. My skull tingled as I set my lips on his neck and breathed in his amazing apple-cinnamon scent which was mixed with chlorine from our impromptu swim in the VC's pool after the YAHN dinner. My other arm went around him; my fingernails lightly ran up and down his bicep. There was a stirring inside my heart. Feelings that had been buried deep inside were stretching and yawning after a long sleep.

Engen had shared with me that the night I went into labor, everything was chaotic at the doctor's office. He'd been so scared having just witnessed everything from the doctor cutting me out of my clothes, to the nurses hooking me up to IV's and bringing in medical instruments, to a woman with a huge syringe. He said he had to leave the room before he fainted. Roughly ten minutes later, he heard a baby cry, and he ran back into the room to see me laying still with my arms propped wide apart and a slit in my lower belly. There was an overflowing tub full of my blood on the floor and it looked like how he imagined a murder scene would. He immediately threw up. A nurse kicked him out to go get cleaned up. When he came back in the waiting room, he was all alone. Lev had gone to change clothes and shower so he didn't smell like smoke when he met the baby, Engen hadn't called Krista and Dee yet, and the doctor and nurses were still working on me, so he had no one else around to focus on to keep the vision of me bloody and split open from his mind.

Then another nurse came out, handed him a pink blanket, and said, "Hold the baby, we need all hands on deck in there."

The moment Victoria was placed in his arms, a warm feeling passed over him. She was the tiniest person he had ever seen, yet somehow with her in his arms, he became comforted, for she was the one person he had while his entire world was in the next room getting stitched up. More importantly, *he* was the one person she had while *her* entire world was being stitched up.

My favorite thing that he told me with respect to that night was, "If the only purpose I had for being put on this Earth was to keep your baby safe while you were being operated on, then I'm fine with that."

Touched to the point of tears at the thought of that, I ran my lips along his neck. His breath caught, and the wall around my heart crumbled. My heart was exposed, and it was reaching for the person I had denied loving for the past year.

"Engen," I whispered, almost painfully.

"What?"

"I--" my throat closed.

I thought back to when we were thirteen, when I'd told Janelle that Engen and I had kissed, and how much I had enjoyed it. Janelle's response flooded my mind: "There's no point, we both know he's going to end up with a cheerleader. Plus, you're too full of darkness; he deserves someone full of light.

My stomach boiled with fury. Why had I been so stupid to allow Janelle to get under my skin? Why had I, essentially, cut Engen loose? Freed him up for the taking? I never wanted another girl to have him, but I also never wanted to disappoint Janelle.

"I see those wheels turning. Talk to me," Engen pleaded.

Janelle was gone. Engen had screwed up, and so had I. It was in the past. We could start over.

"I'm..." I trailed off, lost in his gray eyes.

Something extremely intense was going on inside my body, but I was reluctant to give voice to it now that I'd made the decision to keep myself and my baby out of his way while he attended college. My windpipe felt like it was being crushed.

"Please just say it," Engen urged. "You *have* to be the one to say it, because I am completely at your mercy here."

Seeing him with my daughter, all those negative, unfair feelings from our missed opportunities at a relationship melted away. He was my everlasting friend. I told myself that there were many things I was willing to jeopardize, but not that.

"Shall we put her back in her crib?" I asked, standing.

Engen looked away from me, dissatisfaction at my cowardice etched in his features. "Sure," he said.

Victoria's crib was in the living room so she could be near the air conditioner, not that there was any space in our bedroom. Engen set her down, but not before kissing her cheek. I felt my heart tear, conflicted over the fact that pretty soon there wouldn't be an 'our bedroom' to go back to.

Engen turned around and saw the mixture of sadness and lust on my face. He lifted his hands, and I pressed mine against his, palm to palm, entwining our fingers.

"What's going on inside that sick, twisted mind of yours?" he wondered.

"You're tall," I said, noting the electric zing that had struck my chest at his touch.

"Hey, thanks." He smiled.

"And muscly."

He winked. "I try."

This was one of our favorite bits over the years and I always modified this part to change things up. "And I think I'd rather be cut open, have a baby removed, and be stitched back together one hundred times--"

"That's graphic," he interrupted.

"--rather than go ten minutes without seeing your face."

"Wow," he sighed.

◆ ◆ ◆

The next morning, the new batch of volunteers arrived. My

resentment was shoved aside because Cam needed me. Cam was sixteen and from California. His parents made him apply so he could beef up his college resume. They owned a restaurant, and by the sounds of it, they had taken care of filling out his YAHN application.

I can't describe how it felt to meet my replacement any more than I could describe Victoria's sweet scent. I'd been answering questions for Cam when he broke down crying. I held him, his face pressed into my shoulder, wetting my shirt with his tears. I explained to him that I was just like him once, scared and unhappy to be here, but now I would give just about anything to stay.

When I got back to the apartment, I fixed Victoria two ounces of formula and sat down next to Engen on the purple loveseat to feed her. Engen put his arm around me, and I snuggled into his side.

"I did something for you today," Engen said.

"You bought me a present and then buried it?" I guessed.

"Nothing nearly as cool as that." Engen ran his pointer finger up and down the bottom of Victoria's soft foot. "I saw Lev. I'd left word with Omo a week ago to ask Lev to come see me at Buv's house," he explained. "I didn't expect him to show, but he did today."

"Why did you want to see him?" I asked.

"So I could tell him that you and I didn't sleep together," Engen stated. "He told Omo and all his friends that you cheated on him. He tarnished your name, and now he has to clear it." Engen wrinkled his brow. "Plus, I thought you might want to say a proper goodbye to him, considering you plan on returning one day.

I put Victoria over my shoulder to burp her, and suddenly realized that there was a goodbye I needed to say. I stood. "Will you watch Victoria?"

Engen nodded. I handed her over, and walked toward the door. I paused with my hand on the doorknob and looked over my shoulder. Engen had my daughter tucked into his arm, brushing kisses against her forehead.

I made my way behind the couch, and threw my arms around his neck. "Thank you for every day of your life that you've shared with me." I kissed Engen's cheek and whispered, "If I was forced to choose between you or air, I'd pick you."

Engen stood, set Victoria in her crib, and joined me behind the couch. "Since I'm so great," he said with a smirk, "how come you went for Lev, the polar opposite of me?"

I gave a light laugh. "Because there's no universe where *I* win the jock over the cheerleader."

"I only started something with Brittany to see if it would make *you* come around," Engen said sternly. "Each night I go to bed and pray that when I wake up, we'll be fifteen again. There are *so* many things I'd do differently."

"Me, too."

Engen brushed the hair off of my cheek, and leaned down. I held onto his biceps and looked into his focused eyes. My gaze dipped to see his tongue wet his lips, which were quickly approaching mine. I gripped his arms tighter, and my heart raced. I saw the deep want in his eyes and I felt it, too. Just as his lips met mine, the apartment door burst open, and Krista and Dee entered. I backed away from him, and made my leave.

I had my doubts on taking that rickety, bumpy matatu after the surgery, but how else was I going to get to the lake? I paid my fare and scanned for a seat. The only one available was next to the African goddess that Lev sat next to on our first trip to Lake Victoria. She lifted her eyes from her book and tilted her head gracefully. I sat next to her, noticing she smelled like coconut.

When we neared the lake, I leaned over her to take in the view. The lady cleared her throat, and for some reason I looked over and saw a white piece of cardboard shoved in the collar of her black blouse. I sat back and noticed her book. It was a bible.

"Are you a priest?" I asked her.

"Yes. My name is Oluchi."

"Megan mentioned you. Are you really psychic?"

She nodded, dignified. "This will not be the last time we

meet."

Her all-knowing tone reminded me of when Asya had come to say goodbye to me just before she was adopted, when she mentioned the pretty girl inside me. At that moment, it hit me: Lev knew Oluchi, but he couldn't tell me how he knew her because it wasn't his secret to tell. Adoptions were confidential.

The matatu came to a halt. I gave Oluchi a small smile before exiting the taxi. I walked to the shore, shielded my eyes, and took in the vast expanse of lake. Man, I was going to miss it here. I walked up and down the beach and then, exhausted, I said a silent farewell to Africa, and took a matatu back to my daughter.

LEAVING

The morning, our last in Mukono, dawned bright and hot. I was outside, waiting with the baby things that I was donating. Becky said she'd be over with the truck to pick the stuff up before I left. New Beginnings wouldn't need infant items, but they could get them to an orphanage that did.

Megan and Stuart were the first to come out and wait for the bus. We sat at the picnic table and the two started to rehash the events of last night. From what I gathered they had gone to Lev's house for a goodbye party. I looked at Megan, questionably.

"Lev was going to knock on your door to invite you, but you four sounded like you were having your own party inside," she explained. "We agreed to leave you to it."

I nodded in understanding. Engen, Krista, Dee and I were indeed having a great time. We hung out in the living room all night, talking and playing games.

Pretty soon, the building was empty, and all its previous residents were outside, waiting for the bus. Engen set my luggage down on the ground beside me.

"Thank you," I told him. I had been too preoccupied bringing the baby things outside that I had forgotten my own bags.

"You got it," Engen said.

A few minutes later, the orphanage's truck came into view. I rose to meet Becky. We loaded the crib and the bags in the bed of the truck, and hugged goodbye just as the bus pulled up.

"Miss Denmark," Akiki greeted me, shrewdly.

I nodded and made my way to an empty seat toward the middle of the bus. Victoria and I sat closest to the window, and Dee sat next to us. The bus lurched into motion. We'd only driven for a few miles when a horn blared.

"She's on the opposite side!" Stuart yelled and gestured.

I craned my neck to see an orange pickup truck driving in the ditch alongside us. It slammed on the brakes, waited for the bus to pass, then swerved into the oncoming traffic lane on my side. I handed Victoria to Dee, lowered my window, stuck my head out, and waved.

"Stop the bus!" Dee yelled.

Lev pulled up next to me, and shouted, "I need to talk to you."

"Akiki told the driver not to stop," Krista informed me.

"The driver won't stop," I told him anxiously.

Lev stared determinedly ahead, shifted into fourth gear and sped up. He drove off-road roughly an eighth of a mile ahead of the bus, made a wide turn, and stopped so the pickup horizontally blocked the two narrow lanes. I stepped over Dee and made my way to the head of the bus. The driver braked in front of the pickup. I looked out the large windshield and saw Lev pacing.

Akiki reached out and grabbed my arm. "You will not hold up this bus for your personal affairs."

Engen came up behind Akiki and tapped him on the shoulder. "You *will* remove your hand."

Akiki turned to face Engen, got the full measure of those mad eyes of his, and let go of my arm. The driver, who seemed amused by all of this, opened the door.

I exited the bus and walked toward Lev as fast as my post-surgery body would allow. I noticed all the baby things were still in the bed of the truck.

"I thought about it from your point of view," Lev said when I reached him, "and it all makes sense; you're going to have your hands full with the baby and school. Why would you want to deal with a long-distance relationship?" Lev reached out stroke my cheek, but pulled his hand back. "Don't we always understand each other?"

"Well, there *is* one thing I don't understand," I admitted. "Why did you tell Baba you and I were *finally* done?"

"I was only trying to get on her good side so I could find out if she set that stalker on you, and she did," Lev said, proud of his work to get to the bottom of the case. "Thanks to your description of Rocky, the police were able to pick him up. He confessed to starting the fire, and that Baba blackmailed him into following you because she was so crazy jealous of you. I hope they'll both go to jail for a long time."

I closed my eyes, thankful for that news. "I've decided to come back after I graduate high school," I told him.

"That's not for six months," Lev said contemplative. "We didn't get a chance to make things amicable between us, and I don't know how we can with you gone."

"We'll figure it out," I said, and started walking backwards toward the bus.

"Wait. You still haven't cashed in on that football bet you won." A tear slid down his cheek. "Order me to come with you, Ida."

"People need you here," I said, waving goodbye. "I order you to stay."

◆ ◆ ◆

My roommates and I had retrieved our baggage at the airport in Minnesota and were making our way toward the exit doors leading outside to a row of cars picking up their loved ones, when Krista came to a halt. She let go of the handle on her luggage and with a quivering mouth asked, "Can I hold the baby?"

I passed Victoria to Krista.

"I know the four of us agreed to get together one weekend a month to hang out, but it's not enough," Dee cried.

Engen pulled Dee into a hug. "It'll be fine."

Krista grunted. "Easy for you to say. You and Ida are practically neighbors."

Engen left one arm around Dee, and pulled Krista, still holding Victoria, to him with the other. "Considering I'd travel anywhere in the world for you girls, Duluth will be a piece of cake."

Dee brought me into the hug.

"Our families are waiting," I rasped after a few minutes.

"I can practically feel your skin itching for Paul," Krista said as we broke the hug.

Engen turned to me and engulfed me in his arms. "Your hands are full with VJ, so I'll load your bags into Marilyn's car for you," he offered.

My nerves suddenly took over, and I hugged him harder. "Promise me it won't go back to the way it was, right after Janelle died."

"I promise." He took my face in his hands. "Can I see you and VJ tomorrow?"

I looked at my daughter, who was now being passed along to Dee. "Yes, please."

Engen gave me and Victoria a kiss, and then walked through the exit doors with our luggage.

I collected my daughter, gave Krista and Dee a final hug, and walked briskly toward the revolving doors.

"Ida!" Paul ran up to me and threw his arms around me. "Engen came out forever ago; what took *you* so long?"

Marilyn gave me a sideways hug and squealed, "Give her to me!"

I handed Victoria over, and embraced Paul. "I missed you so much," I exclaimed.

"I missed you!" Paul jumped up and down, eyes on Victoria.

Marilyn threw me the keys. "You drive; I want to sit in back with my niece."

I took Victoria and belted her into the car seat that Dan had told me he'd dropped off at my house less than a month ago. I closed the door and walked to the driver's side, which was not the driver's side here in America, so I traveled around the car again.

"You must've grown two inches, Paul," I observed.

Paul got into the backseat with Marilyn and Victoria. "Does the extra height make me look more manly?"

I nodded. "Definitely."

"She's blowing a bubble with her spit!" Marilyn shrieked. "I volunteer to be her nanny while you're in school."

"Forward me your resume," I jested.

I kneaded the wheel as I reflected on returning to my life at school, which had been rough once the news was out that I was pregnant. The teachers had almost been more cruel than the students. My chest started to vibrate, and my stomach felt ill. I opened the window two inches, put my mouth up to the opening and got nothing but icy air.

Marilyn threw her body over Victoria and cried, "What are you doing?"

"I'm...drowning," I panted.

I pulled into an abandoned gas station next to the freeway entrance. I got out of the car, slammed the door, and placed my hands on my knees and bent over, feeling like I was eight feet deep in freezing cold water.

Paul's hand touched my back. "You can't leave a baby in a car!" he admonished.

"Not...now," I gasped, feeling the panic attack coming on.

"Your breath is gone."

My eyes started to burn with tears. My nose stung with the air that I was gulping. "It...hurts! Help...me."

"Okay, let me think. I'm standing on the shoreline watching my sister drown. What do I do?" Paul snapped his fingers. "Scream for help! Scream, Ida."

I focused on Paul and clutched my head. "I...can't."

"Janelle died too early," Paul said for motivation. "You're gone away from the orphanage. Doesn't that make you mad?"

I threw back my head and bellowed at the top of my lungs. My throat ached, and I was light-headed. Paul and I made eye contact, opened our mouths at the same time, and both yelled again. After awhile, I found a steady rhythm of breathing.

"I think you just saved my life," I said affectionately.

Paul shrugged one shoulder. "It's what I do."

I glanced up and saw a genuinely concerned Marilyn in the

driver's seat. I walked around to the passenger side door and got in, feeling embarrassed. Paul had the backseat with Victoria all to himself.

"What happened out there?" Marilyn asked, watching me carefully.

I avoided her eyes. "I got cold."

"That's not what I meant."

We merged onto the freeway. I closed my eyes and listened to Paul singing to Victoria. When we got home, my parents greeted me happily, and then pounced and gushed over their grand-daughter. I watched them, delighted to see how much they adored her.

Gramps surprised me when he pulled me aside and said, "I told you you'd be in good hands over there."

I wrapped my arms around Gramps. "What did you tell Lev to make him fall in love with me?" I asked curiously.

Gramps chuckled. "That was entirely you."

"After I graduate, I plan to go back," I shared.

"I'd love to go with you." Gramps' eyes cut away from mine. "Let's not tell them just yet."

"I agree." I followed his gaze to my family. "Not yet."

It was 11:00 p.m. on my first night home. Victoria was asleep upstairs, and I was pacing in the dark living room trying to fig-ure out what exactly was missing. I decided it was fresh air I needed. I put on a jacket, grabbed the baby monitor, and left. I went down to the end of the walk, turned right, and saw a famil-iar outline walking my way. My heart skipped as we stopped in front of each other.

Now eased, I reached out to touch Engen's cold cheek. "How did you know I needed you?"

"It's a mutual need," Engen said and held out his hand. I took it in mine, and led him to my house.

He followed me to my room, removed his coat and asked, "Where's VJ?"

I kicked my wet shoes off. "My mom converted her sewing room into a nursery."

Which I felt slightly ashamed about, considering Victoria and I would be moving to Mukono soon.

"Did VJ ask you to come get me?" Engen joked.

"Yes, her first words were, 'Where has that super tall hunk been?'"

"And she said it in that strange Russian cowboy accent, did she?"

"Yep," I chuckled silently.

"My only excuse is that I missed you like crazy," he admitted.

I blushed. "It's only been a few hours."

"Didn't stop the fact that I was crawling out of my skin."

"That's a pretty serious condition. It's called Akathisia."

He looked at me with romantic eyes. "I know what being without you is called, and it's not that."

"What is it called?" I asked.

"Suffocating," he said, and removed his shirt.

"I concur." I hungrily took in his appearance. "Turn your back while I change into my pajamas?"

"Good one," he laughed, and stripped down to his boxers.

NOT ADJUSTING

"Engen Scott Malone," Paige, our security system, announced on this most dreaded back-to-school morning.

"Let him in," my mom commanded.

The door clicked open, and Engen stepped inside. "How do, Gretchen?" he greeted my mom.

"Good morning, sweetie." Mom checked her watch, perplexed. "You're early. School doesn't start for forty-five minutes."

I unstrapped Victoria from her baby swing, lifted her out, and gave her a goodbye kiss.

Engen contemplated his snow-covered boots. "Bring VJ to me."

I obliged, despite my mom's protest of, "She'll catch a cold."

I shoved a pair of shoes in my school bag, and tightened the laces on my winter boots.

"It must be coming down hard if you're already covered in snow." Mom peeked out the window. "Where did you park?"

"I didn't drive," Engen replied, and bobbed up and down with Victoria.

I gently took Victoria out of Engen's arms and handed her to my stunned mother. I gave them both a kiss on the cheek, jammed a dark blue knitted hat onto my head, and slung my backpack over my shoulder. Engen stepped aside to let me pass.

"Ida Natalya," Mom said sternly.

I turned around. "We have a two-and-a-half kilometer walk ahead of us, what do you need?"

My mom's eyes were aghast. "You said he was picking you up."

I grabbed a fistful of Engen's jacket. "And here he is."

Engen shut the door on my mom's frowning face and inquired, "What's with her?"

I shrugged. "She's been acting strange all weekend."

Our boots crunched on the snow-covered sidewalks. The streetlights were still on, and the sky was gray.

"My mom's acting weird, too," Engen informed me. "I yelled at her for throwing half a bottle of water away, and she *cried*."

"My dad yelled at me because I sang to Victoria in Swahili last night," I said angrily. "I'm already sick of everyone except you, Victoria, and Paul."

Engen didn't say anything for a while.

"What's up?" I asked.

"Brittany came by yesterday."

I tripped and almost face-planted onto the snowy sidewalk. "Oh, yeah?"

"She wanted to get back together," Engen shared.

"I knew--" I hated how shrill my voice sounded, so I made it deeper, "I knew she would."

"You're adorable." He pulled my knit hat down so it covered my eyes. "*I* didn't want to, though."

I scrambled to pull the hat back up. "Why not?"

"It'd be pointless. I never loved her. I never could." Engen rubbed his lips together. "You still single?"

Lev had made it clear during our last conversation that he wanted to get back together when I returned to Mukono, yet I was unable to give him hope. I had been pondering my future recently, and no matter what stage of life I envisioned, Engen was involved.

"Single as the day I was born," I answered, staring at his hypnotic mouth.

Engen laughed. "You."

"That's not a complete sentence." I slipped my cold hands into the back pockets of his jeans. "Hey, what do you want for Christmas?"

His arms encircled my waist. "The same thing I want every year."

"Which is?"

His eyes sparkled. "Whatever you already got me."

"Good answer."

Engen put his frozen nose to mine. "I'm obsessed with you."

"I sorta dig you, too."

I heard a honk and the sound of tires stopping on snow. Engen let me go, and I turned toward the noise to see Dan waving maniacally out of the driver's side window. Dan made a U-turn and pulled over to the curb, facing the opposite way into traffic. I noticed Amelia sitting in the passenger seat, staring moodily ahead and blowing bubbles with her gum. Dan got out of the car and dashed over to us.

"Morelli!" I greeted.

"Hey, Idle."

I no longer believed that nickname applied to me, but refrained from telling him so. The videos that we watched in Mukono on readjusting did warn us that while we have changed, those at home most likely did not.

I focused on the guy who had given me Victoria. "It's great to see you."

Dan ran the palm of his hand under the bottom of my hair, and then shook Engen's hand. "Amelia and I are going to grab some coffee, wanna come with?" he invited us.

I glanced at Engen. His eyes shifted infinitesimally, telling me that he was uncomfortable with that idea.

"No, thank you," I said.

"I'll see you at school then. We have first and sixth period together," Dan informed me.

Impulsively, I reached out and took his elbow. "Tell me Amelia makes you happy," I said hopefully.

Dan pulled his arm back and got into his car without answering my question.

"What was that?" Engen asked.

"I wanted to know if he was happy," I explained as we continued on our way.

"Of course he isn't happy!" Engen said emphatically. "Amelia is a distraction. Guys need those, to take their mind off the one they genuinely want."

I picked up some snow and packed a decent snowball. Engen did the same.

"Give me a head start?" I asked.

He gave a somber nod of consent and I took off running, gathering more snow along the way to pelt him with.

As soon as Engen and I entered the school, considerably wet from our outdoor escapades, we saw a small group of students milling around underneath a banner that read "Welcome back, Ida and Engen!"

"There they are!" Principal Andrews exclaimed. He was wearing a black and gold Dashiki.

"I'm not ready for this," Engen said and grabbed my hand. "Let's leave."

I could feel his heartbeat through his hand. "Okay."

We turned around and ran smack into Dan and Amelia, and their iced coffees. Dan had excellent reflexes, so he was able to raise his cup in time. Amelia wasn't as lucky when Engen ran into her. She screamed as the cup slammed back against her chest, and coffee exploded all over her. Amelia spared me a dirty look and ran for the bathroom.

"You're leaving," Dan accused us.

Engen made a noise to indicate we were running out of time.

Andrews clapped a hand on my shoulder. I gave Engen a "Save yourself" look. He stayed.

"Check out those tans," Andrews remarked. "There's an assembly this afternoon, and you two are the star speakers."

"Do we have to?" Engen asked.

"Yes. The school is looking forward to hearing about your time in Africa," he boomed, and then added lower, "Do your best to encourage students to sign up for the program, got it?"

"With all due respect, sir, we don't want to discuss it," I said. "The students wouldn't appreciate it."

Andrews shook his finger at me. "I think you underestimate your classmates."

I thought back to the cafeteria the day before Engen and I left, and the jokes people were making about malaria and HIV. "I don't, sir."

"C'mon, Idle, I'm sure the school is dying to hear of your love affair with a native," said Dan.

Engen stepped in front of me and warned menacingly, "Lay off her."

"Or what?" Dan asked.

Engen cracked his knuckles. "I'll make you."

Dan reached out with both hands and pushed Engen's shoulders, hard.

"Hey!" I shouted and dropped my bag. I charged at Dan and shoved him. He stumbled back. I made up the distance and shoved him again. "Keep your hands off of him."

Dan looked wounded. "Still fighting each other's battles, I see."

"Enough." Andrews extended his arms between me and Engen, and Dan. "You two *will* address the school."

"What if we have nothing good to say?" I challenged, eyes still on Dan.

"How could you not?" Andrews responded. "Thanks to the extra YAHN credits, if you play your cards right, you'll both be graduated before winter break."

The bell rang, announcing we had five minutes to get to class. "Stop by my office after lunch."

"Do we even have lunch together?" Engen's voice cracked as he glared at Andrews' departing back.

"Give me your phone," I said. He handed it to me and I scrolled through it. I knew we didn't have any classes together, but would the world really be so cruel? Apparently so. "We don't have lunch together."

"Absolutely perfect," Engen grumbled. He grabbed his phone and took off down the hallway toward the gym.

I clenched my jaw and went the opposite way, Dan following close behind. I stopped in front of my locker. It had been my locker for three years, but I'd be damned if I could remember the combination to it.

"How's Victoria?" Dan wanted to know.

"Wonderful." I smiled at the thought of her. "She can hold her head up for five whole seconds."

"Is that supposed to be an accomplishment?" Dan asked uncertainly.

I slammed my hand against my locker in defeat. "It means her neck muscles are getting stronger."

"That's cool," he said. "Everything set on your end for the meeting with the lawyers next week?"

Dan was signing a pile of paperwork to relinquish all parental rights to Victoria. He wouldn't have to pay child support, and most importantly, there wouldn't be anything he could do to keep me and Victoria on this continent.

"Yep, all set."

I followed Dan to the classroom and peered inside. I saw Tawny and Trish taking pictures of themselves on their phones, a few cheerleaders laughing while shooting snooty looks at Clara, a self-proclaimed Sci-Fi geek, and Jared Rogers bouncing a mini basketball off the backs of student's heads.

Dan's brow creased. "You coming?"

"No."

I continued walking past the classroom door. My boots made high-pitched squeaks on the waxed floor. I turned down the hallway toward the gym, just as Engen came bursting through the double doors carrying his coat and backpack.

Engen slowed when he reached me. "I tried."

"Let's get Victoria, take her to meet Janelle's parents, and then return for this stupid assembly." I held out a fist.

Engen bumped his fist against mine. "Deal."

PROMM

A few days after Christmas, Engen and I got a call from Principal Andrews informing us that we had each earned enough credits from the first semester to graduate. Gramps, aware of that fact, started to apply pressure about leaving for Africa. I was wishy-washy because Engen wasn't starting college until August, and the idea of having eight more months with him was sublime. As it so happened, Engen was doing some applying of his own, as I'd found out on New Years Day...to the University of Minnesota.

"I thought we had an understanding," I said, agitated. "You're going *away* to school and I'm going to go back to Mukono."

"It's a horrible plan," Engen stated. "We belong together."

"Separate to unite, Mrs. M. told me." I swallowed deeply. "I think she meant that we'll grow to appreciate each other more if we spend some time apart."

I watched his hopes and dreams fizzle from his eyes. "In that case, I think we need to reduce our sleepovers so I can start weaning myself off of you."

"Reduce? Why not just quit this friendship cold turkey?" I suggested, even though inside I felt like little gashes were being sliced into my heart.

"Don't be ridiculous. I have lots of things planned for us yet." He took my waist and pulled me to him, "Plus, we have our trip to Duluth on Friday."

"What trip?" I asked.

"We're meeting Krista and Dee, remember?"

I took a step back. "This is a plan?"

"Dee suggested that you leave VJ with your parents," Engen said. "You deserve a night away."

My chest rose and fell rapidly. "What do you mean?"

Engen's eyes turned panicked. "Krista said she called you."

"She didn't." I continued to back away from him. "Anyway, it sounds like it's just supposed to be you three."

"Why wouldn't you be invited?" he asked, confused. Then a realization passed over his eyes that this was reminiscent of the safari incident, and that maybe Krista was excluding me on purpose.

"I'm going up to my room to take a nap," I said, and ran a hand through my hair. "Due to your snoring, I didn't get much sleep last night."

"Going back to Africa is *truly* what you want?" he asked in disbelief.

I nodded.

"Why do you want to be away from me so badly?"

"Because when you're old and gray, looking back on your life, I don't want you to be able to associate me with any regrets."

"I didn't want to believe her," Engen said, walking backwards toward the front door, "but apparently Mrs. M. was right when she told me that a love as deep as ours wasn't meant for the young."

Engen left, and I went straight into the garage to inform Gramps that Victoria and I were ready to return to Mukono. Gramps searched online and we booked our flight. In just two weeks, the three of us would be departing.

True to our nature, Engen and I made up shortly afterward. Turned out the reason he had left my house the day of the argument was so he could contact SDSU to accept their scholarship. He also placed a call to Dee to tell her that he would not be visiting. Too bad my plans weren't so easy to cancel. Happy to have made up with Engen, I kept that fact to myself for a week and a half. Now that time was up.

Gramps and I had broken the news to my family that we were

moving the same day we booked our flight. Mom had held Victoria and wept silently; my dad was comforted that I'd have Gramps, and Paul cried and ran to his room. I went to his room later that evening and we had a heart-to-heart. He didn't understand why we were leaving, and I couldn't make him. But I did promise that we would talk often.

I had said goodbye to Janelle's parents and Janelle's grave yesterday. Engen was the last goodbye.

Paul was on his winter break, so Engen and I were taking him and Victoria to the zoo. It was an uncharacteristically warm day for Minnesota in January, and I was looking forward to an outdoor outing with my daughter. The outfit I had put her in, lilac and white striped leggings and a white long-sleeved shirt with an elephant on it, were in a newborn size, yet still baggy on her.

I'd just greeted Engen at the front door when Paul came running down the stairs, exclaiming, "Did you tell him yet?"

I scratched my head sheepishly and wagered a glance at Engen. "You and I should talk later," I said.

Engen sat down on the couch. "Now's good for me."

"Hold on." I ran upstairs, pulled open the top drawer of my bureau, and grabbed the jewelry box I had stowed there.

When I returned, Engen had Victoria out of the playpen and was bouncing her on his knee, talking to her in babynese. Paul watched on, patiently awaiting his turn to hold Victoria.

Engen nodded at my hand. "Whatcha got there?"

"A present. Here, let's trade."

"I have a surprise for you, too," Engen said, and gave me Victoria. As he took the box, Paul was immediately at my side relieving me of my baby.

I sat down on the arm of the couch and ran my hand up and down Engen's back as he slowly opened the box. When he saw what was inside, it was as if all the bones in his body had melted.

"This is Janelle's half of the best friend necklace," he said miserably.

"No, it isn't." I held out my necklace, which now had three heart halves on it. "Flip yours over," I instructed.

Engen turned his piece of the jagged heart over in his hand. "It says 'I.'"

"And mine says 'E.'" I picked out the half with the etching on the back. "Will you be my best friend forever?"

"Done." Engen put the necklace on, pulled me off the arm of the couch and sat me on his lap so I was straddling him. "Is that all you wanted to say?"

"No. Victoria and I are leaving for Africa in a few days."

He wrapped his arms around me. "How fitting then, you giving me a broken heart."

"You aren't going to insist I stay?" I asked, surprised.

"I know you won't." Engen leaned forward and kissed my lips. "This doesn't mean we're over."

"I know." I hugged him, liking that I now had his scent on me. "You're taking this way too well. Who spilled the beans?"

"Your dad told me a few days ago. He made me promise not to go to extremes to get you to stay, then we shared a good cry in my kitchen."

I looked at Engen, and realized that after I left, I may not see him in person again for many years. I hugged him tighter.

"I have something planned for us tomorrow night," he said.

I worked my hands under the bottom of his black and gray-striped sweater, and rested them on his abs. "What is it?"

"You'll find out when I pick you up."

I set my lips on his earlobe. "Can I have a hint?"

"Sweet Jesus, you're irresistible." Engen shivered, giving in. "When your mom takes you shopping tomorrow, heed her advice and get something fancy."

Based on the stores Mom took me to, I was pretty sure I had Engen's surprise figured out. First there was the outfit: a knee-length gray halter dress with a gray beaded belt, and gray sparkled, strappy pumps. Next, it was to a lingerie store for a gray leg garter. Lastly, we went to a flower shop. At Mom's insistence, I waited in the car while she ran in.

When a limo pulled up outside my house at seven p.m., I knew for a fact that we were going to prom. I just didn't know how he meant to pull it off. I excitedly held my breath as my dad opened the door. While he and Engen exchanged pleasantries, I waited patiently by the fireplace.

My mom swayed with Victoria on her hip and watched me closely. "You look lovely, darling."

"Thanks, Mom."

Finally, Dad stepped back, revealing my date wearing a tuxedo. Engen peered into the kitchen first, and then into the living room where I was standing still as a statue. When he saw me, his face erupted into a huge smile. My heart was practically leaping out of my chest as he walked over to me, took my hand, and slipped a corsage onto my wrist, all the while keeping his eyes on mine.

"You're wearing my favorite color on you," Engen said, and placed a kiss on my knuckles.

I smiled shyly, and took in Engen in his tuxedo: black pants with a white dress shirt, and a black coat. The vest, bow tie, and pocket square were all gray.

"You look *so* gorgeous," I breathed.

Engen stared dreamily at me. "And there are no words to describe you." He then walked over to Victoria and placed a mini corsage on her wrist. "Can I borrow your mama for the night?"

Victoria cooed and stuck her tongue out.

Engen's eyes lit up as he laughed. "Thanks, VJ."

The wall was officially demolished. All defenses were down. My heart was filled to bursting with love for him. Engen met my eyes, and I swear he could see it by the way his eyes changed color. If my mom hadn't shouted, "Picture time!" I never would have taken my eyes off his.

"Not yet," Dad said, coming into the living room with a boutonniere. He handed it to me. "Left side, honey."

My hands shook as I reached to pin it to Engen's left lapel. They were shaking so anxiously I couldn't pin the stupid thing.

"Ouch!" Engen hissed.

"Very funny," I said, knowing I hadn't come close to hurting him.

I made a few more attempts before exhaling in frustration.

"Hey." Engen reached a hand up and lightly touched my wrist. "Take as long as you want. I enjoy having you this close."

Now feeling more calmed, I got it pinned on the next try. We were posed for pictures when Gramps came in from the garage, wiping his oily hands on towel.

"Gramps," I called, and motioned for him to come in.

Gramps took off into the direction of his bedroom. I didn't want to pout, but what the hell was his deal?

"I'll get him," Engen offered, and started after him, but Gramps returned, holding a jewelry box in his greasy hands.

"These belonged to your Grams." Gramps opened the box to reveal a precious string of pearls. "I'd put them on for you, but my hands are dirty."

I turned my back to Gramps, and lifted my hair. It didn't seem right for anyone but him to do it. I put my hand to my throat, touched. "Thank you."

We took pictures with and without Victoria. Then we had to stop by Engen's house to take pictures. His mom and dad, three sisters, and brother-in-law Doug were there. His mom was practically bursting with pride over having such a sweet and handsome son. His sisters exclaimed over my outfit while Doug and Engen chatted.

Fifteen minutes later, we were back in the limo. Engen and I didn't talk much; we were content just taking in the other's appearance. It wasn't long before we arrived at our destination, which turned out to be the golf course Dan worked at. We pulled up to the main building, and Engen got out to open the door for me. When we approached the entrance, arm in arm, I saw that the marquee board read: Ida and Engen's promm.

"How did you do this?" I asked Engen.

"Wedding receptions and birthday parties aren't common on a Thursday night, so Dan's boss was able to rent the room to me at a decent price."

He held the door open for me, and then led me into the ballroom. All the tables in the room had lit floating candles sitting on top of white linen tablecloths. The table he was leading me to, in front of a large, roaring, stone fireplace, was decorated with a balloon arrangement of our school's colors of red and white. It was our own, private prom.

Engen pulled out my chair for me. I sat, and he sat next to me. He took my hand in his and brought it to his cheek just as a waiter came out. The young man's eyes widened, and he blushed as he set a chocolate milkshake, cheeseburger, and fries down in front of me. He then set a bottle of root beer and the same meal down in front of Engen.

"You're a lucky guy," the waiter commented to Engen, cutting his eyes over to me. "Since you're underage, I can't serve you the bottle of champagne that you requested," he told Engen, but conspiratorially added, "so I'm going to sneak it into the limo for you."

"Thanks, Tim."

I admired the large, romantic room one more time. "Why did you do all this?"

Engen smiled at me dotingly. "Because you're smokin' hot."

I took a bite of cheeseburger. "That can't be the reason."

"You're right, there are two real reasons. Remember when we were eleven, and you and Janelle came over to watch Kaylee get ready for her prom?"

"Of course."

"Your eyes were so huge as you took it all in, the clothes, the limo, and the couples laughing. When Kaylee and Doug were taking their couple's picture, I remember you took your eyes off of them for one reason, to look at me." Engen paused, a faraway look in his eyes. "Before they left, Doug pulled me aside and asked, 'Which one of those girls are you taking to prom?' I pointed to you. Doug said, 'Good choice.'" He pulled out his wallet, reached inside, and took out a worn bill. "Doug told me that prom was expensive and I'd better start saving now, and gave me a five-dollar bill."

Engen handed it to me. Written across the bill was: "Save for Ida and Engen's promm." I laughed, now understanding why the sign outside was misspelled.

"That's insanely adorable," I said, and handed him back the bill.

"Three years later, at Kaylee and Doug's wedding, Doug gave me this." Engen patted his gray pocket square. "But I'll save that conversation for another time."

"That was a fun wedding," I hedged, keeping in mind that I was getting on a plane for Africa tomorrow, and there wouldn't be many more chances to hear the story.

Engen looked like he was lost in a trance, and asked, "Dance with me?"

"Sure, but you haven't eaten yet."

He stood and extended his hand to me. "I'm too wired to eat."

I wiped my mouth with the cloth napkin, took Engen's hand, and followed him to the dance floor. He went over to the table where a computer was hooked up, and pressed a few buttons. Soft music filled the room, followed by a woman singing, "The first time ever I saw your face."

Engen enveloped me in his arms, and we began to move. We danced to all different types of music. We didn't go without some form of skin contact for at least three hours, until the waiter announced our time was up.

Engen reluctantly let me go, and led me to our table. He set some bills on top of it, and excused himself to go to the restroom. I took a last drink of milkshake and noticed that one of the bills he'd left was the five from Doug. I rifled through my purse and found a five to replace it.

Because it was now freezing out, Engen draped his tuxedo

jacket around my shoulders. We had the limo until midnight, so Engen told the driver to take the long way home. We sat in the back, my legs draped over his, and drank champagne.

"Oh, hey, this is for you," he said, and unclasped his bow tie.

I immediately fastened it around my neck. My garter was showing, so I nodded toward it, "And that's for you."

Engen set his flute down, leaned over, and took the garter between his teeth. I leaned back and lifted my leg. He removed the garter, brought it to his nose, and inhaled. I lifted back up and wrapped my arms around him.

"Engen, what was the second reason you put all this together?"

"I thought that was rather obvious," he answered.

After studying his eyes, I no longer needed to hear the reason. I set a hand on his face and brought it to mine. As we kissed, his hand rubbed the inside of my thigh, driving me wild the higher it traveled. Without breaking the kiss, he picked me up and settled me onto his lap. His hands were under my dress, grasping my hips. Our bodies rocked together, and clothes were dangerously close to coming off when the limo stopped.

"We're at the young lady's house," the driver said through the intercom.

"Can you keep driving?" Engen asked, breathless.

"I cannot, sir. I have a VIP pickup to make."

Engen swore. "I'll see you later?" he asked me.

I nodded and climbed off his lap. "Thank you so much for tonight."

"No, Ida, thank you."

Engulfed in Engen's apple cinnamon scent, I made my way up the driveway and into my house. I checked on Victoria before heading to my bedroom. My parents had left me a note that said her last feeding was at eleven, so I set my phone alarm for 3 a.m. and lay on my bed, still in my complete outfit, including the heels and Engen's jacket, and stared at the bill that I took from the table, a souvenir from one of the greatest nights of my life.

Suddenly, I heard a sound on my roof and looked at my window in time to see Engen open it and crawl through. I knelt on the bed, pleased to see that he was still wearing his tux, the shirt untucked and the vest unbuttoned.

"I need that jacket back," Engen announced. "I have to return this tux in the morning."

I removed the jacket and regretfully handed it to him.

He took the jacket, and then let it fall to the floor. "What's that in your hand?"

I lifted the bill for him to see, and then tossed it onto my night stand. "I figured it would be a nice story to tell Victoria one day."

Engen walked toward me, purposefully. When he got close enough, I unbuttoned his shirt starting from the top, while he undid it from the bottom.

"I'm glad you're still wearing that dress," he remarked, as he removed his shirt and vest.

"Why?"

"Because the moment after I saw you in it, I've been consumed with the idea of taking it off."

He crawled onto the bed so he was kneeling with me, and covered my lips with his. He unzipped the back of my dress and pulled back just far enough to ease the dress over my head, and then he was back on my lips, kissing me hungrily. After a few more minutes, he stood to remove his pants. I stood also, set a foot on the nightstand, and started to undo the clasp around my ankle when a growl from Engen made me look up.

"The heels stay," he said, and sat down on the bed.

I raised my arms to remove the necklace.

Engen shook his head. "The pearls stay."

I placed my foot on the floor and a hand on my waist. "And the rest?"

He appreciatively took in the black, strapless, lace push-up bra, and black tie-side bikini panties. "Goes," he whispered.

I removed the bra. Engen reached out both hands and pulled the ties on the panties. They fell to the floor. He took my waist and pulled me to a sitting position onto his lap. He brushed the hair off my face as we held each other's gaze. As often as I had denied it and hid it due to my injured pride, there wasn't a doubt that I was in love with him. But there was also something there that somehow felt more genuine than love:

"I like you, Engen. A whole lot."

"I'd need an eternity to show you how much I like you." He flipped us over so he was now propped up on top of me. I could tell from his eyes that his mind was racing. "I know you're leaving tomorrow, and it's fully going to shatter my heart..."

He trailed off when I buried my head into his neck and inhaled deeply. "But?" I asked.

"I want to lose myself in you," he sighed. "Even if it's just for one night."

Two hours later, still in my bedroom, I untangled myself from Engen's sleeping body, and turned off the alarm a full minute before it was going to alert me of Victoria's 3 a.m. bottle. Since I needed something to wear, I chose Engen's white dress shirt. As usual, the feeding went smoothly and she was asleep twenty minutes later. When I got back to my room, I sat down at my dresser and watched Engen sleep. Before I knew it, I had my flight information called up on my phone. I pressed "edit my flight" and was presented with four options: reschedule, change destination, cancel flight, exit without making a change. I didn't want to change my destination, and I was pretty sure--

"What are you doing way over there?" Engen asked sleepily.

I got up and set my phone down on the nightstand. "Just resetting the alarm for Victoria's next bottle."

"You should've gotten me up to do this one."

I started to unbutton the shirt I'd borrowed. "I needed you rested," I explained, and wiggled my eyebrows suggestively. The shirt slipped off my shoulders and down my arms. "Do you forgive me?"

Engen shook his head as he took me in. "Nope."

I sauntered over to his side of the bed, and laid down on top of him. "It kind of feels like you forgive me."

Engen smiled. "I can never stay mad at you."

"That's too bad." I leaned over and whispered in his ear, "You have no idea what I was going to be willing to do to make it up to you."

"You've already given me more than I could ever hope for."

My lips parted and I felt a warmth around my heart.

After an hour of indulging in each other's bodies, I was sure Engen had drifted off again, so I flipped over onto my side, reached for my phone, and turned it on. I was immediately faced with those four flight options. Engen stirred behind me, and threw an arm around my waist. I knew Engen would give up everything for me and Victoria, but he shouldn't have to miss out on experiences a guy his age should have, on account of us.

Eyes focused on the four flight options, I thought about how it would be selfish to entertain any other possibility. I pressed the corresponding button and set the phone down.

To be continued...

Acknowledgments

Thank you to my wonderful husband, Matt, for this book's beautiful cover artwork as well as the inside illustration of Lev's parents' memorial cross. Massive thanks to my editor, Lissa Roberson, who truly turned good into great.

To my mother, Barb, thank you for the encouragement as well as reading the first draft of New Beginnings which was around 180,000 words. To all of my other beta readers: Matt Olson, Jen Nystrom (who also provided additional editing advice), Sarah Petersen and Justin Atkinson, thank you for supporting Ida and me on this journey.

Finally, thank you to my son, Tanner, just because he rocks.

About the Author

Janet lives in St. Paul, Minnesota with her artist husband (who designed the cover of this book), charismatic son, and three neurotic cats. Janet is a lifelong fan of reading and writing stories. New Beginnings may be her debut novel, but she has several projects in the works. Unlike some of her characters, she has never been to Africa, although she does dream of going one day.

Made in the USA
Columbia, SC
17 February 2020